THE REPUBLIC

THE REPUBLIC

Joost de Vries

*Translated from the Dutch
by Jane Hedley-Prôle*

OTHER PRESS / NEW YORK

Originally published in 2013 as *De republiek* by
Uitgeverij Prometheus, Amsterdam
Copyright © Joost de Vries 2013
English translation copyright © Other Press 2019

The right of Joost de Vries to be identified as the author of this Work
has been asserted by him in accordance with the Copyright,
Designs & Patents Act 1988.

This publication has been made possible with financial support
from the Dutch Foundation for Literature.

N ederlands
letterenfonds
dutch foundation
for literature

Production editor: Yvonne E. Cárdenas
Text designer: Jennifer Daddio / Bookmark Design & Media Inc.
This book was set in Bulmer MT and Trade Gothic by
Alpha Design & Composition of Pittsfield, NH

1 3 5 7 9 10 8 6 4 2

LIBRARY OF CONGRESS CATALOGING-IN-PUBLICATION DATA

Names: Vries, Joost de, 1983- author. | Hedley-Prôle, Jane, translator.
Title: The republic / Joost de Vries ; translated from the Dutch by Jane Hedley-Prôle.
Other titles: Republiek. English
Description: New York : Other Press, [2019] | Originally published in 2013
as De republiek by Uitgeverij Prometheus, Amsterdam.
Identifiers: LCCN 2018039409 (print) | LCCN 2018059718 (ebook) |
ISBN 9781590518540 (ebook) | ISBN 9781590518533 (pbk.)
Classification: LCC PT5882.32.R55 (ebook) | LCC PT5882.32.R55 R4713 2019 (print)
| DDC 839.313/7—dc23
LC record available at https://lccn.loc.gov/2018039409

Publisher's Note
This is a work of fiction. Names, characters, places, and incidents either are the prod-
uct of the author's imagination or are used fictitiously, and any resemblance to actual
persons, living or dead, events, or locales is entirely coincidental.

THE REPUBLIC

PROLOGUE

"These are very nice landscape drawings, Asterios, but everything is made up. Why don't you try doing some from life?"

"I don't like drawing from life. Things are always in the wrong place."

– David Mazzucchelli, *Asterios Polyp*

"I understand the music, I understand the movies, I even see how comic books can tell us things. But there are full professors in this place who read nothing but cereal boxes."

"It's the only avant-garde we've got."

– Don DeLillo, *White Noise*

There's not a whole lot you can hold against a man like Josip Brik. With fluctuating regularity he would attend a few lectures, get his hair cut, eat a sandwich at the campus bistro so everyone could see he was there, and at the end of the day he would always saunter into the offices of *The Sleepwalker, Journal of Hitler Studies, Since 1991*, set up by, among others, Josip Brik.

– Tell me honestly, Friso, are you my Dauphin or my Robespierre?

His presence required that you immediately drop everything you were doing and focus your full attention on him like a stadium floodlight. For me, as editor in chief of *The Sleepwalker*, he was an inexhaustible gold mine, unfailingly submitting a five-thousand-word essay every two months on any topic you cared to name. My office was on the ground floor, and its doors gave onto a courtyard. Whenever he dropped in I would throw them open and improvise a sidewalk café in the form of two wrought-iron chairs and an occasional table. He would always start the conversation himself, talking about his sandwich, about the Yankees, who'd had an amazing summer, about the Obamas, of whom the same could not, alas, be said. I would twiddle the knobs of my magnificent espresso machine, with its built-in grinder and foamer, while he did terrifyingly good imitations—he nailed the gestures as well as the voices—ranging from Hugo Chávez fulminating about the U.S. to the fluty Oxbridge indignation of Emma Watson, whom he'd just seen in the latest Harry Potter franchise. "We could all have been killed, Harry—or worse, expelled!" He'd ask after Pip, inquire about my health, want to know what he could contribute to *The Sleepwalker*, whether I'd seen any interesting films, and then the conversation would gradually start moving inexorably toward something that needed to happen, a small request, varying from looking after two schnauzers for a weekend to, in this case, going to Chile for a month.

– I've been to Chile and while I was there I met a man called Hitler, and you know, Friso, I think there might be a nice article in it for you.

He always reserved places for Pippa and me in the front row of his evening lectures, which he gave once or twice a month to packed auditoria. Whether he was talking about Freud or about Hitlerian Revenge Plays (a genre I suspected him of making up), however often he stood in front of an audience, he always seemed nervous, with patches of sweat blooming under his armpits like gunshot wounds. Physically he resembled Jabba the Hutt, 250 pounds of condemned meat, his head, his eyes, his arms, his hands were large, his belly and shoulders colossal, there was enough cotton in his shirt for a duvet cover. I exaggerate. The minuscule microphone on the lectern only reached up to his nipple, making him bend over, which interfered with his breathing, so that he talked even more wheezily than usual.

(His speech, or speech defects, were the subject of speculation: he spoke rapidly, shlishing inconsistently, in some Czech-Polish-Yiddish accent you just couldn't pin down—he'd been born in Belgrade, Yugoslavia, but since the age of eight had lived in Brooklyn, Chicago, Groningen, and Paris respectively; in theory the accent had no right to exist.)

Josip Legilimens Brik. April 2, 1955. Middle child, two brothers, two sisters. His surname was actually written with an acute accent: Brík, but somewhere in the mid-nineties he'd dropped that to make it easier for publishers, journalists, and Americans in general. Professors mostly couldn't stand him; their PhD students, by contrast, were crazy about him. Together with the late Jack Gladney, he was one of the founders of Hitler studies, but he had many more strings to his bow: qualified psychoanalyst, Lacanian, secretary of the Anti-Derridian League, late Marxist, slightly-more-than-occasional TV host. His most popular and hated work was a comparative study of Robespierre and Hitler entitled *The Red Machine, or Why Things Cost Money* (2005), whose underlying theme was that the West has been lulled into such a torpor it can't carry out the social and cultural changes it knows to be necessary. We want revolutions without revolutions. Wars without victims, racing cars without accidents, beer without alcohol, Coca-Cola without sugar, coffee without caffeine—the degeneration of the free market on all psychological levels. We want to have as much as possible for the lowest possible price and will therefore be helpless when new Robespierres or Hitlers arise.

Technically he'd been exempted from teaching duties, he could do whatever he wanted, but his lectures were faithfully attended by a hard-core group of students, youngsters who hung on his every word, something the university bragged about in its brochures—that its flourishing intellectual climate transcended "mere contact hours," an impressive spin on the fact that their most famous teacher did not teach. He himself had an unshakable confidence in his influence and liked to tell how the father of a student had once come up to him and said: "If you turn my kid Commie, I'll sue you!" He roared with laughter at that kind of thing in his own delightful way, his head thrown back as if he was gargling with mouthwash. His whole body shook in sympathy.

My girlfriend, Pip (God bless her), had given rise to one of the most popular Brik anecdotes on the campus. One day, when he was holding forth on Oedipus and sex in the films of Hitchcock, she'd stood up and asked the legendary question of whether he himself still had sex, whereupon he'd fired back the even more legendary reply:

– Sex? No. *Never.* It's far too cognitive a pursuit.

So there we were, sitting on the wrought-iron chairs outside my office. There was something sharp and heavy in the September air, a harbinger of the first chill since spring. Brik, absorbed in spooning out the last remnants of foam, was trying not to look me in the eye. Anyway. Chile.

– This Mr. Hitler makes murals. Great big paintings with a socialist theme.

I didn't say anything.

– Lots of workers, farmers, children, Indians. Bright colors, red and yellow. Terrible art, in my view, very un-aesthetic, but no less interesting for that.

I still didn't say anything. He fidgeted, looking at his hands, his nails, his feet, shoe size 41 at a guess, so small that the toes scarcely peeped out of his trouser legs and I sometimes wondered how he kept that huge upper body in balance.

– I've spoken to this Mr. Hitler and he's willing to co-operate on an article. There are a lot more Hitlers in Chile, he said. You could stay at the local university, I know some people there and . . .

Here I interrupted him, calmly:

– But, and this is something we've talked about before, won't it end up being the kind of article whose only amusement value consists of using the name "Hitler" in trivial, day-to-day situations? "Hitler awaited us in the doorway of his home, with its stylish Scandinavian interior." " 'Would you like tea or coffee?' asked Hitler."—The joke's getting tired. The joke *is* tired.

He shook his head:

– It would be about living with history. Friso, your name is the most direct, most personal history you have— will *ever* have.

– Hitler's father changed his name.

– Herr Alois Schicklgruber.

– Stalin wasn't really called Stalin, Trotsky wasn't really called Trotsky.

– Lev Davidovich Bronstein.

– Michael Keaton changed his name. Do you know what his real name is? Michael Douglas.

– Incredible.

– And Heydrich changed the spelling of his name to make it more Aryan.

– Yesh. Hitler's sister Paula—she changed her name after the war.

– To "Wolf." Clearly a mark of homage.

– There you go: the very masks we select reveal the depths of our souls.

His voice grew low and honeyed, almost theatrical:

– Here we have a man who, far into the twenty-first century, is still signing his larger-than-life paintings with his own name. No initials. His own name, in full, in the corner, clearly legible: "Hitler." This man isn't frightened of history—or has completely disconnected from it. That's our theme, there's the story!

I smiled back at his smile.

– You know what's good? To have a son. Yesh. It's your only chance to undo damage, have a counterlife. It's as if you get to rename yourself, to do a restart: *Yourself 2.0*. I'll give you three guesses what this Hitler's father's first name was. You got it: Hitler.

– Oh, by the way, Pippa sends her love, I said, and conjured a plastic-wrap-covered bowl out of my desk, containing a dozen homemade shortbread cookies. Brik polished them off in two bites, and when, after a while, no less a person than Dean Chilton put in an appearance, he offered him the last biscuit as if he were Justin of Nassau handing over the keys of the city of Breda to the Spanish general Spinola.

– Gentlemen, gentlemen, Chilton greeted us, grasping Brik's hand with his long fingers, and holding it slightly longer than necessary.

Walter Chilton was a few years older than Brik and had a great fondness for him—a feeling that was reciprocated.

If he was (as many at the faculty suspected) the type of man who preferred the company of dogs to humans, then Brik was the exception. He laughed at everything Brik said, and sat, perpetually entertained, drumming his fingertips together when he spoke ("Just like Mr. Burns in *The Simpsons*," Brik had once remarked).

– What are you two chuckling about? he asked.

– Nazis, I said.

That raised a hearty laugh. Chilton had a narrow head and a thin smile. He came from one of those old families whose roots might or might not stretch back to the *Mayflower*, the type of New England aristocracy that regarded making a career as rather vulgar, and whenever I saw him walk past my office, in the kind of tweed suit favored by the cartoon bear Sir Oliver B. Bumble, he looked as though he, too, was astonished to find himself here.

– I was taught by a man who once shot two Nazis with a single bullet, Chilton remarked in a blasé tone.

Brik and I fell silent.

– Seriously. At Remagen. They were running down a little street, side by side. He told me that at my graduation party. They didn't just exist in movies, you know.

I laughed, but Chilton's repertoire didn't include cozy chitchat. With a wave of the arm more common to professional bouncers, he summoned Brik out of his chair— he was to come along on some PR mission or other. Brik turned around one last time:

– Chile, Friso. Think about it.

We were friends. I'd sat next to him on intercontinental flights, driven across the Alps with him in tiny rental cars, gone with him to visit his mother on her eighty-fifth birthday. As far as I knew he didn't possess a tie. I might not have provided him with an intellectual sounding board—he had a coterie of philosophers and other thinkers for that—but I was the first to read his texts, and if I thought something was vague or careless, he took it seriously. I wasn't an academic; my talent lay in reshaping paragraphs, improving punctuation. The depth of my affection for him took quite a while to hit me. It was after I'd moved to the States at his suggestion and had been living there for about six months. One cold winter's morning we were walking across the campus, when he seemed to stumble. After his second or third slipped disc he'd suffered damage to his left foot, a kind of neurological crossed wiring that made his foot hit the ground oddly at unpredictable moments. It sounded like a hoofbeat or a mousetrap snapping shut—suddenly his foot would move faster than his calf, clack!, making it seem as if he'd twisted his ankle.

I'd immediately grabbed him, one hand under his armpit and the other on his shoulder. It was all right, he wasn't really falling—but I had him in my arms and was suddenly struck by how good that felt, his body, his physical humanity—the fact that he existed, as a being in the world.

From: Fr.Devos@cornell.edu
To: J.L.Brik@cornell.edu
Date: January 11
Subject:

Dear Brik,

You said there was no need for an email, but I'm sending you one anyway. To say this: You were right and I wasn't—aren't you astonished that after all this time this still surprises me?

You warned me, and I didn't listen to you—dumb, dumb! Against your advice I started my speech with some jokes, a lot of jokes. You'd said I was perhaps too high up the order of speakers, and indeed, I came after a rabbi who talked about the jokes he and his brothers and sisters would tell each other in the Warsaw ghetto, a man with piercing blue eyes and a baritone voice so melodious he could have read a whole orphanage to sleep.

Then it was me, not pulling my punches, because at a conference whose theme is "Hitler & the Sick Joke: on Holocaust and Humor" you have to call a spade a spade, I mumbled, before I got started. So I kicked off with: Why did Hitler commit suicide? Because he got the gas bill. Did you hear about the Hitler-based rom-com? He's just not that into Jew. That isn't funny; my father died at Auschwitz. He was drunk and fell out of the guard tower. A few days ago I went to a fancy-dress party dressed as Hitler. Everyone thought it was hilarious. Until they found three dead Jews in the broom closet.

You could have heard a pin drop. Two hundred fifty faces stared at me. I'm not blessed with your body language, Brik, your intonation, your timing. Your theatricality. What the audience must have seen was not someone ably demonstrating how passé Hitler is as an object of shock, but a little boy desperately trying to talk tough.

Afterward the blue-eyed rabbi was mobbed, weeping women fell into his arms, and men pressed his hand as if he'd just set a world record. I, meanwhile, was avoided like the plague, and walked into the buffet room on my own. I'd hardly picked up a plate before the lady in charge of the catering, while looking ostentatiously in the other direction (as if she were signaling to her accomplice in a casino), pointed silently at a small sign instructing people not to take more than one chocolate croissant, thank you very much.

We first saw each other in Utrecht, in the cloisters of the academy building on Domplein. He'd spoken at the opening session of the academic year. I was there to hear my kid sister perform; they'd let her sing an aria, something by Handel. We got into conversation later, during the train journey back to Groningen, where I was still studying and where he led the pampered existence of an extraordinary visiting professor. At some point I told a joke: A rabbi asks his student, "What's green, hangs on the wall, and whistles?" The student ponders for a while, then gives up. "A herring," the rabbi answers. The student protests, "A herring can be green and can hang on a wall, but it can't whistle." "Okay," says the rabbi, "so it doesn't whistle."

He couldn't stop laughing. So it doesn't whistle. What made it really funny was the shrug.

From: Fr.Devos@cornell.edu
To: J.L.Brik@cornell.edu
Date: March 2
Subject: Whoops.

My dear Josip,

A quick scribble. Don't feel obliged to reply. I found your ring binder in the office, with what I took to be your lecture for the O'Neill thing at Harvard in it. You probably left it by accident, but perhaps (I thought) you felt hesitant about asking me to read it (because I had a lot on my plate, having to get *Sleepwalker* to the printer next week) and you decided to leave it to chance. Anyway, I read it, very

quickly. Would you like me to edit it? I could get it back to
you the day after tomorrow, tomorrow if it's urgent.

Terrible faux pas, yesterday. You probably know already,
but yesterday morning I just popped into your place
on my way upstate, to find the DVDs you mentioned
(Pip's on standby to put your PowerPoint presentation
together), well, I was rooting around in the kitchen when
I heard a noise upstairs—one of the cats, I thought—so
I went upstairs and opened the bedroom door and saw a
bare back with a butterfly tattoo, anyway, you probably
know the somatics better than me ... I turned and ran out
of the room, blurting out "Sorry, sir!"

I think—I hope—this salvaged the situation. I'd suddenly
found myself in that scene in Truffaut's *Stolen Kisses*
(which you lent me two years ago, remember?!) where
Delphine Seyrig explains to her younger lover the difference between politeness and tact. Suppose you walk into
a bathroom to find a naked woman in the shower. If you
quickly shut the door saying *"Pardon, Madame!"* that's
politeness. But if you shut the door saying *"Pardon Monsieur!"* that's tact. It's only in the latter case, by implying
you didn't see anything—not even the sex of the person
in the shower—that you display true tact.

However you look at it, it's embarrassing, but I hope it
won't cause any awkwardness between me and the lady

(and by extension you!), as long as we trust in the paradox
of the public space: everyone can be aware of an unpleas-
ant fact, as long as no one actually comes out with it.

That *had* been true tact, in fact: the tattoo on her back
hadn't been of a butterfly but of a dolphin, and it confirmed
the best-kept secret in academe, that Brik did indeed have
a love life. If my eyes hadn't deceived me, the lady in question worked in the French department. How trite. Two
days later Pip and I were sitting in the sun in front of my
office when she walked past, ostentatiously ignoring us.
Okay, be like that.

Great ass, actually.

That evening I strolled off the campus, past the auditorium, the library, and the administration building.
All built in a Federalist, symmetrical style and doubly reflected in the pond at the center of the manicured lawn the
college liked to call the Quad. Then came the dormitories,
arranged around two or three courtyards, which some
foresighted architect had designed in reinforced concrete
to muffle loud music and student screeching.

Pippa had moved to the little town that was associated
with our university, but which in reality lay two miles away,
one and a half if you took a shortcut through the woods
and crossed the footbridge over the river. It had been in

these very woods, in December 1776, that the revolutionary forces had first routed the British invading army, commanded by Cornwallis. Walkers and amateur historians still found musket balls and knife blades here. A place of ancient trees, big game, too, though you never saw any. I was surprised at how dark it already was—winter was approaching. Too cold for my loafers. I stuck my hands in my pockets and hurried on.

Pippa opened the door silently in her pajamas; she had her glasses on and her strawberry blonde hair was tied up in a bun. I threw my arms around her and picked her up. She smelled of herself, the sweet aroma of licorice and banana-flavored candy, which I always noticed when I was doing the laundry or randomly going through her stuff. She took off her glasses, put them on the dresser and rubbed her eyes, puffy with reading, then hugged me again, a long hug that turned into a kiss on my cheek. I kissed her neck, which—to my surprise—she offered to me by tilting back her head. I kissed her face, right on the spot where her hairline formed a peak on her forehead, like a little heart. She led me into her bedroom and, sitting on the edge of her bed, slipped off her pajama bottoms and panties in a single movement and I crouched down and searched with my mouth and tongue for the kernel of her smell.

I hadn't intended to spend the night there, but afterward I lay too long in our familiar, languid warmth to get up. She brushed her teeth (as she always did afterward) and then crept back into bed, pressing against me, her white buttocks cool and judgmental.

– Will you tell him?

– Shall we tell him together?

– Together, she said.

I pressed my mouth very softly and self-consciously against the delta of laugh lines around her eyes, framing a kiss, as if I were miming. The soft light in the room made her eyes look darker than they really were.

The rest of the week I thought about Hitler in Chile, reasonably convinced that this time I'd refuse Brik's request. It was the kind of resolve I formulated with some regularity—I, not he, was the editor in chief of *The Sleepwalker*, hierarchy, stand your ground, etc. Of course, I owed him. He'd brought me to the States, he'd recommended me to the faculty board as *The Sleepwalker*'s new editor in chief—and thus effectively appointed me—it was thanks to him I'd got an apartment in the middle of the campus, rent free, and the contents of his Rolodex filled our columns five times a year. I exchanged emails with Daniel Mendelsohn, Bernard-Henri Lévy, and Jonathan Littell. One Sunday morning I'd answered the phone to find Steven Soderbergh on the other end of the line, wanting to consult Brik about a possible biopic (Von Stauffenberg). Don't do it, Brik said. Our subscriber base mushroomed from two thousand North American and European academics specializing in Hitler studies to almost ten thousand, fanning out into cultural studies and literary markets—and still Brik allowed me to reap the accolades, though, as everyone must have known, I was no more than a little wagon, hitched to the Josip Brik locomotive.

Then the weather changed suddenly, pale banks of cloud rolled down from the mountains like avalanches, piling up on top of one another, and to the surprise even of the locals, the first snow fell before October. It wouldn't settle, the weathermen said, but two days later it still covered the ground. I rang Brik to ask whether I should pick him up if it got worse. I was worried the provincial roads to his upstate farmhouse might get snowed up and the buses stop running. It might have been projection, but he seemed taciturn and remote, and I began to babble, trying to coax him into amenability. I made some remarks about the change in the weather that riled him at first—"You and your weather, what are you, a Victorian authoress?"—but I suggested just in time that extreme shifts like this could be due to climate change, and he took the bait:

– Oh, give me a break! Meteorological determinist! Did you know there was a mini–Ice Age in the Low Countries in the sixteenth century? Of course you did. You can't fit every little rain cloud into a climatological teleology!

He was spoiling for a fight, already looking forward to his debate with a professor from the London School of Economics, the author of a weekly column in one of the more conservative dailies.

– I just love British academics, Friso. Whatever you say to them, they always respond with "Oh really?" I'm going to tell him I did most of my research while I was locked up for child molesting. And he'll say: "Oh really?"

Three days later the weather changed once more—back to late summer temperatures that made the snow melt away. I didn't go to Chile. That Saturday I sat on a bench at the bus station with my jacket on my lap and my shirtsleeves rolled up. The other benches were mainly occupied by retirees, older men and women who were reading the paper or eating ice cream. Others just sat there, with their eyes shut, contentedly warming their bones in the sun. It reminded me of my father, how he'd sit waiting for me when I came back home on Friday afternoons on the long-distance bus. Wearing sunglasses, holding a newspaper. He always claimed he used my return as an excuse to leave work early, and only later did I wonder whether that was really true. I would nestle into the familiar stuffy smell of his car, while he held forth triumphantly about news stories, showing how clued in he was to current events, so much better informed than me, the modern son. He rubbed his knowledge of world affairs in my face, just as he talked endlessly about computers and internet stuff and made far too many references to popular culture. He was so keen to show me he was keeping abreast of the times. Parental pride works two ways.

Brik's bus turned into the station, and long before it got near I could see him waving at me through the tinted window, like a child coming home from a school trip. The bus disgorged a stream of mainly elderly people, then he appeared in the doorway, in a lightweight linen suit that already showed faint patches of sweat under the armpits.

– Friso!

He looked left, then right, and crossed the street toward me. There was something darkly humorous about his gait, the kind of walk taught at a school for butlers, erect back, deliberate steps, as if he wanted to demonstrate to a police officer that he was sober enough to walk in a straight line. He swapped his briefcase from his right to his left hand and extended his right hand toward me, unaware that his briefcase had banged against the bumper of a parked car. Its alarm went off instantly, just as Brik stepped onto the sidewalk—the shock caused his foot to slip, and he twirled around in a semicircle, like an ice skater, falling forward but landing on his behind. A single shoe, the left one, shot up skyward and was plucked out of the air by a passerby in an overdose of slapstick.

I leapt forward to help him up.

– What the heck are you playing at, sonny?

Brik burst out laughing. He drew looks from people sitting at sidewalk cafés. The slapstick moment reminded me of something a journalist had written about him in *De Groene Amsterdammer*:

> *You almost can't help resorting to the cliché of Brik as the absentminded professor and bracketing him with Timofey Pnin or Moses Herzog, "thoughts shooting all over the place." Or the comic-book character Professor*

*Barnabas, who's so lost in thought that he's constantly
at odds with the real world around him—slapstick
lurks around every corner.*

It's the kind of prose Brik would have corrected aloud for
my benefit: "'You almost can't help resorting to . . .' No, it's
the journalist who 'almost can't help resorting to,' it's the
journalist who reduces reality to a cardboard stereotype."

Or: "Those literary allusions might give the appearance of being well read, but don't they also suggest a lack
of originality?"

Those close to him knew his awkwardness was partly
an act. I'd seen him spend hours in the office, silently reading, writing emails, and having serene telephone conversations, then some overzealous colleague would come in and
he'd suddenly start stammering and knocking over piles of
paper. He had his defense mechanisms, he knew what he
was doing.

As we walked down the shopping street toward the little restaurant where Pippa was waiting for us, I saw our
reflections in the windows of the boutiques—in the bright
midday sun his suit took on the hue of a golden retriever,
and his little legs made him look like a gigantic vanilla ice
cream cone going past.

– What do you think of that one?

He had stopped in front of a mannequin in a shop window. Until recently he'd worn easy-iron shirts. Exasper-
ated to see him yet again in one of those faded, shapeless

affairs, Pippa had dragged him into a duty-free shop at the airport (I wasn't picking him up for once) and had bought four Brooks Brothers shirts for him. He was so delighted with them that he regularly tugged people by the sleeves of their jackets, wanting to know what make they were.

– Wouldn't that shirt go well with this jacket?

The jacket he was wearing was vanilla yellow; the shirt had vertical purple stripes.

– You mustn't be guided by candy wrappers when it comes to color combinations, I said.

Once again he burst out laughing.

(In a profile of Brik, a journalist from *The New Yorker*, a breathless, birdlike woman who must have been nearly eighty, referred to me by name:

> *During most of our talks in Brik's apartment at Cornell, Friso de Vos, tall, handsome, wickedly blond, patrols the offices downstairs like a one-man Praetorian guard, primus inter pares among Brik's academic entourage, always at the ready to supply coffee or tea, or any paper, article, or book Brik might require. "My private little Schutzstaffel," Brik says with a smile.*

End of quote. Her words. His words.)

Pip and I took him under our wing. He was a member of two think tanks, to say nothing of being a visiting lecturer at two universities (on two different continents), and in this Byzantine complexity of income flows and work permits he needed people who could just watch a soccer match with him (me) or make him a home-cooked meal (Pippa). In the past year he'd twice fallen asleep on our sofa, whereupon we'd spread a blanket over him and retired, to find him at breakfast the next morning relaxed and in high spirits.

That sense of a safe haven must have been there when he hugged Pippa in the restaurant and complimented her on her outfit. "Friso, I hope you won't mind my saying that your girlfriend always looks like one of those composed, elegant Frenchwomen you see passing by from a café on the Boulevard St. Germain. American women just wear layers: bra, chemise, blouse, cardigan, jacket. So concealing, so lacking in confidence. Pippa, on the other hand, has an unmistakably Gallic style. Trousers, blouse, *voilà*."

Our food arrived. After Brik had polished off his steak salad, he took Pippa's plate, shoveled three spoonfuls of cheese flakes over the remains of her risotto, and started scooping it up. Pippa looked at me, flashing a quick signal with her eyes. She seemed calm.

– There's something we have to tell you, I said.

– Yes, she said. Something important.

What would he have expected? What was the most logical: a wedding, a pregnancy? Brik looked up from his plate with the childish trust that nothing in the world could be amiss.

– We, Friso and I, have decided to split up.

– That's right, I said.

Pippa told him she'd already found a little place to live in town, and that the faculty would let me keep our campus apartment. "You won't lose either of us." I realized I was holding my breath. Brik had once been married, in some distant past. It didn't work out, no big deal. But I'd never told him of any domestic ups and downs, and wondered now if he felt I'd kept my life, or parts of it, hidden from him, and whether he felt slighted. He chewed a mouthful of food, perhaps too slowly, as if he was trying to gain time, swallowed, and looked at the tablecloth:

– And you're certain about this?

I looked at Pippa, and Pippa nodded in confirmation. And that was that. Brik mumbled something, yesh, yesh, yesh—he could say it like a spluttering engine struggling to start, his way of getting his brain into gear—and you could see him searching, as he always did, for an argument, for something we hadn't yet thought of, had overlooked.

– Is it because Friso has been traveling so much for our journal?

– Listen, Pippa said firmly, we don't want you to get the idea that this has anything at all to do with you. You couldn't have done anything.

– Really, I stressed, Hitler had nothing to do with it.

– And nothing *happened*, either, Pippa went on, as agreed. She was to rule out adultery for the obvious anti-feminist reason that on this subject you're more likely to believe the woman than the man.

We'd made pacts, Pip and me. We'd had good times and bad times, we'd fought and we'd been silent, and although the last few months we'd been obsessed by the throbbing of our individual hearts, and had examined all our feelings minutely and dissected words like biblical philologists, pouncing on perceived double meanings, we felt a joint responsibility. There were people here and in the Netherlands who had photos of us both on their walls, and wrote our names on envelopes containing birthday cards and New Year's greetings. The two of us had become part of the lives of friends and relatives, and it was now our duty—we felt—to inform them personally of our disintegration. That was, as we repeatedly said, the grown-up way to behave.

Yet I saw Brik sitting there and was overcome by a feeling of shame, of failure to keep a promise.

He nodded. I was almost relieved, until he looked up for the first time and I saw, against all my expectations, two tears well up in his big blue eyes, and in a voice that creaked like an old door he choked out a single, crucial, intelligent word:

– Why?

Why? Like a knife in the dark. Pippa was sitting nearest to him and put her hand on his shoulder, apparently unsurprised, and explained it all to him, the various points at which we found ourselves in our lives, and I listened with half an ear or not at all and watched Brik's face, which slowly lost its questioning expression, lost any expression, as if he was staring at a deep emptiness, and I had forgotten why.

From: Fr.Devos@cornell.edu
To: J.L.Brik@cornell.edu
Date: September 16
Subject: Chile!

Dear Brik,

I hope we didn't shock you too much last Friday. And I trust you're not offended I didn't tell you about my/our situation earlier. Anyway, I saw you speak that evening in the auditorium, and a feeling slowly welled up in me, pleasant and familiar, like when your appetite comes back after a long illness: Chile! Of course I must go to Chile, change of scene, I can be of more use there, etc. Are you still okay with me going?

In one of his first BBC documentaries about the war in films, there's a great shot of Brik. He's in a little boat on a Swiss lake, just him, bobbing up and down against a backdrop of friendly, snow-capped peaks, a gentle breeze ruffling the remains of his sandy-gray hair, and you can see he's trying to look amiable and peaceful. He's trying to keep his face calm, trying to smile passively. But the

corners of his mouth are twitching and you can see something behind his eyes, a machine that's running. He remains Brik. The camera is filming from a great distance.
His hawklike nose, his broad, firm jaw. His face looks
like something you could lash to your bumper and plow
through snow with.

This is what happened:
Moments after arriving in Chile I slipped on the
aircraft steps, and although my fall was broken by various
items of hand luggage and the elderly couple in front of me,
I still hit the tarmac with considerable force. I mostly felt
embarrassed. A stewardess hurried over and took me to a
first-aid post at the terminal, where a young doctor cleaned
and bandaged the graze on my upper arm. Sorted. A mere
ten minutes later I was in a taxi.

Three days afterward I woke up much earlier than
usual, feeling feverish. The graze was fiery red and tingled
icily when I touched it. The faculty secretariat gave me
the name of a doctor who could see me that afternoon. I
waited for three quarters of an hour in an otherwise empty
waiting room before my name was called. The doctor, an
older man with a bow tie, shrugged his shoulders when
he saw my arm. "It happens sometimes," he said, and sent
me away again with a strip of acetaminophen tablets. I
felt shortchanged but relieved. That evening I rang Hitler
Lima junior to arrange a lunch date, but he invited me to

come for a drink in his local bar that same evening. Its walls were painted green and yellow, there were woven baskets with tortilla chips on the counter, and the guitar music on the radio drowned out the sound of the television. It was exactly how I'd pictured Chile.

We sat down under an enormous painting of a purple horse that was being watched from a distance by blue Indians—not Incas, but North American Indians, as in cowboys and Indians. There was a low, persistent humming noise; it sounded like air-conditioning, but it was hot and all the doors and windows were open. Hitler junior told me the painting had been donated by an artist friend of his who often came here, like many other émigré members of the urban intelligentsia. He pointed out the people at the bar: she was a journalist, he was a lawyer, that person was a writer, the other a former actor, that man was a university lecturer, that woman taught singing at the music academy. The renowned Chilean poet López Truijla had been a regular here, too, he told me, but he'd hanged himself the week before, from a fig tree in his neighbor's garden. The news had raced through that little world like an escaped predator.

I asked if there was anything specifically unhappy about Truijla's circumstances, but Hitler shook his head. Nothing special, he'd just been washed away by life.

He talked a little about the artists who'd influenced him and the things that inspired him, and asked me who my favorite artist was. As a Dutchman, I must surely love

Rembrandt's warm luminosity or the celestial serenity of Vermeer? I thought about it and said that I liked Vermeer, not for his serenity, but because his paintings always resembled a backdrop from which something had just been removed. I said that, leaving nationality aside, I'd always been a great fan of Damien Hirst.

– But tell me: Is that art? Or is it art about art?

He told me more. He was divorced, had a little daughter whom he was allowed to see once every two weeks. His ex had cheated on him, with someone she'd met online—and now *he* wasn't allowed to see his little girl! And his ex was living in the house that *he'd* bought, with the new guy! A telemarketer! He told it all with infectious good humor and no shame whatsoever. He said he'd met Josip Brik and was "deeply, deeply" impressed by him. The one time he stopped talking, his face seemed to retreat: instead of giving it volume, his beard accentuated his hollow eye sockets, his bony cheeks. From a distance he looked like the corpse of Che Guevara. I told him I'd already rung up a few Chilean Hitlers. We arranged that I'd visit him in his studio later that week, so I could see his paintings, and when I stood up it was as if my head was three times heavier than the rest of my body and I fell forward like a complete idiot, sprawling across the table, crushing beer bottles, tortillas, and table legs on my way to the dusty floor. Hitler and the lawyer (or was it the former actor?) helped me up. I said I'd gotten up too quickly, the beer hadn't agreed with me, tired, jet lag, etc., but nevertheless,

Hitler placed a concerned hand under my arm and led me to a taxi, instructing the driver to take me back to my lodgings.

The apartment was on the edge of the campus, in the east of the city, and I had to share it with a Frenchman of about my age, whose only visible presence in the first few days consisted of an atomizer on the kitchen table. He used it to blow marijuana into a plastic bag, so that he could smoke without really smoking. Jean-Philippe scarcely if ever left his attic room, and his PhD thesis was, guess what, "Hitlerian Revenge Plays," based on a grand total of two one-acters by obscure playwrights that Brik had put him on to. He'd drawn a little face on the plastic bag or balloon with permanent marker. When the bag was inflated it smiled cheerily, but when it was empty it turned shrunken and geriatric.

The apartment was small, and I'd told Pip in an email that it was cozy, but it was too cozy, too small. My bed was only two yards from the toilet, whose cistern dripped audibly all night long like a small child with a perpetually runny nose. In the days that followed I hardly got out of my damp bed, even to draw the curtains or open the window a crack. The first night I had a feverish dream in which a procession of large geometrical shapes advanced on me relentlessly, which I had to push away one by one, as if in some living game of Tetris. During another dream I wet the bed, like a moron, and when I woke up I lay there for a few hours, miserably stewing, before I could summon the energy to get up. I listened to the dripping of the toilet for hours, focusing on it to the exclusion of all else. My heart rate suddenly shot up to 120, 130 beats a minute, though I lay as quiet as a mouse in bed, like someone in hiding, as if my heart had rejected the rhythm indicated by my body, suggesting it wasn't my body.

The second day I dragged myself to the sofa and spent hours staring vacantly into the distance. I was aware of my delirium and became obsessed with the idea that I had to play along, to take on the role of the sick, delirious patient losing his grip on reality, and I began to intone softly: Where am I, who am I, where am I, who am I—two questions whose answers I knew—Chile and Friso—but that I couldn't stop asking, because there was something addictive and mesmerizing in that thumping repetition of where am I, who am I. I was alone.

On the third day Jean-Philippe came to see me. I'd stuck a Post-it on the door of the fridge, asking whether he had any antibiotics, but he'd been unable to read my writing, the squashed handwriting of a child, with letters flattened like empty Coke cans. The Frenchman got me a glass of iced water. "Are you going to be all right?" he asked, and I answered that I had to be, because on Thursday I had a date with Hitler, the one and only, and Jean-Philippe knelt down next to me and felt my forehead. He appeared to be transparent. That's how it seemed to me, so close up. I thought I could see right through him.

– But it's already Saturday, he said.

In the hospital I hoped to be stripped of my identity, and to exist at most as a medical case or a patient number, relieved of reason or independent will. My doctor was a Susan Sontag–ish woman with a mild, pained face. A long, melodious "Ayeee" escaped her lips when she saw the red irritation around the graze, which now covered an area two or three times the size of the wound. In the wound itself you could see deep purple spots. There seemed to be an egg under my skin, level with my elbow. She asked me questions and told me I had all the time in the world to answer, and I wanted to answer in proper sentences, God knows why—to prove that I was educated, that I was linguistically competent, or that illness just wasn't my thing?—but a jumble of words emerged from my mouth before I realized I was just jabbering away. I knew I was jabbering and yet I couldn't stop, and Susan Sontag looked at me kindly, *illness as metaphor*, and I was too exhausted to go on talking. She wanted to know where I came from and what my date of birth was, and I knew these were easy questions, but I had to grab my passport out of her hands and take a sneaky look before I could answer them.

– I'm here to see Hitler, I said.

Procedures, tests, and diagnoses followed. I was too sick to be repatriated, a doctor told me. My next of kin would have to be notified; the embassy was being informed. Another doctor told me I'd be given a course of intravenous treatment that sounded exactly like chemotherapy. Susan Sontag said that if I wanted, I could have a skin transplant later to camouflage the scar tissue of the wound. Everyone confirmed that this was a very rare infection. Extremely rare. I nodded, yes, yes, yes, and was grateful and scared to death because I had no idea exactly how scared I should be. I do remember someone from the Dutch embassy coming to check on me, a youth with prematurely gray hair and round spectacles. He told me my emergency contact person had been informed of the situation and that the embassy had arranged a flight for her, paid in advance. Everything was going to be fine, he assured me. There was one thing I should know, he said, and he added that he'd hesitated to tell me this, but felt it would be wrong to hide it from me: Josip Brik was dead. He'd fallen out of a window in Amsterdam. The circumstances were still being investigated. To establish whether or not it was an accident. It had been in all the papers.

That evening, the blitzkrieg between my white blood cells and the infection escalated, my temperature soared even higher, and during a long period of delirium I couldn't remember Pippa or Brik, only the boy from the embassy, and I couldn't recall whether he'd told me that I'd died or someone else had, because everything had fused in my head.

I got through the weeks that followed, though looking back, I can't think how. Most of my hair fell out, to the extent that a nurse finally shaved my whole skull with clippers, to be rid of the tufts drifting everywhere. Every day I had to drink four to five liters of water, with a salt tablet in every glass. I had to sweat out the infection, I was told. I stopped asking what would happen now, and what would happen next, and what would happen after that. I lost eighteen pounds. I remember looking up and seeing Pippa's dear, familiar, shocked face in the doorway, and she walked toward me slowly and sat down on the bed and we both cried uncontrollably.

I tried to remember when I'd last seen Brik. It was just before I left for the airport, and he'd stuffed a wad of Chilean pesos into my hands. *"Hasta la victoria siempre, Friso!"* He'd stood there for a little while, as my taxi drove away, and made a little waving movement, as if he were gesturing to a waiter for the bill.

ONE

THE FIRST WORLD

ONE

The day after Obama's reelection someone from the Onondaga county sheriff's office rang to say there'd been a break-in at Brik's place. The back door had been forced and there were tire tracks in the garden. Not much had been stolen, apparently, little more than the television and some DVD equipment. The Lincoln stood untouched in the garage. Probably kids, the officer said. No serious intentions, he added, and I wondered what he meant by that. A neighbor had heard boisterous yells from a passing pickup truck and seen lights on in the house, which he knew to be unoccupied.

– If you could come by, the officer asked, without really asking, we can draw up a list of stolen items.

He'd rung early in the morning. It was still dark outside, but I'd been lying awake for some time, as if I'd been expecting the call. My voice was primed and clear, and I surprised myself by jumping out of bed without a moment's hesitation and throwing on my clothes. Three minutes later I was driving Pippa's Prius down the deserted provincial road that meandered through whispering forest for exactly a hundred miles, door to door.

A colossal man in a hat was leaning against a green police car on Brik's driveway, his hands wrapped around a mug. When I got out he didn't greet me, or if he did, it must have been with such a minuscule nod as to be imperceptible to the naked eye. Much of his face was hidden behind the fur collar of his uniform. Only when I got up close could I see that he was younger than me, perhaps twenty-five, with a smooth face whose only notable feature was a monumental chin, an American chin, the kind that could serve as a bridge between two tectonic plates. His bumper sticker read: SMITH & WESSON IS MY PRESIDENT.

– Good morning, I said, emphatically.

– Nice Prius, he said.

– Nice election result, I said.

He didn't smile. By now I'd gotten his number. This was the type of guy Brik had often talked about: the townie, the local, the provincial who didn't really try to hide his view that New Yorkers should stay in New York and that all those university folks shouldn't stray too far off campus. Conversations fell silent when Brik entered the local supermarket. Everyone was friendly and polite to him, his bacon and eggs were promptly served in the local café—Mickey's or Marcy's or Marshall's—but he could see them looking at him out of the corners of their eyes. Once, as he was leaving the café and had halted briefly in the doorway to straighten his jacket, he overheard a regular say to the others: 'Those lard-assed professors, huh? All they care about is getting their cock sucked by nineteen-year-olds. No way am I sending my daughter to a school like that."

Sure, that'll be the real reason your daughter won't be going to an elite university, but opting for a career as what? Shelf-stacker? Garage receptionist? Yeah, right, bro, that'll be it. But Brik didn't share my cynicism at all. He enjoyed his overhear. "All they care about is getting their cock sucked by nineteen-year-olds." It was a snippet of un-polished, pure Americana, you never heard them talk like that when you were in their midst. He loved this country.

– Do you mind if I go inside? I asked (I hadn't dressed for the cold). Or does a team still have to take fingerprints?

– This isn't *CSI*.

– So no fingerprint team?

– Just paperwork, a lot of paperwork. I've got a big stack of forms for you.

– What's the damage?

– The TV's gone, probably the stereo and DVD player too. There's some torn-up books lying around. Geez, there's books everywhere in that house.

Just the way he said the word "books" spoke volumes.

– Are those forms for the insurance company or the forensic specialists?

– The "forensic specialists," huh? Yeah, I'm sure they'd love to get these forms. I'm guessing you're not from around here, right?

For a moment I considered saying Germany, rather than the Netherlands. Germany is something Americans can handle: strong industry, disciplined people. But I said the Netherlands, adding that I was from Amsterdam.

– You don't say. *Am-ster-dam*. Again, it was the way he said it.

– Have you ever been abroad?

– I was in the army.

– No kidding? Were you in 'Nam?

Without saying another word he got into his patrol car, flung his coffee through the window into the flower bed, and hit the gas. He drove off without giving me any forms, and I stood there laughing, went on laughing for as long as I must have been visible in the rearview mirror, even though I didn't exactly know what my victory consisted of.

Brik's house was a Victorian pile à la Norman Bates, on a few hundred acres of land. The first thing he did after buying it was to have a covered swimming pool installed. The neighbors had protested before the contractor could even put a spade in the ground, scared that their rural view, especially at night, would be spoiled by a glass light box. This wasn't the America of pools in the backyard, this was the America where Indians had lived, where the seasons still really meant something, where nature still ruled. Here there were foxes, deer, badgers; here you still saw wolves and bears. Who do you think you are?

When the contractor had finished, all that could be seen was a slight incline in the lawn. Brik invited his nearest neighbors, who lived a good hundred yards away, to come and have a look. Only the sloping roof poked out above ground level, but turf had been laid over it. The pool itself, a darker blue than normal, could only be seen from the rear, right up against the edge of Brik's land, where the ground had been excavated. From the adjacent woods you looked straight into the ten-foot-high glass front. Brik swore to his neighbors, and later to me, that as he lay bobbing about in the water, a stag as big as a rhino had plodded straight past the glass, stopped and looked in—looked him right in the eye—and then darted back into the woods. Whether his neighbors believed him or not, they stopped complaining.

– You should have heard them: wolves, bears, badgers... yesh. They made it sound like the list of animals hunted to extinction in that gallery in the Museum of Natural History.

The front door clicked open promptly when I turned my key in the lock—had I not expected it to? Perhaps. It didn't feel 100 percent kosher being here alone. I felt a weird adrenaline rush I perhaps hadn't experienced since I sneaked up the creaking attic staircase as a ten-year-old to play with my father's model trains, a collection worth a small fortune, Forbidden Territory without parental supervision. The same exquisite tension as when I turned the switch that set the trains going, with their nostalgic chuff-chuffing sound, as if I were switching on my own electric chair—at any moment my father might catch me at it, just as now at any moment Brik would surely pop out of the broom closet, grinning broadly in his denim suit. "Ha! Gotcha! April fools!" There was a glimmer of the childish incomprehension of death that I'd felt when my first grandparent died. She was in the coffin, but surely she wasn't *really* in the coffin? I couldn't help tiptoeing through the house, along the hall, past the kitchen to the living room, which indeed looked like the Sack of Jerusalem: every piece of equipment had been torn out of the wall, here and there cables dangled uselessly from sockets, like infusions next to a vacated hospital bed. There were muddy footprints on the sofa. Any investigator worth their salt could easily build a case. (Exhibit A: footprint, size 44. Next, find out how many neighborhood kids had pickup trucks. Then simply wait until Brik's ten-thousand-dollar state-of-the-art flat screen 3-D TV turned up at one of the local pawn shops.) But hey, let's not expect too much! "This isn't *CSI*." Wait for the insurance. What would I know about police investigations, I wasn't "from around here."

He had an L-shaped sofa that a family of six could have lounged on, ordered from the only furniture store in the area. A local carpenter had been hired to construct custom-made bookcases for his library. He had a regular order with the local florist, who once a week delivered two bunches of fresh flowers that sat around wilting for the next twenty-five weeks or so, while Brik was off abroad somewhere for TV recordings or lectures. Once a week a neighbor's boy mowed the lawn for a princely twenty dollars an hour. All that goodwill he'd cultivated! All those ties with the community! What good had it done him?

The marks on the sofa were easily removed, the lamps put upright again. I got the curtain back on the rails in a jiffy, and the vase that had been knocked over wasn't even broken. The two antique topographical maps, of the Hudson (c. 1800) and the state of New York (c. 1850), still hung in neat symmetry on the wall, untouched. It was the living room of a successful man, someone with top-quality furnishings, who took his decorations, his comfort, and his TV watching seriously. It was enough to drive you crazy, if you thought about it. Why did he need this? All these things? The drawer with all those remote controls? The ten-speaker Dolby Surround sound system? What family of six would ever flop down on his couch? Brik never entertained, preferred to watch movies on his laptop, with a headset. Fast-forwarded through half the film because he was impatient. What was he trying to prove to himself, with this set piece of a room? That for him, too, simple happiness could lie in a sofa, a TV, and a bowl of nacho chips? So naive. The idea that this was enough. For someone like him.

I walked cautiously to the study, much bigger than the front room, and a much bigger mess. It was as if they'd had a snowball fight with books. Volumes lay everywhere, pages torn loose, dust covers stained. One bookcase was leaning away from the wall, as if they'd swung from it. The frame of the *Great Dictator* poster lay shattered on the floor. And yet at the same time I felt something like relief. This was no longer *his* place; strange hands had touched it, making his presence more remote. So coming back here became more impersonal, less Brik-ish, and thus less burdensome, easier.

I thought. I maintained. I told myself.

Brik's two salt-and-pepper schnauzers were no longer there—Dean Chilton was looking after them. Pippa had picked up all the desktop computers, laptops, and other data storage devices and put them away safely in the office of *The Sleepwalker*. This, too, went through my mind: I would clear up everything here, I would arrange books, I would label all his possessions, I would read all his unfinished, unpublished texts and I would map his legacy. Me. My task. When I got back from Chile I found a sheet of watermarked writing paper waiting for me, signed not by Mr. but by Mrs. Chilton, who looked forward to talking to me, to "resolving a few issues regarding Brik's estate." I was curious about her. She had been a professor in some economic discipline, later getting a job in that rarefied world where finance meets law, the kind of job that sounds like a series of abstract concepts, so you haven't the foggiest what it actually entails. During the financial crisis of 2008 the Senate had forced her out of office. Worth about eighty million, she received me on her roof terrace with a cool handshake. A helmet of blow-dried hair. Serious mouth. Age impossible to guess. Her breasts seemed to be positioned too high up her body, as if a child had put on its mother's bra, filled with tennis balls. Friso, *so* nice to meet you.

– I love this place, this university. The students are like... like furniture that changes every season, while the trees, the old buildings, the staff, stay the same, year after year. Untouched by the hand of time, don't you think?

– A rarity, I said.

She stared at me, openly sizing me up. I tried to match the stare, to sum her up in return, but I was thinking of myself, not of her. My thin rib cage, my sunken cheeks. She laid her hand on my face as if it were the most natural thing in the world, and stroked my temple with her thumb.

– I saw your photo in the new *Sleepwalker.* A young Edward Fox.

– Perfect, I said, as I slowly broadened my smile. Just how I always see myself.

– You may call me Liddie. I see you sitting there, sometimes. Your office is in one of the nicest spots of the campus. Always with the blinds half shut. In the dark. Like a little spy.

– History is made by men in little rooms.

– You're a sort of *Portable Josip Brik*, aren't you? *The Quotable Brik?*

– You give me too much credit.

– What a pity you couldn't be at the funeral or the memorial services.

– What's it like to be a celebrity? I asked quickly. Brik was a celebrity, in his way, to his circle of colleagues and readers. You're famous among subscribers to *The New York Times*.

She drew on her cigarette.

– Sometimes I'm standing in the kitchen, frying an egg or pouring myself a glass of orange juice, and I see my hands moving, my body obeying impulses from my cortex. And then I think: yes, I'm famous, even now, when there's nobody else there.

– It was always nice to see how close Brik and your husband were. Surprising, really, since their temperaments seem so...

– ...dissimilar? I ran into Brik, once, about five years ago, in a hotel lobby in Chicago. I wasn't alone. It was useless to deny anything. My first husband worked in advertising. An Adonis. I hadn't intended to look him up, I was in town for other reasons, but suddenly there we were in my hotel room. You feel a loyalty, a kind of patriotism toward your past. You want to go on feeling that link, to those people, those things, those places.

– That feeling only grows stronger, I said.

– I've always been very discreet about my affairs, very careful. More careful than I was with my marriages, at least the first two. Have you ever smashed up a really expensive car? I really can't explain it.

– And Brik?

– Afterward I had a drink with him at the bar. He had a faint twinkle in his eye. My fault really; by going on the defensive I played into his hands. I told him it meant nothing, that he shouldn't tell anybody, that it had been a brief moment of madness. He sat there grinning, and instead of falling discreetly silent, he started to ask me questions. About what we'd done. Physical acts. How it had been. Had I had an orgasm? I was dumbfounded that he should ask. I sat there blushing like a teenage girl, scared witless— the sweat ran down my back. And then suddenly I nerved myself and told him. I certainly hadn't intended to. But I told him all about it, in detail, and he enjoyed it. And I got it: If you share a secret, share it properly, stretch it out, deepen it. It made us both laugh, we were in fits. It's always been our secret, something the two of us shared. As if I'd had that affair with him.

– A shared secret is the best secret.

– It was as if we had our own world, a second world known only to us.

– And your ex-husband.

– He died soon afterward.

– Natural causes? I asked. She laughed.

– They never found his body.

This, too, went through my head as I wandered round Brik's burgled home. The feeling that I might stumble across a body among the chaos—eyes rolled back, blood spatters on the wall like an Expressionist painting—but the guest room at the back of the house was spic-and-span. I couldn't help it, I watched too many movies. In the past, a whole league of mothers, aunts, girlfriends, confidential advisers, mentors, and tennis coaches had pointed out my talent for exaggeration. I sat down at the foot of the bed and had a sudden vision of two big, stiff arms shooting up out of the sheets, like zombies rising out of their graves. "Got you, Friso!" His roaring, echoing laugh. I looked at my watch—time to call Mrs. Chilton. As I listened to the ringing tone, I noticed some stains on my shirt, and while I tried to work out what they were—grease spots?—I saw they were getting bigger. Even then it took a moment before I realized it was me, sweating right through my T-shirt and shirt. My forehead was dripping with sweat.

Liddie Chilton didn't bother with preliminaries.

– What's it like there?

– Okay. A mess, but okay. Could be worse. Lots of books strewn around, lot of papers. Some electronic equipment's been stolen.

– Do you get the feeling that anything specific was taken?

– Anything specific?

– Were they looking for something? You said there were a lot of papers strewn about.

– I don't think so. They were just kids in a destructive mood.

– Is the damage serious?

– Not as far as I can tell. It's more ... pointless vandalism. Trashing someone's things while they're away. Who gets a kick out of that? You know who could write a very good four-thousand-word essay on the subject?

– Josip Brik, we chorused.

She laughed, went quiet for a moment, and then asked, in a different, softer tone than I'd expected: And how are you doing, Friso?

– I have to clear up here. That's the least I can do. Just tidy it all up, as he would have wanted.

I held the receiver away from my ear and allowed my head to drop. From a distance I could hear her voice saying:

– Don't stay there too long. You sound terrible.

– In a minute, I said, as I coughed away a sudden obstruction in my throat.

– And check your mail. I've forwarded you a nice little freebie.

I found the following email in my inbox:

From: ldmhchilton@usaonline.com

To: Fr.Devos@cornell.edu

Date: November 7

Subject: FW: participation in End of History conference

Dear Mrs. Chilton,

Firstly, may I once again offer you my sincere condolences. The news of Josip Brik's death came as a shock. He was an inspiring man. We spoke every year at our

End of History conference, and I will certainly miss him. I wish you strength at this difficult time.

It was good to talk to you briefly at the memorial service in New York, where there were some interesting speakers, not least Philip de Vries, a student of Brik's, with an original take on his vision of history and Hitler studies. We are of course considering how we can honor Brik at our conference in Vienna from December 3 to 11. We're thinking of having a panel discussion, pitting your Friso de Vos, editor in chief of *The Sleepwalker*, against Mr. De Vries—does this strike you as a good idea? Or do you consider them unequal luminaries? If you approve, perhaps you could send me Mr. De Vos's current email address (I get an out-of-office reply whenever I try the *Sleepwalker* address), so I can put him in touch with our administration and finance department to discuss travel costs, accommodation, et cetera.

I look forward to hearing from you,

Maria Karsch, M.A.

Call it intuition. A few days earlier I'd had an email from Felix Westerveld, an old friend with whom I sometimes worked; we'd met during my fleeting membership in a fraternity.

Hey old friend!

I thought you were in the hospital, at death's door, with
some super-rare infection racking that utterly vile body
of yours? The thing is, I saw that Indonesian visiting
professor, Patiradja something-or-other, today. He was
just back from New York and said that some guy called
"Frisian or something" had spoken at the Brik memorial
service there. Sounds like it was you? Well anyway. Hope
it went well. (What's up with Pippa?)

All the best!
Felix

The only person who'd been here since the break-in
had been Pippa, to secure some valuable items and look
through the mail. She'd sat at the kitchen table (I could
picture her exactly: frowning, back erect, legs locked in a
wrestling hold) and copied out the addresses of the send-
ers at the top of the letters in a pale blue felt tip, to make it
easier for me to archive them. Most cards were thoughtful
and short, she'd said, only the odd one ventured into an
anecdote. Usually they amounted to no more than a signature under a preprinted message. And why not? They
were addressed to the corpse itself. Who else could you
send them to, in the absence of a wife or children? Pippa

had read only one aloud to me over the phone, her voice unexpectedly breaking a little. It was from a well-known Australian art historian: "What a terrible fucking waste."

The kitchen. Everything was still in its place. They hadn't even come in here, by the look of it; they hadn't pillaged anything to dump on a booze-fueled bonfire. Two neat piles on the kitchen table, exactly as Pippa had left them: letters and papers. She'd also made a selection of newspaper sections with items on Brik's death. When I'd left that morning, she'd said: Don't forget to look at the papers.

That had been a signal, because Pippa wasn't the type to rub your nose in things. So I ignored the fresh crop of black-bordered cards and started going through the papers like a dog digging up a bone. Within a quarter of an hour I'd cut out fifteen items and laid them on the kitchen table. I took off my shirt, made coffee, took off my T-shirt too, put it on again, then installed myself in the rocking chair by the window with the papers on my lap. According to *The New York Times*, the unexpected highlight of Brik's public memorial service had been a speech by a Dutch researcher called Philip de Vries. "Among so many leading lights of the intelligentsia, the young De Vries perhaps succeeded best in capturing Brik's sharp but jovial tone, in recalling his observations—as playful as they were profound—and his general joie de vivre." The article described the mourners gathered in the public library on Fifth Avenue as a veritable Who's Who of philosophers, novelists, independent and Hollywood filmmakers, editors in chief of national and international publications; in short, an assembly of heavyweights that would long remain unparalleled.

At first glance the *New York Post* seemed to have no more than a small photo of an ivory-faced Anthony Hopkins and a fleshy Bruno Ganz at the lectern, with a caption stating that both actors had been interviewed by Brik in marathon sessions about their roles as Hitler (in *The Bunker* and *Downfall*, respectively). But buried inside was a column in which the author reminisced about his student days in Paris, when he and Brik were on an editorial board together, rounding off with a quote from—here we go—one Philip de Vries, who "had hit the mark superbly" when he summed up Brik in his speech as someone "with the energy of a wasp in an upturned lemonade glass."

The Wall Street Journal didn't mention this Philip de Vries once in its report, which was noticeably shorter and more superficial. The article featured a large black-and-white portrait photo of Brik, and a smaller one showing a few people standing together a little awkwardly, but with a giggly, conspiratorial air, like schoolchildren corralled together for a class photo. In its caption, the *Journal* identified them from left to right: "Walter Chilton, dean of Cornell University; his wife, Liddie Chilton; Orhan Pamuk, Nobel Prize winner; and Philip de Vries, a student of Josip Brik's."

In the photo De Vries was looking slightly away from the camera: he had a long nose that was perfectly eclipsed by his pronounced cheekbones and his big blue angel-of-death eyes. He was smiling absently, wore a knitted tie, and had a high 1950s forehead and ash-blond hair that stood up effortlessly, as if someone just out of view had directed a wind machine at him with great precision.

Why was he mentioned at all in the caption? His name didn't appear once in the article. I'd never heard of him. He'd certainly never written anything for *The Sleepwalker*. He didn't have a Facebook page (who doesn't have a Facebook page?), and a Google search only threw up two hits. One was the website of a fraternity, the other of *Blondie*, a journal of Hitler studies published by the Universities of Groningen and Leuven, for which he'd once written a short piece, a review that didn't even run to five hundred words, of a book that wasn't even relevant. "Unequal luminaries"? Who on earth knew the guy? Pippa had to clear this up. She'd been to the memorial service in New York, after all. What had he said?

– The usual.

– "The usual"?

– You know. That Brik was such a friendly, inspiring man, such an independent thinker.

– But what did he say *exactly*? *The New York Times* singled him out for a mention.

– It was one of those services full of platitudes, speeches that sound good, but if you copied them out, there'd be nothing of any substance. So no, I don't remember it all *verbatim, Friso.*

– Because it would never for a moment have occurred to you that I might just be a teeny bit interested in what was said there, *Pippa*?

– Be nice, Friso. Be nice.

Be nice. Maybe. The really shocking, really astonishing thing was the amount of mail waiting for me at home that had absolutely nothing to do with Brik. I had 269 emails. Freelancers were offering articles, subscribers were sending letters, staff were asking about fees, I was getting invitations to attend roundtable conferences, get involved in media partnerships, barters and giveaway campaigns, speak at congresses in flyover states. A Swiss PhD student fondly imagined he was the first to submit a close reading of *Inglourious Basterds*; a Canadian journalist proposed an article about the design and construction of the Führerbunker on a film set in Vancouver. For the umpteenth time, the agent of a well-known British TV historian was offering us a reportage on the primeval forest of Białowieża, where Hitler may or may not have once gone hunting with Hermann Göring.

– How did he come across to you?

– Who?

– Philip de Vries.

– Are we back on this subject?

– We're *still* on this subject.

– Sigh. What do you want to know?

– Whether he had a big dick is what I want to know. No, did he have charisma, was he tall, was he an amusing speaker, what did you think of him?

– Well, just, you know . . . ordinary.

– "Ordinary"? Jesus, Pip, "ordinary." Your vocabulary, it's dropping down on us like golden rain.

– *Just like my love, baby. Ooh.*

I left everything unanswered. The emails piled up. I lived between my hunched shoulders, those first few weeks. If I left the house I kept my eyes obsessively on my feet, to avoid as many stimuli as possible. I couldn't process them, campus life forced itself on me like an internet page spewing out pop-ups faster than you could click them away, get laid now!, enlarge your member! My shorn hair grew back, but only slowly, and more sparsely, I thought, than before. Standing in front of the mirror, I studied the areas where it suddenly seemed to be receding, and marked my hairline with a black ballpoint to see if it would grow back in the future. Even when I wasn't thinking about Brik I had a hollow feeling just below my diaphragm, as if I were constantly sucking in my stomach. *When he is sick, every man wants his mother; if she's not around, other women must do.* Pip drew the short straw, dear Pip, who'd temporarily moved back into our old apartment to look after me. She cooked, did the laundry, rang my mother, and when I jerked awake at night covered in sweat—hot flashes were among the predicted aftereffects of my infection—she would be lying next to me, snoring softly, her belly as hot as an oven. I always made sure that I woke her up when I got out of bed and slunk off accusingly to the sofa.

I should have clung on to it longer, this lying on the sofa, this living in bathrobes, this eating like a small child, this zapping endlessly from cartoons to music videos—but my body had had enough, my body wanted to go back to normal and sent me, bouncing with nervous energy, back into the world, where all I could do was contemplate Brik and, like today, leaf through the newspapers.

Who the hell had ever heard of Philip de Vries? I rang Pippa again.

– So how are you doing? Pip asked as soon as she picked up the phone. Have you eaten anything? You know what the doctor...

– It's okay. I'm clearing up here. I'll go and get something to eat in a minute.

– But how do you *feel*?

I decided to interpret the verb "feel" in a physical sense.

– You let me go out too thinly dressed.

– I was still half asleep when you left.

– You were totally asleep when I left.

– And now you're too cold?

– I'm cold.

– Your clothes aren't too thin, Friso. You're too thin.

Many of the articles were the same brief, standard AP report, along with cut-and-paste profiles by cultural editors, practically identical to his Wikipedia page—a page I'd edited more times than I could remember. I came across three other references to Philip de Vries: He was briefly quoted in *The Harvard Crimson* ("That was how his brain worked: while he was giving a speech he could think of a hundred other things, solve puzzles"). A "Talk of the Town" piece in *The New Yorker* merely mentioned his name, but he was referred to in a brief web article in *The Atlantic* ("the promising young Dutch publicist") as proof that Brik had influenced a score of young "up-and-coming" thinkers.

Rarely had anyone merited a comeuppance more than this Philip de Vries, I concluded, and I felt that Pippa should agree with me:

– Sounds like you need a little de-escalation.

– Perhaps.

– *Vosje*, sweetie pie, listen: Who did they call after the break-in? Did they call Philip de Vries? Phil de Vries? Chilly-Philly to his friends? Who did the sheriff call? That's right. Not Philip. But Friso.

This, from Pippa, a walking mass of self-restraint, whose extremes were always veiled in diplomatic ambivalence, who wanted nothing better than to be on good terms with everyone in the world. Pippa the Rose-Colored. Pippa the Long-Suffering. She was such a funny little nonverbal creature. I rarely failed to exploit the way she always halted in mid-speech, giving me the chance to finish her sentences for her—or, our running gag, to finish them by saying precisely the opposite of what she wanted to say. I was a kind of horse whisperer, I sometimes thought, only with Pip. Pippadippapipsqueak. Only rarely did she say what she was really thinking, but whenever she did, like now, it calmed me.

The evening after she'd cleared up Brik's house, when she was showering after having gone for a run, I'd stepped into the cubicle with her and she seemed to understand straightaway, without raising an eyebrow, that her role as nurse had changed into something else.

I now saw that in my heated state I'd Googled his name wrong, PHILPI DE VIRES. I entered the new search term, got 5,720,000 hits (0.9 seconds), and felt a numbing sensation when I scrolled down and saw the video links. I immediately recognized the host, the red backdrop, the illuminated globe around which the name of the TV show revolved like a satellite.

– Friso, are you still there?

– I have to hang up.

I just clicked on it right away, so I wouldn't first sit brooding about what Philip de Vries was doing there, though of course I knew immediately, instantly, in a heart-beat, just as I knew it should have been me sitting there. The show had been broadcast the Monday after Brik's death. There he sat at the oval table, to the right of the host. Hands folded, he waited obediently, like a trained Labrador, for his turn to speak.

Philip de Vries, you're a student of Brik's. You had a lot of personal contact with him. How did you learn of his death?

I'd picked him up from Schiphol airport the previous day. He was going to give two lectures, one in The Hague

61

and one in Groningen. I drove him to his hotel in Amsterdam. The next morning, at exactly half past eight, the hotel manager called me. "I'm really sorry. I don't know how to break this to you, but yesterday evening Mr. Brik had a very bad fall here at the hotel, and he died on the spot..." I felt as if I'd been hit by a thunderbolt.

Can you just tell us very briefly what kind of philosopher Josip Brik was?

A very...rebellious one. Exactly the opposite of your classical, dusty philosopher. He was more interested in— say—Woody Allen, than in Schopenhauer or Wittgenstein. Human fantasy was the thing that preoccupied him—in art, in books, but especially in films. He believed that the workings of our fantasy provide the key to understanding our deepest drives.

Is that where his fascination with the war and war films came from?

Exactly. That's precisely my point: he thought that to understand what lessons had been learned from the war, you should focus on the role it played in our fantasy.

How did you get to know Brik?

When I was a student assistant at Groningen University, I once had to pick him up for a lecture. The organizers were worried he'd turn up late or forget where to go. He had such a terrible sense of direction: they could picture him going through the wrong door, then another, then another, and ending up in the gutter somewhere. (Laughter.) When I knocked on the door of his hotel room, he called out to come in, and there he lay, stretched out on the bed in his underpants, with books and newspapers spread out all around him. "How can I help you?" he asked cheerfully.

And was that typical of Brik?

Absolutely. He was the archetypical *zerstreute Professor*. You know, like Professor Barnabas in the *Spike and Suzy* comic book series. Too cerebral to be aware of what was going on around him.

"Cerebral," "zerstreute Professor"? You sound pretty intellectual yourself—an embryonic Brik, by the sound of it.

You flatter me.

What appealed to me most about him—because I was a huge fan, I should say, especially of his BBC documentaries, you know, about the war and films—was his presence. His way of speaking. His, how shall I put it, dramatic flair. He really made you hang on his every word.

That's very true! I'm sure lots of people can do a great Brik imitation. Of course, Brik was the best imitator of all. We can't rule out the possibility that Brik was an imitation of Brik. I relished his imitations: it was as if he was performing a play just for you. I always felt honored. The day before he died, I happened to mention Marlon Brando and he came out with *"I coulda been a contender,"* without missing a beat. My version doesn't compare to his, of course, but you get the idea.

Now we'll just play an extract from his documentary Gone with the Wife, *about Hollywood and...feminism...*

I pressed the mute button and watched the film clip without sound, as if this would make it all unsaid, as if it therefore didn't exist, was just a little two-actor sketch in a silent film. His hair fell perfectly; his forehead was smooth and flawless. Not a wrinkle, mole, or freckle to be seen. There was something odd about his face, though—its very symmetry made it look strangely vacant, as if the parts didn't add up to a sum. He was handsome, I think, if you went in for very boring men.

I stood up and walked to the conservatory at the back of the house. My T-shirt was drenched—I took it off and hung it over the back of a chair. And as I looked at the swimming pool, camouflaged like a bunker on the tranquil gray fringe of forest, and heard not a single sound in the background, something welled up in me, like someone who's just survived a train crash, or an earthquake, and surveys the destruction around them from a little way off, and only then realizes what a narrow escape they've had.

There was something weird about his mouth, too, I decided. A tautness. The tension of a person trying to show his hand isn't shaking. He was suppressing a smile, that was it, he was doing his best not to smile, because he was of course bursting with pride at being allowed to do his "embryonic Brik" act here with his boyish forelock and his little jacket, watched by his father and his mother and his little sister and his hockey team and the girl or two who'd perhaps once let him finger them at a class party, along with—according to the Dutch TV audience measurement service—1.2 million other viewers. Two days after Brik's death. And so modest. "You flatter me." So they rang him first. "I felt as if I'd been hit by a thunderbolt": the eloquence of a soccer player. Not that anyone would notice, because if "cerebral" and knowing the German for "absentminded professor"—which Brik in fact wasn't—are evidence of intellect, then you can't say much for the target group in question.

Can you just explain very briefly what kind of philosopher Josip Brik was? Why wasn't I sitting there? Brik had a grand total of one Woody Allen essay to his name, dating from perhaps 1981. He could have known that, if he'd read the bibliography section of Brik's Wikipedia entry—which I'd compiled in its entirety. Since then Brik had never written another word about Allen. And he wasn't preoccupied with human fantasy, but with human imagination. Those are two different things. In his view, films were about re-experiencing the past—that was where their immediacy lay—through the depiction of concrete events. Spielberg's D-Day landings or Spielberg's Schindler. *First there was the war, then the story about the war. The war was bad, but the story made the war even worse.* The difference between the war and the story was colored in by our imagination—with all the consequent blowups, blue and white tints, and concealments that reveal so much about us. That was what it was about, as far as he was concerned. Not about fantasy. Fantasy is Quidditch and the White Tower of Gondor and unicorns galloping under rainbows, and Brik wasn't interested in unicorns.

I went back to the kitchen, and this time clicked on a link that showed not just the clip I'd seen, but the whole program. Sadomasochist that I was, I wanted to watch it all. Starting with the introduction, in which the host introduced his guests with the upbeat delivery of a comedian, without a single joke ever passing his lips. Then the other items, so I could see Philip sitting in the background, laughing politely, self-consciously, aware of the cameras. I must call Pip, I thought, while the video was buffering. Why hadn't they called me? Who, after all, was wandering around bare-chested among Brik's family photos? Among his DVD collection? Who could, if he wanted, stick a spoon into one of the fifteen tubs of chocolate and banana-flavored ice cream that lay ready for him in the freezer?

But I walked away from the kitchen, just as animals sense a tsunami before the water advances and flee to higher ground. Instinctively. Though I didn't feel nauseous, I suddenly dived for the toilet, on my knees, clawing in the dust that in the past weeks had caked itself onto the sticky linoleum. I was powerless to resist, the urge was too strong.

With a force that I hadn't felt since Chile, my body knotted itself together and puked out gall of an industrial stench. In the background I could hear the tinny trumpets of the intro jingle and the affected way the host rolled his *r*'s, and in a new shock wave my body expelled the poison like a torrent of abuse—who was it who was hanging here with his head in Brik's greasy toilet bowl? Who could feel his fingers slipping and his nails filling up with what were undoubtedly the dried-up spatterings of Brik's morning pee? Who? Indeed. Not Philip de Vries. But Friso de Vos.

TWO

W hat was the purpose supposed to be? The *pur-pose*? On the face of it, the taxi driver's question, en route from the Vienna airport to the city center, wasn't so strange. Conferences had purposes, certainly when the theme was climate change, disease control, world peace, the Big, Relevant Issues—but us?

To start with, you had the Linz Hitlerists, who perhaps didn't even deserve to be classified as Hitlerists, mostly run-of-the-mill Germanists who published articles on the usual deadly dull socioeconomic topics: "The Postal Services in the Dual Monarchy: An Interpretation," or "Enlighten Our Minds: Paradigm Shift in the Upper Austria School System, 1867–1938," adding an opportunistic mention of father Alois Schicklgruber about halfway through and thus trickling into our movement. Then you had the Vienna Hitlerists, the first serious category of biographers, whom you could still never quite trust entirely: all too often the postadolescent Adolf appeared in their work as a Viennese Leopold Bloom, poverty-stricken, Bohemian, an art school dropout, wandering through the twilight of the Habsburg dynasty, after which they would lapse gratefully into essayistic lyricism about Mahler and Schönberg and Schnitzler and Freud, figures whose impact on Hitler's radar was at best highly questionable. There were the Iron Cross Hitlerists, obsessed with the question of where, exactly, he had earned his medals in the First World War trenches, but they were pretty much a stand-alone category, like the Beer Hall Putsch Hitlerists, or the Bunker Hitlerists, who focused on a single, discrete period in his life, without connecting it to the rest. A day in the life. The two categories that towered above all the others were the Weimar Hitlerists and the Berlin Hitlerists, who faced off against each other like hooligans in two sections of a soccer stadium, chanting at the tops of their voices, vying for dominance. The Berlin Hitlerists, from 1933 to the bunker death, claimed the throne, logically, because theirs was the Hitler of power, of decisions, of consequences, whereas the Weimar Hitlerists, or Munich Hitlerists, 1918–1933, invoked a Hitler who was less powerful but therefore more interesting, because their Hitler was the unfinished version, still undergoing a spiritual and ideological growth spurt, inventing himself, at a time when he was first experiencing power and attracting followers.

There were other X and Y axes on which you could categorize these categories; I knew them all: a grid with a box for the intentionalists, who believed that all the destruction of the Third Reich—the war, the industrial genocide—had been Hitler's intention right from the start (see the origin myth of Hitler studies: *The Last Days of Hitler*, Hugh Trevor-Roper, 1947). A box for the functionalists, who contended that Hitler's anti-Semitism was to some extent a pose, and that the Holocaust was the result of a Byzantine bureaucracy in which ministers, Gauleiters, and subordinates took the initiative themselves, holding razzias and building gas chambers in an effort to please their Führer and climb higher up the Nazi ladder (e.g., *Hitler: A Study in Tyranny*, Alan Bullock, 1952). In between the boxes lay gray areas, the domain of historians who saw evidence of compromise—that Hitler was first and foremost a pragmatist who, when he saw Operation Barbarossa grinding to a standstill in the Russian winter, the Americans mobilizing after Pearl Harbor, and General Montgomery turning back Field Marshall Rommel at El Alamein, realized that the cause was doomed, from then on focusing only on scorched earth and the Holocaust (*The Meaning of Hitler*, Sebastian Haffner, 1978, a book that everyone in Hitler studies had read two or three times and loathed, if only because its casually penned 192 pages were too convincing, thus undermining the entire discipline). And then there was a box that had to stand outside the rest of the grid, the metabox of the "inevitablists," who believed that Auschwitz would have happened anyway, and that if Hitler hadn't been born, someone else would have taken his place (see: *The Origins of the Second World War*, A. J. P. Taylor, 1960).

But most of the hands I would shake over the next few days belonged to the trivia merchants, the hobbyists, the common or garden historians, who sifted through and arranged minutiae with a passion verging on fetishism, without anyone ever really asking them to. You had the genealogists, who could by now trace Hitler sperm cells back to before the Battle of Lepanto. There were the exegetists who pored over every letter of *Mein Kampf*. There were the pathologists, obsessed by dental records and DNA residues, and in their wake the pathological psychiatrists who hoped to deduce something from the physical data—"Did he only have one testicle? How did that affect his sense of masculinity?" There were the Venus Hitlerists, the Immaculate Ones, who speculated about his love of women, about his unparalleled affection for his mother, the question of why four of his six known lovers committed suicide and whether he had in fact ever physically consummated a relationship. There were the Edelweiss Hitlerists, who focused on his role as host of the Berghof, the Alpine home where he received colleagues and friends for soirées and mountain walks. You had the epistemologists, who specialized in every letter and every document he'd ever signed; the cinephiles, who unearthed which films he'd ordered and which he'd actually watched; the bibliophiles, who researched the size and contents of his library in order to draw up a big Hitler Reading List. You had the sartorialists, who made sewing patterns and could reproduce the exact cut of all his uniforms; the hairstylists, who could calculate the dimensions of his mustache to the millimeter by studying old photographs; the watercolorists, who compiled the Hitler Canon from the 1,300 surviving watercolors he'd painted prior to 1914; and the curators, a rapidly expanding group, who approached *The Sleepwalker* every now and then with reports and essays on artworks and sculptures ("Where are they now?") that Hitler had personally owned. A lot of Böcklin, a lot of Julius Paul Junghanns. Of course you had the Hollywoodies, who kept track in spreadsheets and long essays of all the actors who'd played Hitler, and to what effect—Brik loved that. Drawing on a study of Hitler's vegetarianism (inspired less by animal welfare concerns than a fear of getting fat), three women attached to Temple University had written a

Hitler cookbook, which prompted a lively debate in various academic periodicals—we might know his favorite dishes, but did we really know how he liked them to be prepared? And, taking a more overarching view, you had the chronologists, the category to which everyone perhaps belonged in his or her own way, who did nothing more or less than painstakingly order all the available data, until every day, every hour of his life was thought to be accounted for. A press release had been sent, announcing that a hitherto unknown researcher from Humboldt University, a man by the name of Erich Mariah Maier, had signed a deal with a big American publisher to produce a biographical tome describing every day from March 1919 up to 3:30 p.m. on April 30, 1945. He'd secured a six-figure advance. The publisher was aiming at a mass audience. (The period between November 1918 and March 1919 was the domain of the Black Hole theorists, the time between his discharge from a military hospital and his arrival in Munich, the last episode in Hitler's life on which sources contradict one another and when no one can say with absolute certainty where he was—I'd seen every conceivable fantasy aired: that Hitler was on a retreat in an Orthodox monastery, or that he'd gone on a quest with Himmler to find the Holy Lance of Longinus.)

I explained to the taxi driver that the conference was funded by the European Union and that it would be attended by historians from dozens of countries, specializing in every period from the Renaissance to the present day,

leaving out any mention of Hitler. In the semidarkness I could just make out the rash on his neck. I didn't like taxis, I remembered now; I found it a disconcerting idea to place your life in the hands of a complete stranger. Pippa took the opposite view. Surrendering herself to an unknown individual gave her a feeling of detachment, she said, which was the next best thing to feeling safe.

– You like car? asked the taxi driver.

– Yes, very fine cars, Mercedes.

– I play for Fenerbahçe, now I drive this Mercedes from airport to city and back.

– Wow, I said, Fenerbahçe, you must have been very good.

From his breast pocket he produced a folded photograph that he passed back to me. It showed a youth in a soccer uniform, crouching down with his hands on the ball, looking up at the camera with big, childlike eyes that radiated a kind of disbelief, as if he, too, found it inconceivable that he was a professional soccer player, as if someone might pinch him at any moment, causing him to wake up with a shock.

– I play in Turkey, with Fenerbahçe soccer club.

– Yes, I said.

– Twenty-five years. Someone kick on foot. *Kaputt.*

– Foot is *kaputt*, I said.

– Yes, he said, I come from Turkey to Austria. Drive taxi. I never play soccer no more.

He took back the photo and I wondered why he'd suddenly told me this, and whether it was true—did he hope he'd get a bigger tip, because I felt sorry for him? I decided not to talk anymore, and looked out of the window. The landscape made me think of Mordor; the route from the airport was dominated by heavy industry: looming machinery and mountains of industrial waste framed against a fiery setting sun.

Of course, there was yet another category within Hitler studies, an increasingly popular one, that people like Brik and I belonged to, a category that wasn't interested in facts, certainly not ones that had recently come to light. What use is information that nobody possesses? Brik liked to say. *What use is knowledge that nobody knows?* Nightmare visions that everyone perceives as real are much more significant, much more potent than any mere facts. It's all about how ideas find fertile ground and take root in our imagination—who of our

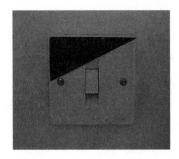

generation could think about D-Day without picturing images from *Saving Private Ryan*? Whether those ideas have any foundation in reality is no longer even relevant.

Josip Brik: "Truths are nebulous and transparent and come in many guises, like ghosts. You can believe in them, but you can never quite put your finger on them."

But I could spend the whole day quoting Brik.

I hadn't seen it coming up, but suddenly we crossed a river and the first horses on plinths appeared. Ringstrasse, said a street sign. Kärntner Ring, said the next. The buildings got bigger and classier and the taxi pulled up right in front of the opera house, just next to the historian Maarten van Rossem, who was talking into a camera, his hands in his pockets.

Once I'd gotten through the revolving doors and past the top-hatted porter, escape was out of the question. The circus had arrived. Two men I vaguely recognized from an earlier conference were standing in the lobby. One of them greeted me. Matthew something-or-other. I saw a man wrestling a lamp into the elevator, TV lighting equipment, presumably, followed by someone lugging at least ten yards of cable, followed by a heavily made-up woman— Mathilda Wilson, BBC host of nostalgic programs about stately homes and aristocratic dynasties. A small, brisk figure straight from the Shires, the icon of provincial lesbians, with her eternal tweed jackets and her short gray hair, which stuck up in permanent confusion, as if it didn't know which way it was supposed to be growing. To be here—in Vienna, in Hotel Sacher! The hotel of the famous Sachertorte, the hangout of the Habsburgs, shahs and kings, and the Allied Command right after the war. To be here with a limitless credit card. It had been Mrs. Chilton, "call me Liddie," who'd sent me here—she'd suddenly appeared in the doorway of my *Sleepwalker* office, surrounded by her husband's Dalmatians, sunglasses the size of twin Ping-Pong paddles. She'd known the hotel manager for years, she said, and I should really treat myself for once, at her expense.

– Friso, believe me, nothing feels like immortality as much as absolute, unassailable wealth.

But that sense of wealth was instantly sullied by the sight of so many other conference-goers, equally keen, it seemed, to escape the fate of the generic hotel chains where the hoi polloi were billeted. I'd wanted to be here alone. The fewer who share in luxury, the more luxurious it feels.

But I realized I was making a fuss. The journey had been tiring. I'd paid extra for a direct flight, and by the time the plane was bumpily descending over the Alps after eleven hours in the air, and a baby in the row of seats behind me started to screech like the Nazgûl, my patience had run out. I noticed that even covering the short distance between the taxi and the lobby made me breathless. The day before I left for Vienna, Pippa, in one of her more grandmotherly moods, had sat down next to me and forced me to think of at least three things I could look forward to in Austria (going straight on to answer for me: "One: you've never been to Vienna. Two: you'll see Felix again. Three: a change is as good as a rest."). To say nothing of Four: a multimillionaire has slipped a credit card into your hand as if you were a corrupt cop, so there's actually no limit to what you can do.

– Think of it as if I were giving you a big green apple bursting with vitamins, Mrs. Chilton had said. You'll feel healthier with every bite you take.

– Didn't they say that to Snow White?

While I was waiting to check in, the revolving doors made a quarter turn, propelling a man in a fedora and a long raincoat into the hotel like a bingo ball in a lottery, and for at least three seconds I really thought it was Sir Ian McKellen—by the flame of Udûn—when just then I was addressed by the youth behind the desk, a boy in a fancy suit, who'd eventually managed to tear himself away from

his young female colleague. My German—or were they speaking Austrian?—was too rusty to grasp the nuances, but the gist of their flirtation was clear. I pushed the printout confirming my reservation toward them:

– I'll just check...

– It's for six nights, I said.

– Yes, here you are in our system, that's right, six nights for Mr. . . . Vos, de, Friso!

The girl behind him gave him a congratulatory pat on the back and shot me an apologetic glance, while struggling not to laugh. The boy continued unflappably, an equally broad grin on his face:

– We've reserved room 262 for you, Mr. Vos, de, Friso.

Scooping up the key and my luggage, I turned around, nearly running straight into the man with the hat and the raincoat, who'd lined up behind me. He wasn't Ian

McKellen, and only now did I see his female companion, a girl who immediately stood out, as beautiful blonde girls with full lips and big blue eyes tend to do. Her wavy hair was cut in an old-fashioned style, level with her jawline, accentuating the length of her neck. If you took the time to look, and I did, you couldn't help but marvel at the flawlessness of her skin, her face, her neck, her modest décolleté in her baby blue sweater. It was as if she were made not of the same mass of dying and renewing cells as the rest of us mortals, but of some kind of warm plastic that had been melted and die-cast.

She halted for a moment and looked at me, a look of recognition. Her mouth opened slowly, as if she wanted to say something—but before she could do so I felt a hand on my wrist, and found myself looking into the excited face of Vikram Tahl.

– Hey, dude, have you read my article yet?

– No.

– And why not?

– I've been really, really . . .

– . . . really busy. Bizzy-bizzy. Sure. That's what you said last time too.

You couldn't overlook him, even though he was about two feet shorter than the average European. Among all the guests strolling or lounging about the lobby, he stood tensely erect, fizzing with energy. I'd met him a few times. His gray hair had a military cut, and his head seemed disproportionately big: his eyes were large and bulging like those of an animal that can see in the dark. His speech was a weird mixture of Oxbridge don and Bombay taxi driver-cool (though I'd never been to Bombay):

– I've just been seriously ill, and of course Brik has...

– ...has just died, his defenestration, such a pity... But a little bird told me you gave a terrific speech at his memorial service, so I thought: Hey, old Friso can't be that sick...!

– That wasn't me.

– ...so he must have read my article too, by now. Perhaps you think me naive for assuming this, but I take it you can at least follow my thought process?

– Will you be in Vienna all week? I asked.

– Holy moly! Is this a pledge to read my article by the end of the conference? Will the mere threat of my physical presence get you reading? Seriously, Friso, if that's the case, I'll take it!

Tahl was not to be fucked around with. He'd set up a Hitler studies curriculum at Delhi University that, despite its complete mediocrity, derived status from the budget with which he flew in Western professors, installing them in Hilton suites (along with their wives or mistresses) while they gave a guest lecture or two. Since then he'd popped up at every conference, peddling his studies and articles that no one was greatly interested in, but that no one wanted to reject too explicitly—for fear of missing out on those three-star invitations. For at least six months now he'd been hawking around an essay that he fondly imagined was original because it compared Voldemort with Hitler.

– Have you got it with you?

– What?

– My article. What else did you think I meant?

– It's in my mailbox.

– But I'm guessing you haven't brought a printer with you, huh? In your hand luggage? Do you like to read seven thousand words on a laptop screen?

– No.

– No, nobody does, Friso. No problem.

Tahl gestured to a serious-looking girl who was standing some distance away, and she instantly hurried up. Twenty, at most, glasses, Asian, but not entirely—had he flown his own PA in?—and she immediately started noting down Tahl's instructions: that she was to print out his article at a copy shop first thing in the morning and give it to me, not leave it at the desk, but hand it to me personally. I gave her a friendly smile, out of a kind of solidarity, because you always feel embarrassed for someone else who's being ordered around, but she didn't smile back. Tahl introduced her, and the girl made a point of ar-ti-cu-la-ting her name very clearly:

– Yuki Hausmacher, how do you do?

– Nice name, I said.

– My father is German, my mother is Japanese.

– Gosh, did they meet at an Axis Powers reunion party?

No one laughed. I tried to move slowly toward the elevator, backward, like a lackey who knows he must never turn his back on the prince. Tahl gradually raised his voice as the distance between us increased:

– Sure, I get it and I feel for you, about Brik and all, but it'd be awesome if you could read my article! So we can talk about it! Because I think it would be absolutely perfect for *The Sleepwalker*! And I said it before, but I gather you really stole the show at the memorial service!

– That wasn't me! I shouted back.

– Are you sure? It was in the paper!

My room was dark and chilly, and it took a while to find the slot to stick my key card into to turn the lights on. I kicked off my shoes and noted with satisfaction that this was indeed the biggest hotel room I'd ever stayed in. The minibar was full—old-fashioned glass bottles of Coke!—and there were framed portraits of Vivaldi and Haydn on the walls. Perhaps it was tiredness that suddenly overcame me, the sight of a bed, after having been awake so long. Perhaps it was a reaction to the parade of well-known faces I'd encountered unexpectedly, unwantedly, as soon as I arrived at the hotel.

It was only now, in a full-length mirror, that I saw how hunched up my shoulders were, making it look as if I was trying to hide my neck. I slung off my jacket, suddenly finding its flimsy weight unbearable, as if I'd been carrying another person piggyback all this time. My neck felt like a solid, unkneadable lump of rubber and I had an overwhelming urge to grab a fold of skin and jab a knitting needle through it—surely that would release the tension? I rubbed and rubbed it until my fingers started to tingle, making me think at first that I was having a heart attack, until I realized I didn't have the other symptoms.

In the bathroom I unbuttoned my shirt and hung it on a peg. Standing in front of the mirror, I noticed something sticking out of my belly to the right of my navel, a swelling that wasn't matched on the other side. I prodded it. The lump was soft, and moved up and down when I poked it. You couldn't see anything in the mirror, but as I looked down, it really stood out. I should just do what Mrs. Chilton had said, treat myself for once and have a masseur come tomorrow. But could massage do anything about my tumor? Because wasn't that what it was, deep in my stomach? Cancer of the esophagus? Very aggressive, apparently. Cancer was something that happened to other people, like sexually transmitted diseases and computer fraud, and I couldn't see myself as one of those cases where you're terminal all of a sudden before you know it. It had to be fat—but why would that heap up in a single place?

It was marvelous, the silence in my room, as if the hotel was deserted. This was what I wanted.

My shoulders were still crooked, like the wings of a banking plane. I straightened my back and aligned them, and the lump in my belly disappeared. Aha. I turned on the shower and, before getting under it, lay down next to my bed and did fifty sit-ups.

The silence was pleasing, it was so delightful lying here, cushioned by the deep-pile carpet, merely gazing up at the ornamented ceiling, merely staying awake, that I didn't want to think about Vienna, or home, or Pippa or Brik. I saw the face of the Chilean Susan Sontag nurse, kind and authoritarian. Relax, Friso. Just close your eyes for a moment. Let the shower run.

Friso de Vos, can you just tell us very briefly what kind of philosopher Josip Brik was?

"Very briefly"? I don't know if I can. I don't know that I want to. Maybe I want to tell you at great length.

In two sentences—come on, you can do it.

A philosopher, Brik always said, isn't someone who has a watertight theory about the world. Someone who thinks like that isn't a philosopher, but an ideologue or a politician. What fascinated Brik was how ideology *appeared* to have disappeared from art and films and literature, but if you looked closely, it hadn't. "The greatest trick the devil ever pulled was convincing the world that he doesn't exist," he liked to quote.

And just who was he quoting?

Come on, you should know that one. It's from ... *The Usual Suspects.*

Very good. You were seen as his right hand. You had a lot of personal contact with him, you often accompanied him on journeys. Do you feel responsible for his accident?

Yes and no.

Why "Yes" and why "No"?

"No" because Brik was a grown man who was perfectly capable of booking trips, arriving on time for flights, and checking into hotels himself. The fact that this Amsterdam hotel had a rotten window frame that broke when he leaned against it was something neither he nor I, nor anyone else, could possibly have foreseen. He could just as well have fallen downstairs, or been knocked down by a taxi.

And "Yes"?

Because if I'd been there he'd never have been in that hotel—I booked better hotels. I knew much better than him the sort of place he'd feel at home. And if I'd gone along he wouldn't have eaten and drunk alone, and would never have been alone in his hotel room at that time of evening. I feel responsible because if I'd been there the circumstances would have been different. But that's pure speculation. Perhaps it was written in the stars, if you believe in that kind of thing. Perhaps his time was up, and fate couldn't have been averted. My mother was a full-time housewife who looked after me and my brother and sisters day in, day out. But my brother still has a scar on his cheek from the time he fell through the glass coffee table, and my sister has a mark on her shoulder where she was scalded by a pot of tea that got knocked over. Things happen.

Do you miss him?

Before I came here I went and sat at his desk in the university building in the evening, after everybody had gone home. No one knows I have the keys. I just wanted to sit there for a minute.

What was it like?

It was dark.

Were you scared?

No. It was a good kind of dark, just like there's a good kind of cold and a good kind of pain.

Where were you at the time of his funeral?

In a bed on the third floor of the University of Santiago Medical Center, in Chile, where a task force of specialists eventually diagnosed a form of septicemia known as the Nubulae-O'Higgens variant and treated me for it.

Did you think about what was happening on the other side of the world at that moment?

I was asleep.

Did your girlfriend go to the funeral?

Pippa went to the memorial service two weeks later. She'd been with me in Chile till then, but I told her she should definitely go back to attend the service. It made sense, I thought. He'd played an important role in our lives, and she had a close bond with him. Of course she should go. But in the end it turned out to be a social event, a "see and be seen" affair. Half of New York turned up. From a professional perspective it would have been good to be there. I, we, could have drawn attention to *The Sleepwalker*'s ties with Brik, to the importance he attached to *The Sleepwalker*.

Were you upset at missing the funeral and the memorial service?

Of course—he was my friend, and I should have been there. Had I not been drugged up and down for the count I'd have been furious, stuck there in that hospital bed in Santiago. But it's pointless to dwell on it. You can't turn back the clock. It is what it is.

Were you jealous of Pippa, because she was there and you weren't?

Up to a point. Just as I was jealous of everyone who was there. Pippa isn't very verbal, she likes to avoid conflict. There's no getting around it, memorial services like that are political affairs, certainly in the case of someone like Brik, who had almost no family. Anyone could claim him, even people who scarcely knew him. So it's handy to be there, and to stand your ground if necessary.

What does Pippa do for a living?

By the age of twenty-five she already had her own little art restoration business. You'd drop in on her to find a sixteenth-century oil painting on an easel, a seventeenth-century gouache under the windowsill, an Impressionist watercolor propped against the sofa. She had all kinds of clients—including museums like the Rijksmuseum and the Hermitage. There she'd sit, for three hours at a stretch, fiddling away at a bit of canvas the size of a postage stamp with a three-haired brush. Her parents had lent her the money for the apartment—her father had a tanning salon empire—but she earned back the money in a flash.

And could she go on doing this work in the U.S.?

That was one of the reasons we went, actually. Through Brik, or rather through his friend, the dean, Mr. Chilton, she was able to get a three-month internship at the Metropolitan Museum. After that, the university's art department got her a lot of assignments. She'd drive to New York pretty much every week to pick up canvases or return them.

How did you two meet?

It's not a terribly romantic story. I'd just moved to Amsterdam, was trying to get a job at a publishing company or a journal. She sometimes went to the café where I hung out, and one evening we got talking. Friends warned me. They knew Pippa slightly, she wasn't the type of girl to go back to someone's place just like that, they assured me, but after the café closed we felt each other up in a nearby doorway as if it was the most natural thing in the world. What did come as a surprise was that a week later I went shopping with her sister, and two weeks later played a round of golf with her father and brother.

How come it all went so quickly?

What can I say? Why do you fall in love? She's very pretty, very sweet. Cliché answers, right? She has this air of being—not childlike, and not like she's a victim—but, how shall I put it, she has a permanently puckered brow. As if the world's an obstacle that she needs a bit of help in dealing with. And because she's so sweet and so pretty all you want to do is protect her.

But she's not very "verbal," you said.

At times it seems as if she doesn't have a one-to-one relationship with words. You can ask her the most basic question, *How was your day?*, and she can ponder it as if no word could possibly exist that does justice to her emotions or experiences. If you ask what she'd like to eat, she pulls a face as if you were giving her an oral exam—you can see her thinking: Shall I say what I'd like? Shall I say what I think he'd like? Would he like me to go for something healthy? Does he mean I need to lose weight? Is he hinting at something I've forgotten to buy? And so on and so on. Meanwhile I'm standing there with my head in the fridge, waiting. If someone at the post office holds a door for her, that's a diplomatic dilemma, as if a brief "thanks" couldn't be enough. The other thing she does is use words that are so much weightier than the occasion calls for. She's not apprehensive about a job interview, but "petrified," her contact with a gallery isn't unpredictable, it's "hazardous." We'll cycle past ten girls in baggy tracksuits being made to collect for charity by their sorority—some kind of mild hazing ritual—and Pippa will say, "Those girls are being intensely humiliated." I'll mention that another Hitler studies periodical is having difficulty getting academic publishers to advertise with them, and she'll just say in a doom-laden tone, "It will be their downfall." Words like that make everything so heavy.

And then you say...

Then I say: "Jesus, Pip, 'their downfall,' they're not getting advertising—it's not like they're sitting in a subterranean concrete bunker, shooting themselves in the head one after the other."

Does that make her laugh?

Hysterically. I always make her laugh.

And does she make you laugh?

Daily. She's brilliant at impressions. Have you ever seen her *Tyrannosaurus rex* walk? She could easily have gotten into drama school. She can sing along perfectly with any song by Burt Bacharach.

You don't have any problems on the verbal front, right?

What I expected of her was very simple, very basic. She'd gone to the memorial service in New York, I hadn't. So I'd hoped she'd be my ears and eyes. But dear, smart, highly educated Pippa, who couldn't tell a joke with a punch line if her life depended on it, doesn't ever give away information just like that. If you want to know something, you have to drag it out of her, as if she couldn't possibly conceive that it's important. Who spoke at the service? What did they say? How did they say it? What was funny? What was moving? Who got a big response?

And you're sure you don't hold it against her that she was there and you weren't?

I already said I couldn't be there, right? It was only logical she should go. I didn't give her any instructions beforehand, no checklist to tick or anything like that. It's just that the things she's struck by aren't necessarily what I'd be registering.

Did she say anything about Philip de Vries?

Nothing! Not a word.

And that doesn't bother you?

No. I already said, I'm not angry.

You realize you're asking these questions yourself, don't you?

I'm calm.

So why don't you give her a quick call then, Friso? Hadn't you promised to call when you arrived?

And precisely at that moment, as if on cue, the phone in my room rang—always louder and more startling than you'd expect. The flashing lights on the display made me realize how dark it had grown. With an arm that had half gone to sleep I picked up:

– Hello, this is Philip de Vries calling.

These were, it seemed, the most disorientating words I could have heard. It was as if a stream of icy water was shooting out of the receiver into my ear.

– I'm looking for Friso de Vos.

The phone vibrated in my hands, impatiently, flirtatiously, because this was the start of something. I'd made plans in recent weeks, about what I would say to him, how I would provoke him, but something in me rose uncontrollably, like milk when it's about to boil. If not fury, then disbelief—or rather fury at myself, for taking everything into account except his actual presence, for failing to realize that he, too, had first-strike capability, that a telephone line goes in two directions. For being oblivious to the reality of his existence. I'd thought myself anonymous and safe in this room, four days before our debate, but all of a sudden he was here—not tangibly, not visibly, but incontrovertibly, an immaterial presence that filled the entire room and demanded a response—a response that I, dammit Friso, didn't have ready. Even *this* was too much for me.

– Hello?

I heard him breathe in with a single deep sniff, like you do when you're walking outside after it's just snowed and you want to savor the cold, in all its sharpness, deep inside your lungs.

– Sorry, wrong number, I answered, in Dutch, *U bent verkeerd verbonden*, and banged the receiver down much too violently on the plastic hook.

I got a bottle of Coke out of the minibar, and emptied it into a glass. I took the immaculate white cotton hotel slippers out of their plastic packaging and put them on, and without knowing why, I walked to the little hall between the bathroom and the door of my room, perhaps to hear the sound of the firm rubber soles of my slippers on the marble floor, and once I'd gotten there, I opened the door for no reason. Left, right, nobody in sight, you could have heard a pin drop.

I'd answered in Dutch. In Dutch. In my high school final exams I'd passed German with flying colors, and gotten nearly top marks for French, *merci beaucoup*. At work I spent much of the day emailing, texting, and making phone calls in English; I sometimes even spoke English to myself—and now I'd answered in Dutch. Like a dimwit. Like a total moron. What did he want from me? Why was he calling me now? I'd known that I looked down on his connection with Brik, his *supposed connection with Brik*, but even so, the fact that a single little sentence from him could conjure up such a wave of unfiltered aggression came as a surprise.

I heard the elevator doors open at the end of the corridor and automatically glanced sideways. Two men in gray suits emerged, nothing odd about that, though one seemed to have something in his ear. Before I could even identify that something as a tiny microphone, a third man got out of the elevator behind them, a man whose face I didn't even have to see to recognize, because he was so much taller that his peroxided pompadour stood out majestically above his retinue. Here, in the wild. The two bodyguards, because that's what they must have been, had seen me standing there; it would have looked suspicious if I'd suddenly panicked and backed into my room, I thought. So I stayed there, half in the doorway, and when they got to within a few yards of me

I smiled affably and gave a little nod. The only person who responded was Geert Wilders* himself, for indeed, it was he. A surprisingly warm smile spread over his tired face.

– Good evening, he said amicably, in German.

– *Bon soir*, I replied.

I went back into my room and watched through the peephole in the door as Wilders and his minders walked down the corridor, and as soon as they'd vanished from sight I instinctively pressed myself flat against the wall, breathless and as terrified as if the Balrog of Moria had just passed by.

---

* Prominent far-right politician, leader of the Dutch Party for Freedom.

THREE

F elix was waiting for me in the hotel café, sitting at a table the size of a Frisbee, his back pretty much in the Christmas tree, but with a magnificent view of the opera house. He was sipping his *Wiener Melange* from a teaspoon, carefully, as if he were feeding a little bird.

– Friso, old buddy!

He gave me a quick hug, which pleased me—I could tick off one of Pippa's objectives for my visit. Felix had an unblemished, delicate face and was slightly built. The twenty pounds of muscle and meat that you put on between the ages of fourteen and seventeen had never arrived in his case. People often took him to be much younger than he was, but he didn't care. He was the most organized and responsible person I knew. When we both lived in the Netherlands he would buttonhole me at parties, telling me not to forget to submit a Declaration of Independent Contractor Status if I was planning on working freelance. "Or better still, just pop into the Chamber of Commerce." He said things like "likewise" when you wished him a nice weekend, and "by no means" when asked if you were disturbing him. When he was eighteen his parents had lost control of their car in one of those classic hairpin bends en route to a ski resort, and he and his little brother and sisters had had to go and live with his grandparents, where he, as the oldest son and at the same time the youngest adult, looked after everyone. He drove his sisters to their tennis lessons, carried his grandmother's heavy shopping. Pippa had known him longer than I, and believed these to be his formative years. In the first weeks, months even, after the death of a partner or parent, I knew, you don't get the chance to mourn—you have to select flowers, music, you have to talk to lawyers, write cards, cancel insurance and subscriptions, and it all provides the perfect excuse, forcing you to concentrate on something other than Death and Absence. It sometimes seemed, Pippa felt, as if Felix had never emerged from that first stage, as if he was still, after all these years, using the organization of life as a way of releasing himself from the obligation to actually live.

Felix Westerveld. Expert on nineteenth-century colonial politics. You could ask him anything about the Fashoda Incident, the Boer War, or Gordon of Khartoum. He hadn't yet gotten his PhD, because what faculty of arts would pony up for that these days? So he taught first- and second-year students and published articles in various journals, hoping to scratch together enough research for a doctorate. Dapper and fussy, he was a bit of a character, but he was well liked—and secretly admired, at least by me. Now, too, he wore gleaming brogues, brown corduroy trousers, and a herringbone jacket, elements that, added up, had no right to equate to the unbearably hip apparition that he was, with his overly long schoolboy haircut and his colossal, black-rimmed glasses. They perched on his thin, pale, probably-never-needed-a-shave face as if he'd bought them in a joke shop, but once again, this was just one of the things he could get away with.

– Good to see you.

– Likewise, I said.

– You have indeed lost weight.

– Enough to fit into Pippa's trousers.

– Do at least order one of the little cakes they have here, they're divine.

After a struggle, a waiter managed to squeeze a chair next to Felix's table. Felix, meanwhile, resumed his fascinated scrutiny of the program booklet—that, too, was nice, the fact that he didn't go in for the obligatory "How are you?"s and "How was your trip?"s, but just started reeling off the events we needed to attend in the next few days, in the most natural and familiar way.

– We really have to go to this, this evening. Listen: "Auditorium, Kunsthistorisches Museum, nine o'clock: European gaming champion Dittrich Hollman (Germany, b. 1998) takes on world champion runner-up Mike Dixon (Canada, b. 1987) in *Medieval: Total War III*, the latest version of the real-time strategy game published by media partner and software developer

Creative Assembly, in which they will replay the Battle of Crécy (1346)."

– That sounds epic.

– It gets better: "Their game will be projected on two screens, while Pierre Declerq, medievalist at the University of Canberra, and Bertrand Cromwell, author of countless bestselling historical novels, provide a live commentary. Will history be repeated, or will the outcome be different this time when arms are laid down? Free admission."

– Do you think we could place bets?

– On Thursday we must go to that gala in Schloss Schönbrunn, tout le monde will be there. Have you RSVPed yet?

– Not yet.

– And then, at the weekend, there'll be the real big guns. "Actors from the new BBC miniseries about the Blitz will be publicly interviewed about—"

– "Publicly interviewed" always sounds like some hideous form of corporal punishment.

Felix smiled and pointed behind me with his little finger:

– Did you spot Pretzel there in the corner?

Turning around, I saw Raimund Pretzel, probably the most renowned, influential German historian since the reunification of his country, a ubiquitous presence at conferences like these, usually as keynote speaker about East versus West, Germany's economic miracle, the future of a united Europe, etc, etc. Now he was tucked behind a table, surrounded by assistants and nurses. The previous year he'd still been able to walk with the aid of crutches, now he was in a motorized wheelchair with a canister on his back that must have held enough oxygen for a fifty-meter dive. Tubes went into his nose. His head and neck were at an unnatural angle, and he was making strange, gobbling movements with his mouth, like a horse choking. Someone had outfitted him with a hat and an eye patch.

– Jesus. What's with the pirate look?

– I'm told that when he dies, they're going to name the disease after him, it's so rare.

– The only thing about him that's still intact is his faith in social democracy.

We both laughed, and then I told him about Wilders, and Felix said he wanted to just fall backward out of his chair, with the cartoonlike exaggeration that the situation demanded. I told him about the bodyguards and that Wilders had greeted me in a friendly way, and that, all in all, it was pretty unfuckingbelievable. What was he doing here? Surely he wasn't going to...? Gripped by the possibility, Felix began to go through the program booklet methodically, following it up with a digital search on his smartphone. Of course there was no mention of Wilders, but we couldn't find any "mystery guest" either, or a program component that had "t.b.a." where the speaker's name should have been, and anyway, what could he possibly talk about? This was crazy, Felix said. How did you manage to get a wink of sleep? Weren't you scared that ji-hadists would storm the hotel? And what would you do if Al-Qaeda rushed the place and Wilders knocked on your door asking to hide under your bed?

– I'd first make him promise to raise the retirement age.

– Wow, Felix said. Of all the things you could have picked, all the politically correct and right-on options, you go for the most right-wing thing on the menu.

This was about as far as Felix could go in silliness. He pulled himself together and addressed me in a business-as-usual tone:

– Tell me, Friso. Friday. Your debate with that Philip de Vries guy. Are you ready for it?

– I've written something, a sort of story about Brik.

– I thought you didn't like writing?

– Not really. I'm happiest editing, arranging stuff, emailing. Writing a thousand-word preface for each issue of *The Sleepwalker* always takes me two weeks. You know that article I was going to write in Chile, about men called Hitler? I spent three days staring at the screen before I could even think of an opening sentence.

– And that was?

– "Chile, the atrophied spine of Latin America, is home not only to Hitler Lima junior, but also Hitler Lima senior, a man so untroubled by the loaded nature of his own first name that he passed it on proudly to his son."

– "Atrophied."

– Indeed.

– Nice word.

– It took me a day just to come up with that.

– Meaning "shriveled"?

– I think so, yes.

– You're not sure what it means?

– Try to keep an open syntax.

– So this story about Brik, what kind of piece is it?

It's a mix of fact and fiction, I told him. Satirical, with a
dash of Dorothy Parker. It's set in a taxi that Brik's sharing
with Jack Gladney, just when he has this brain wave about
how to shape Hitler studies. That much was fact, as Brik
had once told me. I was hoping this piece would make me
come across as witty, intimate with Brik, totally at home
with his thinking. But I didn't tell Felix that Philip de
Vries had rung me up. His highly rational mind made him
a less than empathetic listener; he rarely had the patience
to listen to your own small private battles and obsessions.
He wouldn't have understood why I'd hung up immediately, and would have explained to me in his schoolmas-
terly way that if I'd just talked to De Vries, if only for one
minute, I'd have found out what he wanted and wouldn't
have lain totally jet-lagged and wide-awake in bed for two
hours, as rigid as a board, terrified that the phone would
ring again at any moment—which it *didn't*. When I went
downstairs the next morning, the concierge told me that
someone had indeed called at the desk, wanting to contact

me: he'd personally spoken to the gentleman in question, who had left his card. The man handed it to me. Underneath the printed contact details De Vries had written in ballpoint: "Call me! Let's get together."

– What did he look like? I asked.

– Your age, same color hair, about the same height as you, I'd say.

Let's get together. Why? What did he want: for us to be friends? Did he hope to start up a Josip Brik Fan Club with me? That telephone call had hit a nerve, prompting a deeply instinctive rejection, a sort of primal No. It was all too much for me—like a long-lost biological father calling you up out of the blue, and straightaway wanting to come to your birthday party, be a grandpa to your children, buy shoes with you. In this case not a father, but a brother. Someone who thought that he and I were the same, that we were on an equal footing, fellow Brikians. But there were divisions. Gradations. Brik had contacts all over the place, but they were subdivided into echelons, placed at varying distances: a junta of colleagues, friends, editors, producers, journalists, PhD students, undergraduates, all jostling to get near him, and he, as generalissimo, was very conscious of whom he admitted to his circle and when. And I couldn't even say for certain whether Philip de Vries was among our ranks. Who was he, besides the worst-chosen guest of an overly popular TV show? To put it in Nazi terms, I was at least Martin

Bormann, whereas this De Vries might be, at most, that Dutch SS volunteer who gets blown up on a Russian toilet in the film *Soldier of Orange*.

Felix ordered two chocolate cakes.

In 1346 the English army is drawn up between the hamlets of Crécy and Wadicourt, and it's only in the late afternoon of that summer's day that King Edward III and his heir, Edward of Woodstock, the Black Prince, see the first waves of French soldiers and mercenaries advancing across the hilly landscape of Brittany to be struck down, one by one, as they reach the closed English ranks—first the Genoese crossbowmen, then the French cavalry.

There is nothing the crossbowmen can do about it—it has rained, their bow strings are wet, and their arrows land far too short, yet they are well within range of the English archers, who unleash a deadly rain of arrows on them. Next come the cavalry, who test their swords on their own retreating crossbowmen.

– Treacherous dogs! scream the French knights—but by the time they reach the English ranks their steeds are exhausted, and they fail to breach the wall of shields painted with the cross of St. George. The horses are brought down with swords and axes, the French knights thrown to the ground in their heavy breastplates, making it child's play for the English infantry to skewer them to the wet, sticky clay of Brittany. Later the glory of the

House of Plantagenet gains added luster when the youthful Black Prince, sweet sixteen, joins the fray, sustaining the first proud dents in his black armor with gold inlay. The French nobility are decimated that day, and it will take at least a decade before the House of Valois can once more raise an army of that size.

Now, too, nearly seven hundred years later, the Battle of Crécy began with an advance by crossbowmen. But this time the fifteen-year-old German gaming champion sent his Genoese mercenaries to the right flank of the English army. He was still placing them within reach of the English longbowmen before they could retaliate, but he seemed at least to be opening up the field somewhat, trying to escape the geographical confines of the terrain.

All the audience could see of the young German was a pointed nose poking out of the bilious green hood he'd pulled far over his head. His Canadian rival was a beefy kid in a T-shirt printed with a band logo. Sporting huge headphones, he kept flicking his tongue in and out in deep concentration, like a lizard scenting the wind. A little earlier he'd punched the air when a toss decided who'd play whom—he got the English and was overjoyed, as if history was a law of nature that wouldn't let him down.

Both screens showed a baby blue river and an impossibly verdant forest. Between them lay a crooked green valley, at whose opposite ends stood thousands of small, brightly colored, animated figures, awaiting the orders of their commanders. The author and the historian who were providing a lively commentary on the battle controlled the screens, allowing the audience to float above and look down on the battlefield, occasionally zooming in with a scroll of the mouse. As the pixels contracted you could clearly see the little knights sitting idly on their little horses, surprisingly lifelike, even though they wore identical armor and carried identical weapons, and were a bit too luxuriously outfitted with banners and plumes, like plastic action figures.

The author explained that the Black Prince wouldn't be called the Black Prince until a century and a half after his death, and the historian said that battles like these were a rarity because the Hundred Years War mainly consisted of what the French called *chevauchée*, war by raids, with small bands burning and pillaging their way around coastal areas. These were isolated facts, waiting for a narrative.

The Canadian placed his Black Prince in the foremost ranks very early on—a choice betraying either arrogance or uncertainty. All troops within a certain radius of the prince were boosted to 110 percent hit points, but that was balanced out by the fact that if the prince was killed, the entire army went down to 90 percent hit points (on the French side, this also applied to the Count of Luxembourg, John the Blind). The same happened if the king's banner fell. If the king himself died, the game was immediately lost.

The German had his crossbowmen, perhaps a thousand little figures in black doublets and purple breeches, form a longer line than usual. It meant they were less clustered, reducing the damage inflicted by the British bowmen from +25 to +15, but it increased their vulnerability to cavalry attacks, from +35 to +50. At the same time he cautiously advanced his first line of cavalry, forcing the Canadian to choose whether to allow his crossbowmen to be slaughtered by the knights, so his archers could fire on the French cavalry, or whether to keep his ranks closed and accept the minor casualties inflicted by crossbow fire, so he could ward off the much greater damage the French cavalry could potentially inflict by deploying his own cavalry—

The author: According to the rules of the game, you have to choose between two evils...

The historian:...and he's putting off that choice just now.

—because the Canadian didn't do anything, just waited for the German, who at the last moment had his galloping cavalry swerve aside, heading straight for the archers. They cut through the archers, a vulnerable group on the edge of the English line, as if through a field of corn. At the same time he ordered his crossbowmen to run back to the center of the field, to try to engage the French left flank, which so far had seen no action. A lot was now happening at once. The author and the historian fell over themselves to provide commentary, while the audience grew excited and noisy. Now the Canadian did send his cavalry toward the marching crossbowmen, who were easily wiped out, after which he returned them to the right flank, where the French cavalry had put almost all the crossbowmen to flight. A hand-to-hand battle ensued among the cavalry, just in front of the lines of English infantry, which the Canadian kept closed. The commentators zoomed in, showing us knights on horseback hacking away at each other, and praised his discipline in keeping to his original battle plan in the spirit of Edward III.

The two gamers were positioned so they couldn't see the screens on the wall that we, the audience, were watching. All they could see was what was happening within sight of their own forces, and so the Canadian was slow to notice that as he tried to prevent the thinning French cavalry from retreating, a great mass of French infantry was heading straight for his right flank and getting close to his cavalry. Aware that he could no longer cover himself in glory, he attacked the infantry full-on—but the German had stationed his pikemen at the front, and their long spears inflicted an extra +20 damage on the cavalry.

Now that he'd cleared away the archers, the massed ranks of his infantry could advance directly on the English line, and thousands of infantrymen joined battle. Within minutes all the lines had broken up, everything merged into a fighting, dying, swarming mass—the German leaned back and stretched, while the Canadian pressed his face against the screen and the commentators went crazy, zooming in left, right, and center. They showed us the figure of the Black Prince, sent into the fray by the Canadian in the hope of giving his troops that vital extra boost, but who was very soon surrounded. He hewed at the footsoldiers and pikemen from his white steed with automatic blows, as if hammering in tent pegs, and we saw the health bar above his head turn from green to orange to red, until he collapsed, horse and all, his black became gray and ever more transparent, until his pixels in the end seemed to melt away, a little puddle of oil dispersing in water, until the Black Prince had dissolved utterly into the green earth.

– I grew a beard, not so long ago, Felix said. Early last year or thereabouts, a big bushy Moses-in-the-wilderness affair. At first as an experiment, to see if it made me look more mature. But then from pure curiosity. After a while it began to lead a life of its own: it started to curl, and some of the hairs were very soft and fair and others dark and as hard as straw, and the longer it grew, the redder it got, seriously, I looked like the Duke of Alva! It's one of those things you only find out about yourself by putting it to the test. My cheeks were pretty bare, actually, it all grew out of my chin. It was only a goatee, really. I let my hair grow too. It got to a point where I could tie it back, not in a real ponytail, but a little knot, like samurais have. Only I don't think samurais have beards.

– Hard to imagine you with a beard, I said.

– Indeed, Felix said. But that was the whole point. You grow up and you do things and you slip into a kind of groove or pattern, and the more your past stretches out behind you, the less you think about that pattern and how it's shaping your future—do you follow me?—and sometimes you just need to do something to deviate from it, if you see what I mean, to kind of break from everything you've done up to then.

– So you grew a beard?

– I did indeed.

Felix looked at his glass, empty, once again, with a kind of defeated wisdom. We were sitting in the café of the Kunsthistorisches Museum, on the second floor, between two rooms full of Bruegels and Arcimboldos. It was exactly eleven o'clock, and the strategically deployed security guards were keeping an eye on the young audience that had just seen the French win at Crécy. They were sitting in the café and on the steps of the magnificent marble staircase that led to the central hall, a staircase of the kind that princesses lose their glass slippers on. And actual princesses had descended it, there had been balls here, Sisi had probably waltzed on this very spot. A good hundred feet above the staircase, a chandelier hung from the cupola like a gigantic inverted crystal and gold leaf Christmas tree. I suddenly found myself marveling at the past—the fact that it was still there, so very much in sight.

Meanwhile Felix was going on about Wilders again:

– Do you think there are security services in the hotel?

– Like the AIVD?*

---

* The Dutch intelligence and security service.

– For instance. We need to investigate.

– You're right, Watson. Data, data, I cannot make bricks without clay.

– Funny that you think if this was a detective story, I'd be Watson and you Holmes.

– Isn't that the whole point of fiction, that you automatically identify with the hero?

– But Sherlock Holmes isn't really a hero, he's more a natural phenomenon.

– When I read *Heart of Darkness*, I identified with the river.

– When I read *The Death of Ivan Ilyich*, I identified with Death.

Dancing had started nearby. Two boys gyrated around a girl who was jerking her pelvis almost exactly in time to the music, in a way that lacked grace but radiated commitment. The doormen, used to a rather different public, smiled approvingly. One of the dancing boys did the Robot.

– Something tells me I should go to bed now, Felix said, but something else tells me another Sambuca would go down nicely.

– My round, I think?

If truth be told, I should have let Felix go to bed, but this was all much too enjoyable. Anyway, I'd proclaimed this week the great Renaissance of our friendship, so had to strike during the rare moments that he spoke frankly about himself and/or drank too much. What's more, if I went up to my room I ran the risk of being ambushed by the telephone, tinkling out friendship requests from Philip de Vries or evacuation orders from the AIVD.

Two medievalists were still deep in conversation at the bar, perhaps envisioning how a French victory at Crécy would have affected the Hundred Years War, but apart from them I could only see people in their twenties and thirties. I don't know exactly what I'd expected Viennese students to be like, but not this collection of hipsters, goths, girls with ponytails, and boys in blazers that you could find in any university city in the Western world.

I walked back to the bench on which Felix had now fallen asleep and put his glass down where he couldn't knock it over.

I should have spoken at the memorial service—about our soccer evenings, about his sudden interest in fashion, about the time we visited his mother in Belgrade on the Fourth of July and he pined for America, because he wanted so much to be there on the anniversary of his adopted country. I could have told everyone everything I knew about Brik, things that *I alone* knew, and that would have been it. End of story, nothing that still needed proving. My eulogy would have been short and sincere, and I could have shown that you didn't need to canonize Brik by making sweeping statements about his standing and oeuvre. And Pippa had rubbed salt in the wound, by her stupid remarks when I showed her that TV program, by the stupid way she made allowances for everything and everyone. She couldn't even go along with my anger. In fact, when I told her about Philip, she'd made things even worse by frowning sympathetically and saying that she found it really odd, *really really odd*, after which she'd gone into the other room and called her mother, sounding totally chipper and upbeat—so much for the sincere empathy.

"You don't know what fire is," I'd texted her.

"I'm a volcano pretending to be an iceberg," she texted back. Smiley.

My debate with Philip de Vries could only be painful, I was sure. I already felt embarrassed for him. He must know that I knew that he'd had very little to do with Brik, virtually nothing, dammit, and that this time he wouldn't be able to bluff his way out of it.

Nothing is as annoying as when someone's lying to you and you know he's lying—and he knows you know he's lying, and meanwhile he goes on lying.

There were more people dancing now. I took a sip from Felix's glass and smiled contentedly, mainly, I think, at the sight of the bestselling author, a man of pensionable age, bravely throwing respectability to the winds and, together with a woman who probably wasn't his wife, performing a novel move that involved doing the two-step with his feet and the Chicken Dance with his arms. The conference was already making good on its promise to "bring together conflicting ideas."

I poured the contents of Felix's glass into the dregs of my own and took a cautious sip. The treacly Sambuca was rather pleasing, adding a hint of cough syrup.

It was most unlikely—I'd long since decided—that Wilders was here. The more high-profile program events, particularly the Hitler studies ones, were taking place on the other side of the city center, in the auditorium of the university, where an assortment of particularly eminent professors were discussing Hitler in Vienna, a well-worn topic—and yet I caught myself feeling relieved when someone tapped me on the shoulder and I saw it wasn't him.

– Can I ask you something?

It was the girl I'd seen the previous day in the hotel, and who'd wanted to say something to me before Vikram Tahl intervened.

– You're Philip de Vries, aren't you? I think I was behind you in line at the hotel desk yesterday.

How had the boy at the desk pronounced my name?

"Vos, de, Friso." Of course.

– I'm Nina.

And I, I said, surprised and also, somehow, hugely relieved, am Philip de Vries.

We shook hands. She was perhaps thirty at most, dressed in black tights and a short mint green knit dress, but whatever she'd worn, it couldn't have disguised the fact that she was in absurdly great shape. I also realized that if I tried to explain this to someone else, they would cut in and say I was just describing "a hot chick," but there was more to it than that. It wasn't just her legs, hips, buttocks, belly, breasts, but everything: the fullness of her skin, the clarity of her eyes;

it was as if she'd just been assembled from components so fresh, so terrifyingly healthy, that it gave me an uncomfortable feeling of vulnerability, like when you're holding an absolutely perfect tomato and you know that by the time you get around to eating it, it'll be going soft and wrinkly. But I guess that's just my innate tendency to exaggerate.

– You were on TV, weren't you? Talking about Josip Brik, right?

– *Correctamundo*, I said. And asked if she also had a surname.

– I do.

– But for some sinister reason you're not allowed to divulge it?

She grinned.

– Bart.

– Bart?

– Like the first name "Bart." Whenever teachers saw my name on a list of pupils they always thought I was a boy.

– But you're a girl.

– You were paying attention during biology class.

Leaning back so lazily was a bad idea, I realized—if I wanted to keep this Philip de Vries lie going, I'd have to play a more active role. I sat up straight, closer to her, and asked conspiratorially:

– And do you spell "Bart" with a *t* or a *d*?

– *B.a.r.t.h.* But the *h* is silent.

– Nice name. *Nina Barth*. My mother's called Nina.

My mother wasn't called Nina at all. In another flash of alertness, I indicated the chair opposite me. She sat down and pointed at Felix.

– Is he... drunk?

– Mainly tired, I think. He arrived today. He didn't drink that much, but he did gulp it down.

– What are you guys drinking?

– Sambuca.

– Can I have a sip?

I gave her my glass, she took a sip and handed it back.

– Aniseed.

– I like how treacly it is.

– I've got mascara in my bag. We could draw something on his face.

– A Hitler mustache?

– Don't you ever get the urge to go wild at these big, stuffy conferences? To do something naughty?

I wondered whether she meant it as flirtatiously as it sounded, and apparently she saw me thinking something along those lines, or perhaps she just realized that this conversation could get out of hand too quickly, too easily, because the playful smile vanished from her face and she adopted a different, more businesslike tone.

– Do you know the Burgers Foundation? That's who I work for. It's based in Brasschaat, in Belgium. It's an organization in the international art and antiques sector. We work for private clients, maintaining and restoring historic objects and collections, and mediating in sales. We also host a lecture three times a year, for our clientele and any other interested parties.

Thanks for the information folder, I thought. I asked if she lived in Brasschaat.

– In Antwerp. I used to live in Amsterdam, didn't want to move to Belgium—but actually I really like where I am now. That's my boss over there.

She waved at two men standing a little ways off, who now walked toward us. I'd seen one of them with her in the hotel—he wore an expensive blue suit and leather shoes with buckles, and even indoors he kept his fedora on. He'd draped a raincoat over his left arm, so you couldn't see his hand—if this had been a Hitchcock movie he'd have been hiding a gun. He shook my hand.

– So you're Philip de Vries? Nina said she'd recognized you. Sweder Burgers.

– Nice to meet you.

– This is my associate, Markus Winterberg.

His associate was a corpulent man in a less chic suit. He had a sallow complexion and a kind of reverse baldness: just a circle of sandy hair about the size of a beer coaster on his crown, a hair yarmulke. He nodded at me.

– Do you often go to the End of History?

– We attend this conference every year to strengthen ties with our network of art historians, Nina parroted on behalf of her boss, who now chimed in:

– In our line of work I believe you need to build up the biggest possible mix of contacts, from eminent professors to great philosophers, from bestselling authors to junior Fulbright students. An inspiring diversity.

– Yes, I said. Diversity. It's as if all the colors of the rainbow are coming together here.

– Josip Brik once gave a lecture at our foundation, Burgers said. Very thought-provoking.

– I was just going to say that, Nina added diligently.

I couldn't remember that Brik had ever been in Brasschaat and asked when.

– Once. Years ago.

– Is it difficult for you, Nina asked, now you've lost a mentor?

– When you've just been bereaved, I said, and paused in a way that was intended to come across as contemplative, it's a miracle you don't just dissolve, like a bar of soap in a bathtub, from all the heartache and pain.

"Heartache and pain" had been selected from the soccer player's vocabulary that went with the role. Nina ostentatiously laid her hand briefly on my upper arm, the two men nodded in agreement.

– And now you're ready to succeed him, Burgers asked, to keep Brik's ideas alive and, as it were, preach the true gospel?

– No one can fill Brik's shoes. His knowledge, his bravura, his gravitas were unique.

– Usually when someone says something like that, the next word is "but."

– *But* I would see it as a great challenge to take Brik's thinking a step further.

I said it as devoutly as possible, with disparaging modesty, because I knew for sure the bastard would put it like that.

Nina and Burgers nodded, and Winterberg looked at me with an inscrutable smile, one hand resting on his belly, just like those sixteenth-century dukes you see in paintings, content with the wealth of their own obesity.

– How did you get to know Brik? he asked.

How did you get to know Brik?

That was a question I could answer. A question I'd been ready for since that afternoon in Brik's ransacked house, and I told the story quite naturally, the story Philip told on TV, about how as a student *I* had to pick him up from his hotel for a lecture, and how *I* found him in his room, in his underpants. But I told it better: I had a willing audience, and I didn't want to let this chance slip. I added that I'd found a tray outside his room door with an empty tub of chocolate ice cream on it, and a McDonald's hamburger wrapper—I told them that Brik always said he could only think properly if his jaws were grinding and that unfortunately he never *stopped* thinking. That I found Brik on the bed, with the newspapers spread around him, but also that he had pay-per-view on and was watching a film in which the Earth was invaded by aliens, and it had just gotten to that scene where the spaceship destroys the

White House, and that Brik said how perverse it was that in Hollywood, American patriotism always went hand in hand with the longing for American self-destruction. But it was always a painless destruction in those apocalyptic movies, because the good guys, the people with whom we, the viewers, are supposed to identify, always survive or die in moments of cathartic self-sacrifice—it wasn't for nothing, he said, that the evangelical sects proclaiming the Rapture and the Coming of the Kingdom remained a purely American phenomenon. I told them that Brik had put on his trousers, which he struggled to zip—he made a joke of it, pointing at the fast-food packaging—and that I'd said: "You're your own worst enemy, right?" which felt daring, because it suggested a personal connection I didn't yet have with him, and that made Brik laugh, and he said: "Yesh, my God, I dread to think there's anybody who could do me more harm than I'm already doing to myself."

They laughed and I continued, or rather, I was unstoppable. This was a fantastic role, I now realized. I knew the bare bones of the anecdotes told by De Vries. But I possessed the firsthand knowledge to breathe flesh onto them—I was a better Philip de Vries than he himself could ever be.

I told them I often saw Brik in his underpants. He was like an animal, I said, in that he was never ashamed of his body, or even gave it any thought. I told "one of my favorite stories" about how I was once having lunch with him at a chic hotel on Amsterdam's Dam Square when he suddenly felt unwell, something to do with his blood pressure, and had to be taken away in an ambulance, which he himself naturally found ridiculous. As he was carried out of the busy lunchroom, past the line of tourists waiting for a table, he called out: "It's the food! It's the food!"

Once again, Nina laughed out loud, her mouth stretched wide, revealing a broad panorama of white teeth and gums as pink as her lips.

I'd come across the "It's the food" anecdote in the biography of an English actor, but it was precisely the kind of humor Brik loved, and what's more, this mythologization process was driven by people exaggerating their Brik stories and their personal roles in them, so it would be typical of Philip de Vries to tell the story in this way. Just as it would be typical of Philip de Vries to squeeze Nina's knee very gently just below the table, so her boss couldn't see.

– Did he leave a will?

The question, so concrete and so brutally formulated by Burgers, knocked me half out of Philip de Vries mode.

– That's unclear. He had no children, of course. I believe his family in the former Yugoslavia has the best claim to future royalties. He didn't have much in the bank, as far as I know.

– What about his house in upstate New York?

– There are plans to turn it into some kind of university annex, or a writer's residence.

– Have you ever been there?

– A couple of times. (I was growing unsure who I was now playing, me or the other.)

– He has an enormous collection of old films, books, and art, I believe?

– Indeed.

– Did he keep his entire library and collection there?

– Yes.

– I heard there'd been a break-in at his place.

Felix suddenly woke up with a shock, like someone falling. He rubbed his eyes and studied one of the paintings on the wall with exaggerated interest, probably trying to make it seem as if he hadn't been asleep, but just distracted. Bedtime for you, young friend, Sweder Burgers said with a sardonic smile.

F elix and I walked out into a flurry of snowflakes. We could scarcely see the statue of Maria Theresa. The snow crunched underfoot. By the time we'd taken four steps, fresh snow had already obliterated our first footprints. *Winter is coming.*

Except for us, the square was deserted. It wasn't cold. I held Felix by one arm.

– I keep thinking we're going to run into him at any moment, Felix said.

– I don't think so. I'm guessing he's in the university auditorium.

– Really? *Really?* Felix said, with the exaggeration that went with the role of drunk.

– That's my theory, at least, I said, and explained that since that was where the most high-profile Hitler studies events were, that's where he'd be—it felt good to stress this, the fact that *we weren't* at the important events, as if we formed our own little club of dissidents and decided for ourselves what was relevant and what wasn't. Felix looked at me in surprise:

– Who are you talking about? Did you find Wilders on the program then?

Wilders, of course. Why did I keep forgetting him?

After walking down the palace passageway, past the Sisi Museum, we came out on Kohlmarkt, with its expensive shops. We had to turn left here somewhere, go a bit farther out of the center to get to where Felix was staying, some gigantic hotel building. Felix had gone silent now and his eyes were getting glassier and glassier. Five minutes later he announced that he just needed to stop and rest for a minute.

The city was smaller than I'd expected. No boulevards, only small streets you could easily overshoot if you didn't watch out. Narrow, echoing little streets with cobblestones and closed shutters. If you wanted to make a halfway decent spy movie, this would be the point where you'd have the hero realize he was being followed: the sound of footsteps on wet pavement. I heard them now, in fact, those hurrying footsteps, but I wasn't surprised, I didn't worry about whose they were. I knew, I thought, the trick was not to be surprised.

– You caught up with us quickly, I said.

– It might sound crazy, but I suddenly felt like a swim.

– A swim?

– Yes, there's an indoor pool at the hotel. Quite a big one. But it closes at eleven thirty, I think. So I need to get a move on.

– Aren't you staying at the Sacher? I asked.

– I wish. Only Sweder gets to stay there. We drones are at this place, with all the other conference-goers. It's just around the corner. Your friend's staying there too, I take it?

Nina had tied her shawl around her head, an improvised hood to keep off the snow. I could picture her in a swimsuit.

– Do you swim a lot?

– Forty lengths a day. Except weekends.

– What do you think about during those forty lengths?

– Nothing. It's like reciting the four times table. I do it on autopilot.

Felix had gone gray all of a sudden, and just as I went to hold him upright, he sank onto the pavement. Nina grabbed one arm and I the other, and together we got him on his feet again. I draped his arm over my shoulder, so as to support him better.

– Can you manage, Philip? asked Nina.

– My name's Felix, said Felix.

The hotel had a corporate name and was unmissable. A night porter greeted us as we went through the automatic doors. In the lobby we could go left, toward a bar that sounded very noisy, or right, toward the rooms. Or we could go downstairs, said Nina, to the spa and the pool.

– Would you like to join me for a swim?

This was the moment. I saw she had a narrow band of gold on her ring finger. Had she been wearing it in the museum? She must have been. Felix had wrapped his arms around himself and stood there, his teeth chattering.

– I think I'd better get him to bed.

– Good night then, Philip.

– Same to you, said Felix. I guided Felix to his room, helped him with the key card, and sat him down on a chair. I was prepared to give him a hand with his shoes; the rest he'd have to do himself. It was gratifying to see how much smaller and more impersonal his room was than mine. Mrs. Chilton's money worked. Someone had made the bed so tight and rigid it was as if they wanted to punish it for being soft. He wobbled toward it, fell forward, and went out like a light.

It had all gone really well. Things were under control. I'd left the casino just when my pile of chips was at its highest. I hadn't overplayed my hand. Perhaps the only thing I could blame myself for was *not* overplaying my hand, so for all I knew Markus Winterberg and Sweder Burgers might now be going home this very minute and saying to one another, "A nice fellow, that Philip. Smart guy. Good to know Brik's legacy is in his hands," instead of thinking, "What a self-important little creep." As hatchet jobs went, it lacked punch. Perhaps I should have matched Felix's intake speed, perhaps just one more Sambuca would have gotten me in the mood for Victorian melodrama, with long-lost sons who return, fritter away the family fortune, and then turn out not to be long-lost sons after all. Somewhere along the line I'd failed to make a faux pas. I should have made sure that Philip de Vries could never expect to be invited to Brasschaat.

I was satisfied and yet at the same time I wasn't, and to add an extra layer to that paradox I got another shock when the elevator doors opened and I found myself face-to-face with Nina, in bathrobe and flip-flops. As if I wasn't sure I had the stamina to give it another go.

– Is he asleep?

– Like a baby. Like an exhausted, drunken baby.

She smiled, I did, too, and for a moment we were at a loss for words, until the elevator doors opened again on the ground floor.

– Shame about the crowds, she said.

– The crowds?

– *Clouds.* Cloud cover. Snow. Otherwise we could have seen Castor. It's the brightest it's been in nineteen years. Don't look at me like that, I don't mean anything by it. Castor's just a star. It's only a star. Not a symbol of anything.

– Do you know the whole galaxy by heart?

– You mean to say you *don't*?

I thought, first as Friso de Vos, then as Philip de Vries. It wasn't that I could talk more easily in the latter role, I just had a sense of greater license. I could dig up any cliché in the world and present it as a nugget of profound wisdom. I could link everything to Brik.

– So when you're working away, busy with art, just like me, busy with history, are you never suddenly overwhelmed by the thought of the universe expanding for all those billions of years, and what was there before the universe, and the utter insignificance of what we're doing here on Earth, on our laptops? Brik liked to point that out from time to time, just to put things in perspective.

– The realization that the stars are actually just giant gas bubbles? That the sun will eventually swallow us up? That as we speak, trillions of neutrinos are passing right through our flesh?

– *Neutrinos, they are very small / they have no charge and have no mass and do not interact at all / something something something / like dustmaids through a drafty hall.*

– Very good.

– See, here's the thing, Mrs. Barth, I'm trying not to think of our flesh.

She laughed:

– I'm reading Brik at the moment.

– You are? Which one?

– *The Red Machine.*

– Well well. The Big Brik standard work.

– What he writes about *décalage*—am I saying it right?—is absolutely fascinating: the feeling you're in a different time zone from the one you're actually experiencing. That's the chapter I've gotten to. About the difference between experience and the narrative of that experience. The idea that literature and drama and great films come into being because the characters realize they're the prism through which we experience their adventures. Shakespeare has Hamlet remark: "Time is out of joint." And who was it said his whole life felt like a TV program?

– Warhol, I said. Andy Warhol, after he was shot. The attack so derailed him from his ordinary life that everything he experienced afterward felt like watching TV.

– Do you know that feeling?

– I'm experiencing it right now.

At first I congratulated myself. I'd remembered a good chunk of the Updike poem, I had the *décalage* remark down pat. It was only then I realized something else: she was lying. That bit about *décalage* wasn't in *The Red Machine*, but in the slim essay collection *Herr Doktor Alzheimer*, about sense of self and recollection, 130 pages, light typeface—a book that hadn't been translated into Dutch yet, despite pledges by Brik's publisher. She was lying! It had been Pippa who'd pointed out that quote to me a few weeks earlier, when she spotted it in a Flemish newspaper article and wondered whether the journalist in question had picked it out because the book of essays was so much thinner than *The Red Machine*, so much easier to quote from than wading through 650 pages on Robespierre and Hitler.

This was how things now stood, probably, this was what all the reports of his death and all the obituaries added up to, the fact that everyone knew the one-liners of his oeuvre without having actually read any of it. Perhaps that was what was left of you as a public figure, as a writer, as a talking head. Meanwhile Nina was looking sweetly at me, smiling, as if she expected something of me. And why shouldn't I give it to her, I thought. Because it wasn't fair to her? If she was lying about her knowledge of Brik, then so could I. Because it wasn't fair to Philip de Vries? If he could pass himself off as Brik's bosom friend and heir apparent, then I could pass myself off as an overrated PhD student—and my lie was much more modest. I wasn't impersonating him, he was impersonating me.

– Hey, Nina, I said. You don't by any chance have a swimsuit for me?

FOUR

ondon, 1985:

With an air of fatalism, the pale young man let his pudgy body sink into the back seat, so low that his head hardly came level with the window, as if he were a film star trying to avoid the lenses of the row of paparazzi who were not in fact standing there.

"Oh God," he said. "Oh God, oh God, oh God." His companion must have been a good twenty years older. He wore sunglasses—at this time of day?—a creased black suit, and a black tie, and if he hadn't had the broadest of smiles plastered across his face, you'd think this was some poor guy who'd just come from the funeral of an old friend.

"Really, Josip, it wasn't that bad."

"Are you kidding? It was terrible."

"Good heavens no, it was a ball, everyone had a gay ol' time and you led the revelry."

"Led the Light Brigade is more like it. Jack, I got the distinct impression that Lord Percival Parker would gladly have shot me."

"Gosh no. There may have been a moment, just between the main course and the dessert, when a few people had to restrain Percy, push him back in his chair so he could calm down a bit. But nobody at the other tables saw it."

With a small movement of the hand, like a woman brushing a lock of hair out of her face, the taxi driver adjusted his rearview mirror to check whether his two passengers were both really wearing deerstalkers. And yes, both wore the same checked cap with tied-up earflaps—exactly in the style of Sherlock Holmes. By the time the car had reached the Mall and was passing Buckingham Palace on the right, the younger of the two was leaning his heavy head against the misted window, his hand in front of his face.

"Did Dorothy Pope Loundon walk away angrily?"

"Dorothy thought you were hilarious. You had all the wives of those Oxford dons in stitches. I reckon they appreciate someone who can put on a bit of a show, someone who's not uptight. She walked away, I think, because she couldn't fish that ice cube you'd slipped down her neck out of her dress without more or less disrobing at the table. Honestly, it wasn't a problem."

"What about the man who was tugging at the electric cable?"

"He wasn't even a guest. All the guests loved you. That guy was the maître d'hôtel and he was a little bit concerned because you didn't want to stop singing, and there were other people in the room who probably hadn't expected it to be that kind of party. I think he was just shocked that you'd managed to dig out a microphone from behind the bar."

In the tiniest voice, as if it wasn't himself asking, but a little pixie he kept captive in his mouth: "And was my singing bearable?"

"You have a very nice vibrato, Josip. Charles Trenet would be envious. It seemed—though I could be mistaken—that you got your words a bit mixed up half-way through, I got the impression you sang half a verse of 'Nathalie.'"

"Seriously? What was I singing then?" The man with the sunglasses sat up a bit straighter, placed his left hand on his heart, and gesticulated with the right as if he was conducting himself:

La Mer
Près des étangs
Une bande d'étudiants
L'attendait impatiemment.

In between the phrases, he made trumpeting noises, *On a ri*, tatatataaaa, *on a beaucoup parléeeeee.*

"Oh God, oh God, oh God. I want to go to my hotel room and stick my head in a bucket of ice—those oysters didn't agree with me, I repeat, did not agree with me."

"My dear Brik, of course it was the oysters."

He buried his head in his hands, and for a moment the driver thought he could hear muffled weeping. What the driver couldn't know, of course, was that out of the deep ravines of Josip Brik's despair a little figure was climbing, an idea like a mountaineer, gradually emerging from the sharp, dark rocks to appear bathed in light. It sprang from the Baker Street gala, the annual black-tie do for Sherlock Holmes aficionados, to which Brik had only been invited because he'd recently coauthored an article with Jack Gladney for *The Baker Street Journal* about Holmes's surprising popularity in Nazi Germany. This was the sole occasion at which the two schools of thought on Holmes met: in one corner you had the Doyleans, centered around the Sherlock Holmes Society of London, who researched not only the stories but also the life of their creator, Sir Arthur Conan Doyle, his examples, his epigones, the context of his oeuvre, etc. In the other corner you had the Sherlockians, who met as the Baker Street Irregulars and who ignored Doyle, focusing their research only on Holmes, as if he were a real person.

He looked at his mentor next to him. Jack Gladney had been a Hitlerist since the late 1960s, one of the first to be bitten by the bug. Since 1968 he had headed a department that categorized, classified, and chronologized every piece of data on Hitler, however obscure. As if every fact, every dental record, every diet, every uniform would explain something about the vortex of destruction that enveloped Europe, and the cult around the man who unleashed it.

The question was simple, Brik suddenly thought, unbelievably simple: What if you were to approach Hitler as a Baker Street Irregular? What if you focused solely on Hitler in fiction? Wouldn't that give you, just like Holmes in the case of the Irregulars, a much better idea of what he signified, without the constraint of facts? Brik resolved to shut himself up in his hotel room that evening and use the complimentary notepaper to plan a research project, a department, a series of essays—something! He would order coffee and cake or ice cream, something buttery. His body no longer interested him, forget the nausea, forget the stomachache. I am a brain, Watson. The rest of me is mere appendix.

PHILIP & FRISO

"Until the day he met Philip van Heemskerk, nothing had ever happened in Rink de Vilder's life that had allowed his personal qualities to come to the fore unpunished."

– Marja Brouwers, *Casino*

FIVE

n the morning the low, rising sun shone through the net curtains, and the sheets and wallpaper glowed a warm creamy yellow. She spoke first:

– It's a lovely day today. Outside.

– Outside?

– The weather, the sun, the snow. It's beautiful.

– Really? I hadn't noticed.

– Have you done this before?

– What do you mean?

– Just the way you said "I hadn't noticed." So smooth.

– Smooth criminal.

– I don't know about that. A little too pat, perhaps, as if you've done this hundreds of times before—*have* you?

– A strange question.

– I'd really like to know.

– Why? Supposing I have done this hundreds of times, would it make it easier for you? Knowing you'd walked into the trap of a master adulterer?

– Such a harsh word. "Adultery."

– Never be scared of words.

– I want to know, I think, whether I fell for it.

– Aha, *fell for it*. Into my trap, in other words. Those would be nice extenuating circumstances, wouldn't they? One treachery cancels out another—is that it?

– It would explain *something*.

– And to explain is to understand, and to understand is to forgive.

– I'm not going to ask for forgiveness—I'm not *that* weak.

– I never said you were weak.

– You implied it. But I was looking for an excuse. You're the sort of person who . . .

– Is this the moment where you pick a fight? So you can distance yourself?

– Are you playing at being my therapist? Seriously? Is that what you want?

– No. But I see . . . a pattern.

– Sigmund bloody Freud!

– I'm going to deescalate things now, okay?

– *Fuck!*

– I am the deescalator. I have a cap on, a uniform, and a stop sign. Listen to the deescalator.

– Ooh!

– Okay, okay.

– Fuck. Okay.

– Hey! Are you back to normal?

– Okay.

– Calm again?

– *Yes!*

– Come here.

– Sorry.

– Me too sorry.

– But this isn't the first time you've done this?

– Not the first time.

– Do tell.

– Really?

– Yes, spill the beans.

– She was Greek. Curls, nose. Quite a bit older than me. It was a few years ago, in Istanbul, when the End of History conference was held there. Simon Schama and Slavoj Žižek were keynote speakers, and afterward they came to blows about whether or not Robespierre was a bloodthirsty dictator.

– Is there a case for the defense then?

– The fact that he wasn't power crazy, for instance, that he didn't rule just for the sake of ruling. That he never ruled alone, anyway. That his Terror worked. That in '93 France was bankrupt, torn by civil war and invaded by half of Europe. And that by Thermidor a year later France was thriving, free and prosperous. He understood that you can't have a revolution without a revolution, but these days no one wants to ...

– Wow.

– I'm digressing, aren't I?

– Just a tad.

– I just have this weird thing about Robespierre.

– Go on about the Greek woman.

– She worked in the U.S. too, West Coast. Something in women's studies. Do you want to know what she looked like? Very thick, dark hair with those tight corkscrew curls, big, broad mouth, perfume, very feminine. Anyway, so there were two of those colossal, generic, dime-a-dozen hotels where all the conference-goers were staying. I was at the bar with a few acquaintances and was just going to get something from my room when I ran into her at the elevator. She was annoyed because she couldn't get it to work with her room key. I offered to help and it turned out she was actually in the wrong hotel—she was staying in the other one.

– And then?

– And then, and then. She joined our little group at the bar and at a certain point we were the only two left.

– Okay.

– This is a nice bit of your body, does it have a name?

– "My ass."

– No, this bit, the little triangle where your butt crack stops and your back starts. Or do you find that a dirty word, "butt crack"?

– The skin there...

– ...is soft. And it has a kind of profile. Like orange peel.

– Thanks a bunch.

– No, don't get me wrong, it feels great. As if my fingers belong there.

– Who made the move? She or you?

– I can't really remember anymore whether there was a move. It was more the fact that the two of us were left over. You know how certain magazines always have those Proust Questionnaires on the last page? One of those lists with short questions. "Are you attractive?" "What are you most afraid of?" and "What quality do you admire most in a man?" I always answer "ambition." As a man you need to want something, to get ahead. It sometimes has the odd effect of tempting me to apply for jobs I know I'm not suited for, jobs I really don't want, but that I feel I should aspire to, because otherwise I'm not ambitious enough. Does that sound crazy?

– So you picked her up out of ambition?

– No. Perhaps. But we were sitting there, the two of us, alone, late in the evening, she was there purely to be seduced, I felt—*I feel*. I remember thinking, somehow, that it would be strangely impolite if I didn't ask her up to my room.

– Jesus, you picked her up *out of politeness*?

– You couldn't really call it picking her up. I said something like "Oh, now you have to go all the way back to your hotel..."

– At which she said: "Can't I creep into bed with you?"

– I think what she literally said, and she sounded pretty tired, was "Can't I just join you?"

– Easy.

– Clear.

– How would you answer the question: "What qualities do you admire most in a woman?"

– That's tricky. It sounds so disparaging and sexist if
you answer "ambition" or "intelligence" for a man, and
then, for a woman, put "good looks."

– Almost as bad as "great cooking skills."

– What would you answer?

– For a man? Honesty.

– And for a woman?

– Camouflage.

– Good answer.

– But how was the sex?

– Just now, with you?

– With the Greek woman.

– I could also say what it was like with you.

– Oh, I know where that would lead, young man, thank
you very much. No, let's confine it to the Greek woman.

– Do you really want to know?

– Yes.

– Very, very oral.

– What a slut.

– I knew you'd say that.

– What an utter slut.

– Don't ask then.

– Tell me more.

– How much detail do you want?

– Tell me all.

– Do you know what rimming is?

– Haha, piss off.

– Okay. One of the first things she said to me, and we'd been lying on the bed for, like, two seconds, was: "You can come in my mouth." I immediately thought: forget it, if it's allowed, *if I have your permission*, then it isn't exciting anymore.

– She was just trying her best.

– You reckon?

– It sounds like a woman ending up in bed with a younger man and suddenly falling into a sexual generation gap. All the pornographic images she's ever seen, all the women's magazines she's ever read, are suddenly spinning through her mind like a merry-go-round on tilt. And she's seized by the crazy untenable notion that she has to act easy and casual and pornofied. And the whole time she's terrified you'll think that her labia are too big and natural, or that her pubic hair hasn't been trimmed enough.

– Nice theory.

– We women understand one another. I know a lot of women of that age, who experience sex much more rationally than you think. They tend to be divorced, in their mid-thirties, fortyish, they go out on a date and decide beforehand whether they'll go home with someone or not. A lot of thought goes into this. You men mustn't get the idea that it's all down to seduction techniques.

– What about this, then? You and me? When did you make the decision?

– No comment.

– Sure.

– Have you ever talked to her since?

– Quite often. Run into her fairly regularly at the university and at conferences. We say hello and ask how things are going. All very amicable.

– All very professional. As if it happens by arrangement. Academic Flings, Ltd.

– It's as if you both briefly enter another world. A shadow world or whatever you want to call it. You're together, it's lovely and fun, and then you go back to the real world again. Nobody knows about it. That's the arrangement.

– I wonder whether, in a year, you'll be telling someone exactly the same story. But then about me. And what would you tell? Which acts would you describe?

– No story. Sometimes things happen that don't need to be translated into a story.

– Is that a promise? How well you put it. Perhaps you should become a gigolo.

– Do you think it pays well?

– If you're good at something the money will just roll in.

– Where would I find my clientele?

– Facebook page. Euphemistic ad on eBay. I could introduce you to some of my older colleagues, I know just the kind of women who fit the bill. In their early forties, boring marriages, could do with a bit of excitement. Purses full of children's photos, insurance cards, and a wad of cash.

– Sounds convincing.

– The kind of women you can do anything you want with, who only want to submit... Hang on a minute, do my eyes deceive me, or are you getting a hard-on?

– Huhuh.

– Unbelievable. I talk about male prostitution and you get a boner?

– Come here, you.

– You look different. Your gaze. So piercing.

– *Come.*

(. . .)

(. . .)

– You may *not* come in my mouth.

The week before I set off for Vienna, Pippa and I had gone swimming in Brik's pool, just as a spectacular storm blew up. First, fat drops like disoriented little birds smacked against the glass front, then it got darker and darker very quickly, as dark as a moonless night at four in the afternoon, the rumbling in the sky approached like a wheelie suitcase in a narrow street, and finally, whiplashes of lightning forked through the cloud cover overhead. The individual drops on the glass morphed into a river of streaming water, and I stared out and felt a wonderful madness taking hold of me. It was a special sort of madness, the kind a child would feel, a blend of recklessness and a lust for destruction, and I reveled in every thunderclap as lightning struck farther away, somewhere in the woods behind

Brik's farm, blasting ancient oaks to matchwood. The discharges got louder and more frequent, so close that after every strike you could hear the electricity sizzling for a full second. The hairs on my arms stood on end. For a moment, Pippa seemed to be screaming, but what's the point when the sky above you is one giant shriek?

At first, Pip had felt uncomfortable in this pool, so close to the edge of the forest, the kind of horror film location where teenagers are impaled on meat hooks. But I'd taken off my trousers and dived into the water naked. A minute later, strangely prudish, she jumped in after me in her bra and thong. When the hullabaloo broke loose she swam toward me, her lower lip trembling, and flung her arms and legs around me.

Something disappeared, something was disappearing. We knew this was the last time we'd be here and still feel some trace of Brik, his energy, his atmosphere—in a week's time the removal firm would drive his stuff to the storage facility, and the faculty would decide what to do with the building. Less than five minutes later the storm was as high as the mountain ridge and a few miles away, and then it simply disappeared from view, sliding behind the mountains to be replaced by clear skies.

I climbed out of the pool, walked to the glass facade, and watched the clouds move away, as if I wanted to wave them off. This was an ending. I turned my wet cheeks back toward Pip, who was dangling in the water, holding on to the edge of the pool. She stroked my colorless calves when

I came up to her, pinching my intensely pale skin with fascination.

– What a sweet whitefish you are.

– A trout, I said. A redfish.

– A white fox. *Een witvos.*

Although I'd sometimes slept on Brik's couch if it had gotten late after a meeting and he didn't want to let me drive home after a couple of glasses of wine, I'd never swum in his pool, I told Pip. I'd never felt relaxed enough. And maybe I didn't want to shock Brik with my—then—athletic body. As if my fitness implicitly rebuked his fatness. Pip didn't say anything, she knew it all already. I told her this must actually be the first time I'd swum since an excursion with my student fraternity back in the day. Pippa smiled:

– And you didn't have a swimsuit then either, Monsieur Willy?

When we told Brik that we were splitting up, he'd talked about his own failed marriage. He'd gotten married too young, for a start, but when he started to make a career he lost sight of his wife's love. In his mind she existed as an object, an island, or a wall you could attach planks to, something self-evident that sat waiting for him at home, not a personality that you could preface with adjectives.

– It was only when we were getting divorced that I began to see adjectives for her, *yesh*: lively, intelligent, meticulous, *hair-splitting*, opinionated, legally adept, uncompromising, patient. Aha! Adjectives that apply to your worst opponent in court. Dangerous words. Years later I ran into her, and only then did it strike me how glamorous she was. Big blue eyes, mane of dark, glossy hair. The divorce had done her good, I thought. Only later did I wonder whether she'd always looked like that, but I just hadn't noticed. Will you promise me the same thing won't happen to you?

Nina and I never made it to the pool. It was only now, as I was walking out of her hotel, that I felt the disposable swimsuit in my jacket pocket, still safely vacuum-packed in the plastic in which the clerk at the reception desk had sold them to us for €34.99, a sum that had immediately been added to Nina's bill. Almost as soon as she and I had gotten back on the elevator, one of us had pulled the other into an embrace.

Things happened quickly. Matters progressed.

I threw the swimsuit into a trash can and walked back in the direction of Hofburg, merely because it was my only point of orientation in the city. There was still perhaps half an inch of snow on the ground, just enough to give that timeless feeling that goes with snow. I turned up my collar, stuck my hands deep in my pockets. The cold felt good, open, sharp. It was as if there was extra oxygen in the air.

The funny thing was that now that the mist of lust had more or less evaporated, the images also lost their power. I had to try hard to remember the night, the order in which things happened, the things that were said, the way she growled when I was too slow with the condom, how she wanted to do it standing in front of the mirror, how she wanted to see herself. She had lifted up her breasts and shown me the tiny scars of her operation, two delicate white lines on pink skin—she had been "as flat as a pancake" when she was twenty-one and had treated herself to a full B cup with money she inherited, something that wasn't done in her student circles, but afterward she felt twice as feminine.

What had she smelled like? How did her swimsuit come off? When had I had time to take off my watch and put it carefully in my shoe so I wouldn't lose it? She'd talked to me in bed, but what had she said?

She was indeed married; it had been their second anniversary the previous month and she'd been given a gold chain and pendant. Why didn't that feel like it was enough, she asked herself. What was she looking for? I couldn't come up with answers, could only proffer what I always proffered: the notion that this wasn't taking place in the universe, the real universe of marriage licenses and shared house contents, but in a hole in time that no one needed to know about, a second world.

Who had first kissed the other? To judge by all the things she'd just said, it had been me. I was surprised I'd supposedly seduced her, supposedly encouraged her to commit adultery, rather than the other way around. I'd never been to Istanbul, I'd never ended up in bed with a Greek woman—that would have been totally out of character—but it did seem like something that Philip de Vries might do, glutton that he was. He'd be pushy enough to grab a woman by the lapel of her bathrobe and have his way with her in the elevator, still half in her swimsuit. If I were to do something like that, it would surely only be because she'd been egging me on, as she had done all evening. That urge "to do something naughty," that hand on my arm in the museum. Swimming had surely never just meant swimming, I thought, but perhaps this was the result of spending too much time with Brik: that deep longing for *something* also to mean *something else*, for here also to mean there, yes also to mean no, rage also to mean happiness, always that extra layer.

Call it irony, Pippa once said in a tight voice and with angry tears, whatever you like, fine, but it's as if you're afraid of taking responsibility for a single concrete meaning, a single consequence, a single concern.

Was it fair to Pippa? "Dear Diary, tonight I found myself in a hole in time that no one needs to know about, far away from the real universe of marriage licenses and shared house contents." Was it anyone else's business? Not if I closeted myself in my five-star hotel room today, ordered room service, watched pay-per-view, and waited until Felix had slept off his hangover and we could go and have dinner somewhere out of the loop. Keep a low profile. And how much would Felix be able to remember anyway? Comrade Korsakoff would surely have struck by now.

I'd walked out of the hotel hurriedly, not wanting to run into anybody. Now I relaxed. I craved coffee, I suddenly realized, and something buttery. I'd given her

Philip's business card—"Let's get together"—crossed out his number and substituted mine, telling her it was an old card.

I'd slept with Nina, but she hadn't with me, at least not with Friso. This was the typical inside-out logic that Brik adored.

While Nina was sleeping I'd gazed at her body under the sheet, though it felt wrong. She was ridiculously beautiful, and in repose her body looked entirely natural, like an animal's, whereas mine still felt as if the components hadn't been glued together properly. Everything stuck out. My rib cage. The veins in my wrists, the tendons in my shoulders and my legs. Since losing so much weight, my feet suddenly seemed to have doubled in size, clowns' feet under skinny little legs.

As I walked along I caught myself grinning. Nina and I had done it three times. Three times. Not bad for someone who couldn't climb stairs without getting out of breath—my heartbeat burned triumphantly in the tip of my dick.

I spent the next three or four hours in chain stores and boutiques on Kohlmarkt, where I tried on at least half a dozen pairs of trousers, shirts, jackets, and shoes and paid with the glossy black credit card given to me by Mrs. Chilton, who'd been so kind as to call me that morning and tell me she'd looked at her credit card account and seen that I'd scarcely spent anything yet. *Dear boy, please treat yourself for once.* The connection was crystal clear. She sounded as if she was standing next to me in the elevator.

– What time is it where you are? Isn't it really early? About five a.m.?

– I'm a morning person, Friso, and to quote our former president: Go out and shop.

In a jeweler's shop I watched while an engraver long past retirement age engraved a silver fountain pen with the words "*Für Pippa*" while he told me something in Austrian-German, probably that he'd been doing this for many years. The pen cost the equivalent of a month's salary, and if necessary I could claim that the blue of the barrel exactly matched the color of Pippa's eyes. Deceit and self-deceit. Reclining in a see-through Philippe Starck chair I informed the sales staff of an Italian fashion house that I did not like blucher or derby shoes, nor double-breasted jackets, nor super 120 worsted. It was too shiny. The first thing we agreed on was a gray-brown overcoat in a slightly thicker than normal twill. When it came to suits, two salesmen eyed me up with folded arms and pursed lips, told me that navy blue wasn't really my color, then outfitted me in a soft gray-blue number that fitted like a glove straight off the hanger. I'd never had such a small size before, 46 for just about everything.

When I took off my shirt in the cubicle, one of the salesmen was already standing ready next to the curtain with an unbuttoned shirt, and I held my arms up and allowed him to put it on me as if I were a woman and he my gallant date. I felt a shiver of pleasure run down my spine, caused by the seriousness with which the staff took my sartorial needs, the urgency they seemed to ascribe to them.

With two big bags in my hands (in my calfskin gloves), I headed back to the hotel. Fresh snowflakes already hung in the air, and opposite the entrance to the opera house a chauffeur was hoisting his manatees of passengers one by one into their coach—Americans, by the sound of it, Mr. and Mrs. Airbag, too old and obese to go on a journey without a minder. A stage must come, surely, when you took responsibility and stayed at home.

Brik was perhaps fatter, I thought. Or as fat. But he had earned his weight, like a truck driver; it had been acquired over the years. Their fat was soft, fresh, effortless.

I, by contrast, reflected in the plate-glass windows, looked like one of those businessmen in a CNN commercial: "Live in one continent, work in another." So sharp, so alert. An outfit like that might cost a few thousand euros, but it made you look as if no time zone could get the better of you. The porter held the door open for me, and I nodded in the direction of the Americans.

– How much Sachertorte have they eaten?

– Sir, our restaurant staff are worked off their feet.

I took one step into the hotel and immediately turned on my heel. In the lobby I saw two people on the look-out for someone—that person probably being me, I realized. Yuki Hausmacher, wearing an orange parka, sat on a bench gazing into space, chewing gum and holding a fat wad of paper in her hands: the promised gift from her paymaster Vikram Tahl. Not far from her stood Markus Winterberg, the unspecified associate of Sweder Burgers, his hands behind his back, looking contemplative, like a losing coach during overtime. He seemed to be examining the porter's notice board with concert posters, but I saw his eyes darting above it, scanning the lobby. How I knew he was waiting for me I wasn't sure, but I was quite certain of it. It was me he wanted. Had he said a single word, yesterday? Did he even speak Dutch?

I gestured to the porter.

– Sir?

– I'd like to enter the hotel by the service entrance.

I didn't say please; he had to know that a refusal wasn't an option, and without asking why, as if he was used to this, he led me around the corner of the building into an alleyway, where we reached a heavy door that led to the kitchen. It was just past five, and two chefs stood at a stainless steel cooker from which came the crackle of hot fat: the two gigantic schnitzels in their frying pans resembled undiscovered continents wallowing in a sea of butter. From the kitchen we entered a passageway, and the passageway took me to the stairwell, safely avoiding the lobby.

– Brilliant, I said to the porter.

– Sir.

In my room I found a sheet of notepaper from the reception clerk with two messages. 1: From Mr. Philip de Vries. Could you please ring him back *urgently*? 2: From Mr. Philip de Vries. In case you have lost his number, it is...

This was pleasing. The more I thought about it, the more I felt I'd done the right thing. I hadn't impersonated him; it was he who'd impersonated me, when he appeared on TV, spoke at the memorial service, played Brik's long-lost son. Bastard. Now it was my turn to steal from his plate. *I drink your milkshake.* There was no way I'd call him. I'd discovered the power that lay in *not* doing something, and found it deeply satisfying.

Pippa hadn't called me yet, so I didn't call her either. I called Felix.

He went straight into typical Felix mode. *My dear friend*, I'm so frightfully sorry that I let you down so *appallingly* yesterday. I could tell how he felt just from the effort he put into articulating his words. He sounded tired, but didn't want to show it. His civil servant persona lay in ambush. Everything had to be done correctly. I couldn't tell him about Nina without subjecting myself to his supposedly wise, but inevitably moralizing advice. But perhaps some unconscious part of me wanted to mirror myself against his uprightness.

– Did you have a good night? No raids by the AIVD? You didn't have to hide a populist under your bed?

– I slept like a log. Strolled through the city a bit. What's your take on Vienna?

– I was just thinking about that. I've been walking around it for days now, but have yet to come up with a suitably original observation.

– It's a difficult city to have views about.

– The Heldenplatz isn't as lovely as it should be. All those classical facades give it potential grandeur. But for the full effect it needs huge lawns and boulevards. Instead it's bisected by a busy main road and there are parking lots everywhere, full of tour buses.

– I keep scanning those facades, looking for the balcony where Hitler announced the *Anschluss* in 1938. Because I sort of feel that's expected of me. Perhaps I expect it of myself.

– "The oldest eastern province of the German people shall be, from this point on, the newest bastion of the German Reich." Cheering crowds, perhaps over a quarter of a million people. But you couldn't blame them, the Nazis had shut schools and factories, in those days people had nothing better to do.

– I just stand there and look, and every ten yards or so I see a new balcony that could be the one. I don't have to know the exact spot, it doesn't really matter, and yet I need to know. Apparently I can't visit Vienna without everything making me think of Hitler. Just as in Madrid everything made me think of Franco, in London of Churchill, in Arnhem of Market Garden.

– That's how we were brought up, Felix said.

– Yes, it's a generational thing, isn't it? I'll never get over the fact I that missed out on the Second World War. That I'll never get the same opportunities as Erik Hazelhoff Roelfzema.*

---

* Dutch Resistance figure immortalized in *Soldier of Orange*. The quote that follows refers to a scene in the film where Hazelhoff Roelfzema, played by Rutger Hauer, is forced to sing at a student hazing ceremony while soup is poured over his head—he gives a spirited rendering of the Indonesian folk song "Terang Bulan" (Bright Moon).

– *Terang bulan*!

– *Terang bulan*!

Some sort of Wagner happening was going on in the square that my hotel room overlooked. It had stopped snowing. All the streetlights had been extinguished, and the square cordoned off. Tourists watched from behind crash barriers, as did locals, now also turned into tourists. In the dark the square seemed to move, in the way that still water seems to move when the moon shines on it. Men and women dressed in black held out pieces of black plastic in front of them, shifting them about with calm gestures. The plastic reflected the dark, made it glossy. The darkness moved like a black flag. Music could faintly be heard through the window; I couldn't see the orchestra. The dark plastic now emitted light. The music swelled. The lights moved forward, in V-shaped formations, not quite synchronized, in the way that waves aren't quite synchronized. Perhaps the lights were swans landing on the dark water, perhaps this was *Lohengrin*. Surely we were supposed to read more into it, though, after centuries of Wagner interpretations. It should portray the past in the present, but I wasn't seeing that now.

It was screaming for a metaphor. Forcing itself upon me, begging me to assign a deeper significance to it, a double meaning.

Only now did I see a long procession leading from the hotel to the opera house. It was a performance for invitees, the elite of the conference. I spotted Mathilda Wilson,

Vikram Tahl. A couple of camera teams were filming it all. I looked for Sweder Burgers but didn't see him. Or Nina. I wondered, if Brik had been here, whether I would have been invited too.

I started up my laptop, opened iTunes, and switched the television on. Instead of showing the hotel's selection menu, the screen remained black. I tried zapping, but nothing happened and I threw the remote on the bed. The faint sound of applause came from the square.

I brushed my teeth in the bathroom, took off my socks, and saw that the television screen had meanwhile lit up. The picture showed a room, with a big bed and a little desk opposite it. In the background you could see a small, dark hallway. The bottom right of the screen showed something that was probably a time and date, but the numerals had been made illegible. You could see something moving in the dark, two figures making wrestling movements, something fell softly on the floor, one figure wormed itself out of something. And together they left the darkness, emerging into the light, in full view.

Once again, I was struck by Nina's body. There was nothing accidental about it. It wasn't just her varnished nails and her perfectly trimmed pubic hair, but everything seemed to emanate intent, a physical plot was manifesting itself. Her breasts were cheerful and round, as if drawn by a small child. I was next up. I kicked off my shoes, unbuckled my belt, took off my socks, nearly fell over. My eyes looked so defenseless, I thought, so exposed. My face was gaunt, not a gram of fat left. She laid her hand on my chest and pushed me onto the bed, unbuttoned my shirt, took off my trousers.

Now, as in the recording, I sat at the foot of my bed, my nose nearly touching the screen. I could feel my heart thumping, calmly, but with a force that echoed right up into my palate.

She gave head with a vehemence I'd never before experienced, she attacked my dick like a game show candidate who has to eat a plate of sheep's intestines for fifteen hundred dollars, gobble gobble. This wasn't real life, I tried to tell myself, this wasn't real—but there I lay like an idiot, silent and about as responsive as a corpse, my arms dangling lifelessly, my shoulders drooping. I resembled a toddler at an optician or a real estate agent who wants to show his parents how totally bored he is. She looked up a few times, perhaps to check I was still conscious, but I continued to lie there with my mouth open, staring.

And then—I was reading my own thoughts—I moved my right hand, stretched my arm out to the top of her head, in encouragement. My hand moved gradually, in slow motion, like one of those paintings in which Jesus speaks to a sinner about the True Faith, but I pulled back before touching her. Mission aborted. She then sat on me, guiding me inside her with *her* hand, and I still didn't do anything. She moved her pelvis rhythmically and I placed my hands on her knees, but my contribution ended there, as if I were keen to avoid indecency, not to seem vulgar, while the amazing, surgically enhanced boobies jiggled in front of my nose.

We turned, at her initiative—everything was at her initiative—and I wondered whether this was something women had, an action plan, a little routine that was performed, first this, then that, then finito. A set menu, a preconceived idea of what their partner would be offered and what not. Now I was lying on top. At first I didn't even notice the lack of rhythm in my thrusts, or that I was thrusting in a strange way anyway, crookedly, like a nail you keep hitting askew, I only saw my pathetic excuse for an ass. My pale, shrunken buttocks. What had I left behind in Chile? What part of me had disappeared? Something gaped inside me.

Now I saw myself say something, and I remembered it now, as I read my lips on the screen. "I want you to kneel in front of me like a horse." She rolled over, crouching on her knees and elbows, with her bottom toward me. From the camera's perspective her body took on the shape of a question mark on its side. I had a perfectly medium-sized dick, I concluded. Good to know, I guess. I couldn't work out what tipped the scales, why there was a sudden turning point. My hands gripped her buttocks, her skin rose up between my fingers as if I was clutching butter. For the first time I saw the well-defined muscles running up from my pubis, for the first time I saw my abdomen: I'd never been so ripped. Every time I moved I saw new areas tense, muscles running lengthwise and widthwise. A grill plate from chest to groin.

On the television screen I saw me touching myself, my hands on my own belly, on my own chest. I continued to thrust without letup, a metronome. Work was being done. She laid her face on the pillow. Each thrust made her jolt more violently, pushed her toward the headboard; I saw her right hand clutch at emptiness, reflexively. And I saw my own hands grab hold of something, apparently without being aware of it.

There I was, in Vienna, on television, twisting my own nipples.

For a second, just after I'd come over her back, she seemed to glance aside briefly—just the tiniest movement of the head—and look straight into the camera.

With a click, the screen went black and I saw my own reflection. My expression was new to me: vacant, hollow. The territory was familiar, though. Clips like that are a dime a dozen on the internet, I knew the websites, their appeal lay in their amateurishness: filmed by boys and girls for kicks, put online by angry partners after the breakup. Other emotions should have predominated, other feelings been felt, there were myriad questions I should have been asking myself, but at that moment, in that first instance, self-admiration triumphed over astonishment.

Which doesn't mean, of course, that it didn't come: the astonishment, the blind panic, a frantic heartbeat pulsing so high in my throat that the tension nearly made me throw up.

itler lived. In various places. Chile, the atrophied spine of Latin America, was home not only to Hitler Lima junior, but also to Hitler Lima senior, a man so untroubled by the loaded nature of his own first name that he passed it on proudly to his son.

Shortly after stumbling off the plane, I was received in the spacious, minimalist office of Amanda Romero, extraordinary professor of civil history at the University of Santiago. A secretary brought me a bottle of water; Romero pointed me to a chair that was just slightly too deep. She herself sat bolt upright at a kidney-shaped glass desk and picked up one of her own books, prestigiously titled *The Oxford History of Chile*. She started to read aloud from it: "A Pepsicola Phillipe worked at the Supreme Court, an Adidas Gomez played in the first squad of Colo-Colo, and a Blancanieves Diaz ("Snow White Diaz") sang and danced in the girl band Bailamos. In his novel *The Ground Beneath Her Feet*, the British Indian writer Salman Rushdie calls one of his characters—a Chilean soccer player— Hector Achilles." This name, with its classical overtones, was above all a glossy paradox, she said, of the type that Rushdie had patented—*Hector Achilles*, Trojan and Greek, victim and murderer—and would have lacked all credibility were it not for the fact that the son of the Chilean ambassador to the United Nations, a well-known socialite, was actually called Hector Achilles.

Only later did I read her book, also coming across the reference to *The Lieutenant's Parrot* (1965), the sole novel by Gabriel García Márquez to be set in Chile, in which three rival village youths compete for the hand of the mayor's daughter. Minimaxi Gonzalez and Ivanho Sucre are vanquished, and in the end Donalduk Marinha rides off into the sunset with the lovely Ariel Bulnes. New names, old story.

According to Romero, unorthodox names like these sprang from the wave of anticlericalism that swept Chilean politics and the media in the 1920s and 1930s: "You have to picture the Chilean population in the early twentieth century. Settlers were arriving by the boatload, the big cities were a melting pot of cultures: German, Italian, Spanish, Irish, Greek, you name it. The government didn't want to fan ethnic tensions by favoring a particular religion, so it kept church and state strictly separate. What you see around then is that the traditional names— often of saints and martyrs—made way for secular names, sometimes inspired by political figures, but more often by American pop culture, which had a huge impact from the 1940s onward. Hitler really wasn't such a big deal."

Her theory corresponded with a study carried out by one of Brik's students, who, besides Hitlers, also counted five Stalins, three Churchills, and two Mussolinis in the telephone book. My note-taking speed lagged behind Romero's private lecture, forcing her to pause occasionally. She hadn't noticed my jet lag, I thought, and it seemed wimpy to mention it—but suddenly her expressionless face lit up with a smile and she said: "Hey, Chico, go get some sleep." I nodded, I beamed, always ready to let myself be mothered.

– Tomorrow I have to drive to Aquila.

– That's quite a ways off.

– I've got an interview with someone called Hitler, who's also named his son Hitler. Hitler Lima.

– A notorious name, she said. Be careful.

It turned out he was the most high-profile Hitler in Chile, and the competition was quite stiff. Brik had had a Spanish-speaking student research this. Before I left she'd come to my *Sleepwalker* office, beaming from ear to ear. You could find them simply by looking in the national phone directory. Among all the common or garden surnames, the name lit up like a falling star. Hitler Mendoza, Hitler de la Huerta, Hitler Fazal. She hadn't come across the name on Facebook, because the social network site didn't allow people to set up accounts with the names of serial killers and war criminals. But she did find, on a hunch, phonetic Hitlers: a Diego Ytler Bravo and an Itler Moccadenes.

Hitler Lima lived in Aquila, a little coastal town three hundred miles south of Santiago, in Jauregui Bay. He was easy enough to find, being listed in the telephone book under his full name. It was a six-hour drive. The biggest café on the boulevard had a Coca-Cola logo painted on its facade. Once bright red, it had since been weathered by the salty sea wind, like a tattoo sticker after a few days' wear. Aquila had never been a popular tourist destination. From the boulevard you saw a strange panorama: the seawater was propelled into the bay by streams from the South Pole, making it unusually white and clear, in stark contrast with the sand of the beach, which thousands of years of volcanic activity had turned jet black, so it was too hot to walk on barefoot in summer. White water, black sand: a negative of the natural order.

You could see Lima's house from the beach, beyond the boulevard. It stood just outside the little town, a square box, surrounded by tall, clipped fir trees lined up around it like jailers.

Hitler Lima was no longer young, but he walked erect, his chest stuck out. A proud man. A gaucho. He still had a thatch of silvery white hair and a thick, rectangular mustache. A holster dangled from his hip. It was empty now, but whenever he went out and about he packed his six-shooter, he assured me. He led me through the house and showed me the kennels in the garden, occupied by four lolling Doberman pinschers, their coats black and glossy. He released one of them. It immediately sat up obediently, its ears pricked. Lima threw a treat on the ground, but the dog did not move. Ten, twenty seconds passed before he gave a sign, and the dog pounced on the treat.

Mrs. Lima emerged from the kitchen, bearing a plate of coffee and cookies, which she balanced on her wheeled walker with practiced ease. She'd baked the cookies especially for my visit, and after taking a bite I told her they were delicious.

– We really need some kind of agreement that this conversation will take place on our terms, Mr. Lima said.

– Perhaps you could let us know the questions in advance, so that *he*—Mrs. Lima did not say his name—can decide beforehand what he does and doesn't want to talk about.

– There isn't any beforehand, I said. I'm here now. Mrs. Lima and her husband exchanged glances and it wasn't clear to whose advantage the dialogue had been concluded, but Mr. Lima started to talk. He had grown up in the interior, he said, in a plantation village between the spurs of the Garenta river. Since then the village had been reclaimed by the jungle and was virtually forgotten, except by a handful of archaeologists and historians who trekked to the ossuarium, which, just like in adventure stories, lay some way off, hidden behind a waterfall. It contained the skulls and bones of Mapuche Indians who had been systematically hunted and exterminated by conquistadores as of the sixteenth century. Hitler's father had taken him there as a boy. They would clamber upward for two hours to get to the cave, where the bones gleamed like the moon in the quiet darkness and his father told him not to fear anything, least of all the dead.

Lima was a social climber, he told me. He might be the son of a prominent man where he came from, but in the city he was looked down on as a provincial. When he stood there in his uniform writing tickets on a street in Santiago, parking offenders would snarl at him to piss off back to the jungle. When he was investigating crimes, junkies and prostitutes would laugh at his accent. "Sometimes pimps and killers would give me directions, without me asking. It was downright embarrassing."

The event that had made him famous took place just after he'd been promoted to the security service. One day—just some ordinary day like any other—he and his partner happened to be driving past a bank when they saw a shifty-looking individual in the doorway. There'd been no emergency call, but when they stopped and got out, his partner was shot and died on the spot. ("We must have been instantly recognizable as cops, with our mustaches and shades.") Something clicked inside his brain and without a second thought, he stormed the bank single-handedly, bullets whizzing past his ears, one tearing a button from his sleeve, a second grazing his shoulder pad, until Hitler Lima fired back, shooting four robbers dead with four bullets. The hostages were unharmed; he himself wasn't even out of breath.

– They say that people often black out during experiences like that, can't remember anything afterward. I can still remember everything. The bullets seemed to go past me in slow motion. I still remember how the light fell into the building and how the robbers looked when I shot them.

– How did they look?

– As if they couldn't believe it.

In the living room, Lima showed me the keys of the city of Santiago, given to him on his retirement, and searched for a videotape of the ceremony in which he was awarded a medal for bravery. Your fifteen minutes of fame, I volunteered.

– Oh no, he said without any irony. The tape only lasts two or three minutes.

The recorder accepted the videocassette with a noise like a robot struggling to swallow, and after ten seconds of hiss, pictures emerged. The camera showed a row of men saluting General Pinochet as he prepared to ascend the podium. Sometimes the picture jumped. Loud march music almost drowned out the voice-over as the cameras zoomed in on the men one by one. Lima was third; his eyes were the same steely blue, but the skin of his face was self-confidently taut and only now did I see how broad his jaw was. "H. Lima" came into the shot. His mustache was thick, black, and regal and sat on his lip like a trained animal.

Pinochet, dressed in a white uniform covered in gold frogging and spangles, stopped in front of Hitler Lima, who stood ramrod straight, his chest sticking out. The shot changed to another camera, showing a close-up of the general. Pinochet looked fragile—but perhaps that was because I only knew him from news items as an old man, and this was a case of the future influencing history, a two-way mirror. After having pinned on the medal, the general returned Lima's salute. Even if you hadn't known what he was about to say, you could read the words from his smiling lips.

"*Heil Hitler!*" Pinochet grinned.

That was just the start. Colleagues would click their heels together as he passed and smirkingly retort "*Jawohl, mein Führer!*" when he asked them to get coffee. At times he would have to make his way through an archway of extended right hands, and when, at a weekly meeting, he announced that he had solved a case, his boss said he'd been confident he'd come up with an "*Endlösung*." "But you shouldn't read too much into it. It was just, you know, office humor. Like someone putting salt in the sugar bowl, so you put it in your coffee by mistake. It had nothing at all to do with the murder of the Jews."

I asked what he knew about the origin of his name.

– My father was the overseer of a cocoa plantation. Everyone in the village worked for him, everyone fell under his responsibility. (. . .) The post would be delivered twice a week, on Tuesdays and Fridays. Very few people could read or write. But they were all keen to hear the latest news, so at the end of the day my father would fetch the newspaper and read most of it aloud to his employees. They hung on his words. (. . .) The stories coming out of Germany at the time were inspiring, I won't deny it. Chile, too, had suffered in the Depression, and here was someone—someone from a humble background—who'd taken a whole country by the collar and lifted it back onto its feet. We envied Germany. When I was born, Hitler was an inspiring name.

That was in April 1940, just before Nazi Germany trampled over Western Europe. His father cut a photo out of the newspaper showing Hitler posing in front of the Eiffel Tower. Lima could remember it, which suggested the photo was still on display long after the war had ended. In those days, war was seen differently, he said. It wasn't yet the taboo subject it is now. It went with politics.

He told me a great deal more: about his father, who had difficulty accepting the reality of the Second World War, about his life as the father of four children, about his son whom he'd named after himself, simply because "that's the custom," fathers and sons, never easy, yadda yadda—he talked about the paintings his son did, and showed me one he'd been given for Father's Day. I wrote it all down. He answered every question politely, precisely. His wife brought us two cold beers and a bowl of peanuts. Pinochet wasn't mentioned again.

The strange thing was: I was there because of a name, because of a story that had more to do with human interest than history, and everything he said was fine as far as I was concerned, I didn't think too much about it. And yet one thing did cross my mind, that he'd made a career in the security service during the most notorious years of the Pinochet regime, and that perhaps at some point he'd herded ten

or fifteen people into the hold of a plane—Socialists, dissidents, undesirables—and waited until they'd screamed
themselves hoarse, until their vocal cords gave out, before
dumping them somewhere off the coast from a height of
two miles. I wondered about that, and then I wondered
whether that was in fact the Pinochet regime or some other
South American junta, I always mixed them up, the evil
ones and their methods. Was Chile the country of the soccer stadiums and Argentina the one with the airplanes? Or
was it the other way around? The specifics of totalitarian
excesses have never greatly interested me.

At that point I still hadn't the faintest idea what was
about to happen to me, I knew nothing about the infection
that had already infiltrated my body like the secret service,
Brik was still in the pink of corpulent health, Pippa had
ceased to be my girlfriend, lover, partner, or whatever you
want to call it. Order prevailed.

I thought about how I'd have sat here in a different era,
with my notebook and my questions and my tape recorder,
back when the planes of the junta were still circling the sky.
Less free, more frightened, undoubtedly, but at least I'd
have had a mission: to uncover murky dealings. Amanda
Romero of the University of Santiago had warned me—she
was still thinking, probably, of what a journalist's work
used to be, and the risk it involved. But the man opposite
me was just a retiree, an old gentleman who looked as if
he'd gotten past the stage of serving up little white lies, and
was just telling me what he thought. If this was the last face

that countless dissidents had seen in their lives, it was now looking at me amicably and impassively, and I was returning the look amicably and impassively.

Impassive. Amicable. Calm & Collected.

That was the motto, that was who I was. A counterweight to Brik's permanent revolution of clumsy blunders, his faux pas, his snubs, intentional and chiefly unintentional—I was the diplomatic corps. My tie was straight, my socks matched my shoes, I smoothed out misunderstandings, followed him around like a Dustbuster. I apologized to hostesses on his behalf for arriving an hour late at their dinners, for all the missed deadlines, for all the books and DVDs he borrowed and then left in trains and planes. I dismantled conflicts, I did not create them.

And then there was Pippa, for whom I went through life as a traffic sign. I never cycled next to her, but a bike's length in front, so she could see whenever I indicated, whenever I changed lane. On walks I'd say things like: "When the light goes green we'll cross." All to prevent her from getting stranded in the middle of an intersection, too hesitant to take priority, too stubborn to retreat.

That was my role. Things were expected of me. Calm & Correct.

And yet there I was, me of all people, hurrying along the corridor of my five-star hotel with panic at my heels. To flee: that was the first impulse. A primitive instinct, as old as humanity, to run away from forest fires, from floods, from pterodactyls, from saber-toothed tigers, from bears, from wolves, from invading Mongol hordes. But what was I running away from, exactly? From me-that-was-not-me. From digital cameras. From hacked TV channels, from secret recordings. From someone I'd never met.

Not really running, by the way—that would look conspicuous—but taking great awkward strides, like when you're trying to step over a puddle. Not that anyone could see me in the corridor, but still. Hadn't I thought that no one could see me yesterday evening in Nina's room?

After just managing to get a foot between the closing elevator doors, I ran straight into the mobile bunker of Raimund Pretzel, *Panzer Pretzel*, and a nurse who was sticking her index and ring fingers up Pretzel's nose, V for Victory, probably to position the oxygen tubes better. *Sic transit gloria mundi.* Through his Coke-bottle glasses I could see that the eye that wasn't covered by a patch was sharp and bright, and taking careful note of my face. The elevator doors closed again. I waited until the nurse had finished, and bent down in front of him, my hands on my knees, grinning inanely in a way that was meant to be disarming, the sort of look you adopt for a toddler or an animal at a petting zoo.

– Mr. Pretzel, may I say how inspired I am by your work?

Of course I was trying to prove something to myself: that I could do this, at such a moment, have a little chat, that all the adrenaline coursing through my body could be controlled by my brain. Mind over matter, intellect over gut instinct.

He looked at me with his bright eye and something like a smile appeared on his crooked mouth.

– Thank you, he said, his voice hardly more than a whisper. Are you a historian by profession?

– I work in Hitler studies.

He nodded, he could still do that, and in the forced voice of someone trying to talk through a ball of phlegm, he said: a truly fascinating field of research.

I'd felt a brief pang of embarrassment when I told him my field; this man, whose historical research had shaped current social debate on the reunification of East and West Germany, on European interventions in the Balkan wars, surely he had more important things to occupy his tired head than a bunch of navel-gazing theory-mongers? But I couldn't help being disappointed by his response. He too. Truly fascinating, yes, absolutely fascinating.

– I understand that in your field no topic is too insignificant. Is that true?

What I wanted to prove to myself couldn't be proved: not by me, not there in the elevator, not ten minutes after the TV screen had gone black. A trapdoor opened, a hole in the roof.

– I'm researching Hitler porn, is that something you're familiar with? I asked. It's claimed that no pornography was produced in Nazi Germany—though when we look at

Leni Riefenstahl–type propaganda through today's porn-tinted lens we see plenty of innuendo, all those blond, bare-chested lads—but this gap was filled later, mainly in the 1970s, when Nazi porn became a subgenre in its own right. Did you know that? I've researched the actors, the film companies, the budgets, the reviews, the target groups. I've gone through endless sex scenes. Such a lot of fellatio, such a lot of girl-on-girl, such a lot of sex aids. Naziploitation, or Nazi sexploitation, whatever you want to call it. With a special focus on sadomasochism, there's a lot of that, girls in hiding who have to do things for men in uniform. Or women in uniform who dominate men. A pearl of the genre is *Ilsa, She Wolf of the SS*, 1975, pretty hot stuff actually, about camp commandant Ilsa who every evening selects a male prisoner and rapes him. Because of her insatiable lust, however, she's always furious when her victim ejaculates, and promptly castrates him. In the end she chooses an American POW who can defer climaxing and thus turns her weakness to his advantage. This naturally generates essay questions: What is American potency a metaphor for? What analogy do we find in German insatiability? Everything means something, while at the same time meaning something else. They say that before you can become an expert on anything, you need at least ten thousand hours of experience, and I'm well on the way, Mr. Pretzel. Fascinating, eh?

Pretzel replied with a fit of snorts, in which I at some point made out "Your name."

– My name? What a good question. My name is Philip de Vries. *D.E.V.R.I.E.S.* With a space between "de" and "Vries," they're two words. The spring edition of the *Journal of Contemporary History* features a long article by me. Eight thousand words, in fact. It took me a whole month to write. "*The Cunnilinguist, oral fixation in pejorative language use in Naziploitation 1969–1975.*"

– I look forward to reading it, he said, having gotten his voice back, as he looked pointedly in the other direction, clearly embarrassed. I clapped my hands and stuck up two thumbs, the international gesture of the dickhead, and jumped out of the elevator as the doors opened.

– Splendid. Don't forget my name—Philip de Vries!

The truly bizarre thing was that I was fully primed for this: *Ilsa the She Wolf*, Leni Riefenstahl, I'd read it all somewhere, it had all lodged in some corner of my brain, and, like caked dirt soaking off in soapy water, it all now came loose in my head. Random facts, random ideas. Like confetti. Like dandruff. Theories. *Oh, you Moor, you strange black man, always so full of theses, never a church door to nail them to.*

So full, you mean, of feces.

Poor Pretzel. I needed a drink to recover from the chaos of my imagination. And something to eat. Or money, so I could buy something, something to calm me down and realign me with those thousands and thousands of people in the city who were gradually consuming their way toward Christmas. I speed-walked through the hotel lobby—Don't run! Don't run!—and there, once again, was the pleading face of Yuki Hausmacher, who glided toward me like a ghost in a cathedral cloister, clasping some paper.

– Mr. De Vos?!

That was my name, but Mr. De Vos was temporarily absent, Mr. De Vries now had priority.

– Just a sec!

And before she could grab me I got through the revolving doors, into the late evening. The Wagner show on the square near the opera house was over. The crash barriers had been taken away and the tourists could roam once more. Yet again I went to the Heldenplatz, I was there in a trice, Vienna was ridiculously small. The closer I got to Nina's hotel, the more I felt as if I was missing something. It was an image that was lacking: the picture of an outcome. It's said that top athletes can visualize every move before they make it, in perfect detail. They know exactly how the ball will curve in toward the corner of the net. I couldn't imagine how this might end, what I would be forced to do, whom I was dealing with, or, if there was an "oops, my mistake" solution, what form it would take. I could only picture myself walking into the hotel and pulling out a brace of pistols—the old, round-barreled kind—and one by one blowing away the porters, the janitors, the bell-hops, the reception desk clerks, the cleaners, the guests, Nina, Sweder Burgers, and Philip de Vries like a row of ninepins, like Hitler Lima storming into the robbed bank, in a cloud of gunsmoke, like a one-man Bonnie and Clyde.

Never mind.

It wasn't necessary. No one was lying in wait for me in the hotel lobby, and no one was lying in wait for me in Nina's room. I'd forgotten the number, only knew that it was on the fifth floor, where the corridor ended in a cul-de-sac and there was a big, kitschy painting of a cavalry officer around the time of the *Ausgleich*. It turned out to be room 519. The door was open, the room was empty, the bed had been made with clean sheets. The place smelled of lemon. On the spot where the camera must have hung, just above a lamp, a tiny piece of adhesive tape had been scraped loose, the size of a Band-Aid.

The clerk at the reception desk was as friendly as could be expected: the lady in room 519 had checked out that morning. Unfortunately she couldn't tell me where she'd gone. Her sudden departure was revealing, I thought. Either flight or acknowledgment of guilt.

I stood there at the desk and was overcome by a feeling of tiredness and hunger and boredom, incredible as that seemed, even to me. At first I thought it was the emptiness of an anticlimax, but there was more to it than that—it was as if something had been done to me (and it had!) and just as I wanted to get my own back (revenge!) on whoever was responsible, the bird had flown, forcing me to return to my unnaturally luxurious hotel room.

The hunger was the easiest problem to solve. At the end of the street in which the hotel stood I could see the lights of several little shops and possibly snack bars, and before long I was standing in the doorway of a cheap-looking convenience store. Packs of B-brand tampons and razors dangled prominently in the window, like those displays of top-quality smoked sausages you see in butcher's shops. A bored-looking youth of Middle Eastern appearance sat behind the checkout counter, playing with his phone. The brands inside were reassuring: the familiar logos, the well-known colors and shapes. The chips came in different flavors but in the same tubes, the Coke bottles were of a softer plastic than in the Netherlands, but the brand names gave you the reassuring feeling of being safely cocooned inside the cultural market hegemony of the First World, the sense that nobody could really harm you, or even wanted to. It was the internalization, the personification of the Golden Arches theory: countries that have McDonald's do not go to war with each other.

Kids and grown-ups love it so—the happy world of Haribo. I paid and took my bag of peach-flavored candy outside, flopping down on one of the garden chairs that served as sidewalk seating for the neighboring snack bar, now closed.

The sugar coating was tough, but as soon as it dissolved you could feel the center, soft yet solid, a sort of chemical meat. Peach sweets came in different sizes and this was my favorite—the smallest –which meant more outer layer, proportionately speaking. I loved their hardness, the feel of the rough grains of sugar on my tongue.

Various people walked past, including a woman about the same age as my mother, holding a doner kebab between her thumb and middle finger like an appetizer, as if she wanted to kid herself she wasn't really eating a doner kebab for dinner. She had big dark eyes and short bangs. There was a blob of garlic sauce just below one corner of her mouth. A long shawl was draped around her neck in a complicated way, but her coat was unbuttoned, so I could see her name badge with the congress logo.

– *Bon appétit*, I said.

– Good evening, she said. She was undoubtedly going back to her hotel, where she was undoubtedly staying in a room like Nina's. If only I'd fucked *her*, I thought, smiling, as I went back into the shop to get another bag of peach sweets. I sat down again and felt the muscles in my legs protesting.

I stuffed candy into my mouth, two or three at a time. It made me think of the soldier at the end of *A Farewell to Arms*, who polishes off four or five plates of sauerkraut while the woman he loves is dying in childbed. *I was not made to think. I was made to eat. My God, yes.* Pippa was the only woman I'd ever seen read Hemingway with enjoyment; Brik couldn't stand him. When I'd eaten all the sweets I put my finger in my mouth and ran it along the bottom of the bag so that all the loose sugar stuck to it, then licked my finger. It wasn't a taste that lingered.

– Good evening, said a voice, and I looked up into the loveless, watery eyes of Markus Winterberg.

In that narrow street where footsteps should ring out, I hadn't heard him approach. But I smiled and held up the empty candy bag:

– All gone. You're too late.

– I was hoping, actually, that you were on your way back to your hotel, Mr. De Vries. Mr. Burgers would like to speak to you.

He, too, knew how to formulate a request so that refusal wasn't an option. I smiled again.

– Mr. Burgers won't take up much of your time. He's waiting for you in his suite at the hotel.

– Is this about what I think it's about?

– Mr. Burgers will explain.

Winterberg spoke Dutch, but he clearly wasn't a native speaker. He seemed to give every word much more weight.

– Will it take long?

– That's hard to tell.

His plump, full lips projected patience and authority. Okay, I thought. So this is it. The denouement. And anyway, piss off! It's not my fault, this whole mistaken identity thing. This was supposed to be my moment. Mine. *He* passed himself off as *me*. He was on television and spoke at the memorial service and was in the paper and he must have known very well that that wasn't his role, it was mine. So bring it on—I nearly said it aloud. Bring it on, whatever it is you want of me.

————

When we entered his suite, Burgers was nowhere to be seen, but Winterberg assured me he'd be there shortly. In the meantime, he said, we could consider another matter. From an envelope he produced two sheaves of paper, one of which he gave to me. The text was printed on letterhead of the Burgers Foundation, Brasschaat, Belgium.

– Mr. Burgers wanted you to read this.

– What is it? I asked.

– Just read it. I'll be back in a minute, he said, and left the room. I watched him go, noting his broad shoulders, the three creases in his fat neck.

I was alone. It was a pleasant suite. I'd expected wood-paneled walls, massive sideboards, and all the other things one associated with Habsburg Vienna (ivory table legs, walking sticks with hidden daggers in them, curtains that sucked up the light, and a generally suicidal atmosphere), but the interior was modern and sparsely furnished. The big windows overlooked the opera house. The sandy gray sofa where Winterberg had indicated I should sit was angular and minimalist, with no decorative cushions or frills.

But for the first few minutes I couldn't read. I merely stared at the sheets of paper. At first the letters didn't form words. They floated. Perhaps I was hysterical. (Vienna was, after all, the city where hysteria was invented, right?) I had to read, which shouldn't have been a problem. That was my job, to spend forty hours a week reading, underlining things, improving punctuation, making comments in the margin. I was better at reading than at living. Always had been. Back in primary school I exaggerated or lied about hundreds of things, just to see how far I could go before getting caught, and I was *never* caught—until the time I said I'd read a book in a week. Some tale of knightly adventure. The teacher didn't believe that I hadn't skipped chapters; she thought I'd cheated. But I was telling the truth. I'd really read it in a week. I was furious, felt that my honor had been slighted. A few years later it happened again, in a junior class at secondary school, when my teacher refused to believe I'd read *Lord of the Rings*. I remember his heavy sarcasm: If you've really read it, Mr. De Vos, pray tell us what the giant spider was called? Why did Boromir loathe Aragorn? What do the elves call Gandalf? Who is the real "Lord of the Rings"? *There is only one Lord of the Ring*, I said, *and he does not share power*, and to prove my point and assuage my wounded feelings I made it a point of honor in those years to put the thickest possible novel on my desk and sit reading it ostentatiously during his classes.

I don't know if that's what propelled me in the direction of literature and history and cultural studies, and thus toward Brik and *The Sleepwalker*, but back then, in those unsure teenage years, it seemed such a clear, straightforward way of amassing power. You read a book and then you knew. You knew the characters, knew why they behaved as they did, you possessed that knowledge. You flipped through the pages, you could smell the paper—the older and yellower, the sweeter. I never saw reading as a duty. To me, it was always a means of gaining something.

That helped: reminding myself why I read. I could take myself to task. Read that text, Friso.

It was a fragment of a maquette, an architectural model representing the double front of a building, perhaps a foot wide. Two floors with pillars as high as your middle finger, fronting a facade in whose niches—in the fictitious world represented by the maquette—busts would have stood. From a distance it looked as if it were made of ivory. Brik adored it, had paid a few thousand dollars for it, not because it had been broken off Albert Speer's maquette of Germania, *which stood like a dolls' house in the Reich Chancellery, but precisely because it hadn't. Supposedly looted from the ruins of the Berlin bunker complex in the spring of 1946 by a lieutenant in the Russian intelligence service, the object had been put up for auction at an asking price of over ten thousand dollars. It came with a letter from the Soviet intelligence officer, a man by the name of Arkady Rossovich. Despite all that was going on, Berlin was quiet, he wrote. People avoided eye contact. He told his mother about the winter storms that blew up from time to time, and how everyone went about with red, watery eyes because of the grit and gunpowder that were still wafted along in the chill wind.*

His call to arms had come as something of a
surprise to Rossovich—he taught Latin and Greek
at a small grammar school in Leningrad, and had
been working on a monograph about Achilles myths
when he was called up by the intelligence service. The
war had swept him away from classical antiquity to
the here and now, from art to arms. "Now I must lay
aside my Horace," he wrote to his brother, imme-
diately after Operation Barbarossa, "and turn to
Clausewitz, Machiavelli, and Mein Kampf.*"*

What had brought Rossovich to Berlin was a
rumor, and back then, when the Iron Curtain was
just beginning to take shape, rumors could carry
more weight than facts. It was the tale that Hitler,
the sleepwalker, was still alive, had perhaps even
been given refuge in one of the Western zones. Later
to be dubbed "the survival myth," this persistent
belief that Hitler had escaped from the bunker
where his charred body was allegedly found was a
game, a trail of fictitious information intended to
unsettle the various Allied parties, Rossovich was
sure. No one told him this, but he knew how these
things worked—he was there to provide cover for the
Kremlin.

Winterberg came in with a tray, on which stood cups
and a teapot.

– Who wrote this? I asked.

Winterberg shrugged.

– Read it as if that didn't matter, he said, so I did.

*In that winter of 1945–1946 Rossovich interviewed
the circle of politicians, soldiers, and personal staff
who had spent the last days of Nazi Germany in the*
Führerbunker. *He spoke to Traudl Junge, recovering
from diphtheria in a hospital in the British zone,
a fragile little cow-eyed creature, the secretary who
had drawn up Hitler's last political will. He spoke
to a member of the* Führerbegleitkommando, *Ewald
Lindloff, who had personally doused the bodies of
Hitler and his secret bride with petrol. Lindloff, now
in an Allied prison cell, was unsure whether he had
been right or wrong to do so. He spoke to Albert Speer,
silent as a sarcophagus, save for the occasional calm
utterance that seemed to come from somewhere deeper
than himself. The* Reichsarchitect *was very sure
about one thing: there was something about his gaze.
Hypnotic.*

*Rossovich tried to do all the fieldwork and inter-
views before lunch, so he could spend the afternoon
jotting down his findings on lined index cards, which
he would type up in the evening. He stuck to word
quotas; knowing that the authorities liked precision
and brevity, he set a rule that the typed version had
to be less than half the length of the handwritten one.*

Each day he noted his progress (telephone list, number of words, bedtime) in a logbook.

He wasn't sure what he hoped to find among the ruins of the Reich. There were warnings of booby traps. He didn't set out to plunder, wasn't in search of gold telephones or silverware to send home. It was pure curiosity. From the Volga to Berlin he'd seen his peers, his friends, sometimes, run straight into German machine-gun fire, lives were lost like tears in the rain. Columns of black smoke billowed up from the Reichstag, and now he couldn't not go and look. He had to know what was there, in the nerve center of the war.

He was amazed at how easily he gained access to the place of Hitler's death. At the entrance he encountered two Russian soldiers, gangling lads, bored to tears, who let him enter in exchange for a pack of cigarettes. He went down a dimly lit staircase that reminded him of the stairways in the Moscow underground. Graffiti on the wall, Cyrillic alphabet.

At the bottom he found himself ankle-deep in sewer water. It was difficult for him, with his classical schooling, to suppress a smile, given the heavy symbolism of the situation. He was entering history underground, in the semidarkness, like a grave robber rubbing his hands at the sight of the pharaoh's treasure.

He also thought of the old Norse legend that tells how when great men die, they go into the mountain,

*and that sometimes, during long nights, you can hear
their voices deep under the ground. But the way Hitler had intended it, there wasn't to be any mountain
left standing after him, any voices from under the
ground, any ground, and least of all anyone up there
standing listening.*

– This is a very strange piece of writing. That's not how
you write for one of your foundation's catalogues, surely?

But with a shock I remembered, and stopped myself.
Editorial experience—it was Friso who had that, not
Philip. I was the one with skills, not Philip.

– Read on, Winterberg said again.

So I did as I was told.

*His flashlight beam fell on a rat, which promptly
froze and stared at him. In his coat pocket Rossovich
found a piece of gum, which he threw at the creature.
The rat bounded off into the water and swam—so
that's how rats swim, he thought.*

*A staircase took him to a series of passageways
lined with small, bare rooms. The walls dripped with
moisture; a sickly smell of burning, urine, oil, and
abandonment grew stronger and stronger. Paper and
dirt floated in the water. He should come back with
Wellington boots, storm lanterns, assistants—but
now he was here alone, amid ransacked filing cabinets and smashed tables. A black telephone stood on*

a desk, its cord severed. There had been a time when that cord was not severed, he thought, when it had been operational. Once, that cord had extended into the continent like a tentacle, conveying orders with consequences.

"Mein Führer: a message from the West. The Ruhrgebiet has fallen."

"Flood the mines. It will take the Jews twenty years to get them working again."

There were indentations in the walls that he took for bullet holes. Shades of the Prinsenhof.* He ran his fingertips over them—who had committed suicide here? Who had paced around here, despaired?

He looked at the telephone. Its ring was discordant, a painfully cheerful sound in an underground world of dull thuds and rending concrete. That spring, Berlin had seen three hundred square feet of rubble come down for every one of its inhabitants.

"Mein Führer: the airfields have been hit by precision bombing. The Luftwaffe cannot take off."

"The Luftwaffe, I should have had them all strung up a long time ago."

He waded through the brackish water toward a small room that served as an antechamber to a larger room—you could picture a division of roles, a positioning. Suite and en suite. Leader and secretary.

---

* The site of William of Orange's assassination, in Delft, in 1584. The bullet holes are still visible.

"Traudl, dear child, don't stay here any longer, surrounded by death."

His hands, his fingers trembled constantly, as if he were operating an invisible Morse key. But was anyone still receiving the messages?

The large room was full of chests with open drawers and empty crates. He looked for the bunk beds that the Goebbels children must have slept in—Helga, Hildegard, Helmut, Holde, Hedda, and Heide, aged between twelve and three—but was scared of finding them. A sudden picture: Magda Goebbels throws herself at his feet. "Don't do it, think of us, of the National Socialist dream!" He waves her away brusquely—no drama!—because he knows he can only dream this dream a little longer. Meanwhile, twenty-seven feet above them, Berliners are screaming in desperation, not knowing where to hide. The Red Army is approaching, house by house.

"Have Axmann mobilize the Deutscher Jugend!"

A new antechamber, another desk. Another telephone, Fegelein!, and a typewriter with its keys smashed, its ribbon torn. A chair next to it, perfect for if you want to dictate to the typist.

"Above all I order the leadership of the nation and all staff to rigorously enforce the race laws and ruthlessly oppose the great poisoner of all peoples, international Jewry . . . Can you read that back, Traudl?"

*There was a second desk in the antechamber,
again with a shiny black telephone in the center, like
the bust of a deformed person.*

*Speer appeared, to make his farewells. Minister
of Armaments and War Production. He saw it, he
said, as his duty to report that in the past months he
had systematically ignored Hitler's Nero Decree. He
had sabotaged the scorched earth strategy, he had shut
down munitions factories. "I had to tell you."*

*Hitler listened calmly, abstractedly, his thoughts
with the ash factories in the east, which had gone on
operating. He was silent.*

Speer left, and the telephone rang.

*"Führer—we've lost contact with Wenck! The
Russians..."*

*"Don't worry, don't worry. I always know the
right thing to do."*

*Here he would slam the door behind him, with
such violence as to shatter it.*

*The door wasn't locked. The walls of the room
were scorched black—he had been told that, too, by
the two indifferent soldiers. Bormann, they said
(how did they know?), had wanted to destroy Hitler's
private apartments, but the fire had gone out. Too
little oxygen. Bormann had been the first to enter the
room. Gunsmoke. The scent of almonds. She had lain
against him, her curled locks on his shoulders, her*

habitually tight smile gradually vanishing. At last.
She had nearly written her new name wrong on their
wedding certificate, a few hours previously. She had
written "Eva B" and then crossed out the "B," she
was now Eva H. "Eva Hitler, née Braun." As always,
she'd done what he had asked her—he felt her growing
heavier on his shoulder, her breathing becoming more
labored. This had been less than a year ago. And then
he had targeted himself, with his Walther PPK. Made
in Germany, since 1931. The feel of the pistol. The
solid weight in his right hand. The sharp ridges of the
grip against his fingertips. The short barrel, scarcely
longer than an index finger. It had been the subject of
discussion: Mouth or temple? I always know the right
thing to do. Temple. Into the mountain.

– Countless films have been made about Hitler, but did
you know that only a handful show his actual death? Why
is that? I asked, just to make conversation, because we
must have published at least sixteen hundred *Sleepwalker*
articles on the subject.

– Cowardice.

– It's really more a form of self-censorship, prompted
by...

– The mistake you make is that you talk to me as if I
were Brik. I'm not Brik. Brik is dead. I'm not interested in
film scenes. I'm alive—he described a circle in the air with
his finger—in this world.

What could you say to someone who said things like that? Who then looked at you sweetly, poured you a cup of tea, and asked:

– One lump?

– Two, I said.

– My my, haven't you got a sweet tooth.

It sounded so flagrantly gay that I looked away, immersing myself in the text again.

Arkady Rossovich: *"Suddenly I threw up. As I've never thrown up before. At first I thought it was the surroundings, the stench, the sickly water. But it was me. It was as if I'd realized something without formulating it, as if a vacuum had suddenly been pumped full. The bunker. The Reichstag. This end. This story—it existed in a different world from the one in which we existed."*

As Rossovich's account went on, it became harder and harder to follow. He described how he had passed his hands through the water, like a sieve, that he kept thinking he heard voices, and that in the end he had seen the piece of the maquette floating in the water and had fled outside with it.

Years later, when he was transferred to the Russian-occupied zone in Vienna, Rossovich met an antiques dealer who was interested in the item. It was at the latter's request that he'd written the letter. The Viennese dealer sold it to an Italian dealer and

via Venice it ended up in the hands of an American
tourist, which is how it entered the collectors' market.
Experts examined it and concluded that it was one
of the houses on the seven-lane Prachtallee, between
the Brandenburg Gate and the Volkshalle. It was sold
about ten times, each time for a higher sum—until a
simple test proved it to be a forgery. Somebody from
an auction house had doubted the authenticity of
Rossovich's letter, not the story itself, but the typeface.
It seemed to him that the letter had been written on a
too-modern typewriter. The forgery was ultimately
proved by a sample taken from the maquette: it con-
tained some kind of plastic composite that had only
been invented in the 1960s. The object wasn't even
fifty years old. Arkady Rossovich had never existed.

That only increased its value as a relic, Brik said
cheerfully. Not because it had really stood in Hitler's
private apartments, but because the ten previous
collectors had been so keen to believe it.

That was where the story ended, though there were still
three words underneath it, three words that somehow
sealed a fate: "Philip de Vries." Who writes like that?
Philip de Vries writes like that.

– I'll let Mr. Burgers know you're ready.

He knocked on a door and Sweder Burgers slipped
into the room, looking relaxed. He wore corduroy trousers, a gray linen jacket, and loafers. His face was friendly

enough: a perfectly straight nose, sharp eyes with soft bags underneath them, and cheeks that were beginning to sag. The sort of face that presents the *News at Ten*. It was the first time I'd seen him without a hat. From a distance it looked as if someone had branded him with an iron, level with what must once have been his hairline; a clear red triangle stood out on his forehead. Only when he got closer could I see it was composed of a few dozen bloodred dots, beautifully symmetrical, undoubtedly the expert handiwork of one of Austria's finest private clinics.

– Philip. Nice to see you. We need to talk.

There was no wounded look, no sarcastic tone when he said my name, *his name*. He didn't know anything about Nina. Nina, Nina, Nina. The recording had to be a mistake. Hold your horses.

I decided to say nothing: wouldn't raise the subject of Nina, wouldn't apologize, wouldn't volunteer information, wouldn't do anything to prematurely end this audience. I'd either fail as Philip de Vries or hear what this Sweder Burgers wanted from him. I would remain serious, stay in character, and I would not stare at his hair, repeat not stare, because suddenly I found myself wondering whether this brand-new hair implant was in the right place, whether Burgers's new hairline wasn't going to end up too close to his eyebrows, making him look simian.

Winterberg closed the en suite doors of the room as if he were formally concluding the introductions and the real conversation could now start:

– Philip, might I tell you a story?

He might.

– Picture the following. Perhaps you know the facts. I assume you know the facts. But this is about their interpretation. So listen. In 1954, Simon Wiesenthal got a postcard from an old acquaintance in Argentina, who wrote that he'd seen "that filthy swine Eichmann." It's a well-known story. This is how it goes. Eichmann works as a foreman in a Mercedes-Benz factory. Lives in a suburb to the north of Buenos Aires. Has a false passport in the name of Ricardo Klement. Immediately after the first sightings, Mossad and Shin Bet set up shop in Argentina, building up a team of eleven secret agents who tail him and keep him under surveillance for the whole of April 1960, unobserved. May 11, 1960. The Mossad team plan to seize him on his way home from work, as he walks from the bus stop to his house, number 14, Garibaldi Street. Facts, Philip, facts. But Eichmann doesn't get out of his regular bus. Where is he? One of the Mossad teams is in a car that has supposedly broken down—friendly passersby offer assistance, the agents manage to wave them away. The tension mounts, should they abort the mission? I love telling this story. Half an hour later Eichmann at last emerges from a bus, putting his head in the noose, as it were. One of the secret agents heads toward him, quasi-nonchalantly, imitating the swagger he's seen on South American beaches, where boys and girls frolic, oblivious to the recent past, to destruction, to the people in their midst who are trying to outsmart history; he walks with an exaggerated swing in his step, perhaps snapping his fingers, and addresses the bald old man with his briefcase in Spanish: *Hola!*, or *Buenas noches, señor.* The headlights of a parked car snap on. Eichmann finds himself looking straight into a cold sun. Wham! He puts a hand over his eyes, too late, a spider's web of light flashes on his retina. Two men overpower him, bundle him into a car. He's driven past a police blockade, taken to a kind of shed. Someone shoves him into a chair, ties him up, removes the damp wad of cotton from his mouth: Are you Eichmann? Are you Eichmann? *Herr Klement*, the game's up. You can choose. A bullet in the head now or stand trial in Israel? This story can be told more elaborately, more excitingly, hunter and prey, concealment and discovery. I've heard it done. Speakers who dragged out Operation Klement for two hours, until a collective sigh of relief went through the audience when the old SS officer had finally been drugged and led on board the El Al plane dressed as a steward. A sigh of liberation. We did it! So, is any of this new to you?

– I know the story.

– Of course, of course. A smart boy like you. This isn't much more than the Wikipedia entry, I suspect, padded out a little by my imagination. Suppose Eichmann had opted for the bullet in the head. Suppose the Mossad agents, instead of Eichmann, had gone for Mengele. That's what I keep thinking about lately. Last year, in an interview in *Der Spiegel*, one of the agents said that his team hadn't only been watching Eichmann, but also Josef Mengele. They soon found out that he, too, lived in Buenos Aires. The head of Mossad put the team leader under pressure: Couldn't they kidnap Mengele while Eichmann was being held in secret, and take him to Israel too? Josef Rudolf Mengele, date of birth March 16, 1911. I'm sure you know all about him. The Angel of Death of Auschwitz. *Hauptsturmführer.* Awarded the Iron Cross for valor in Ukraine. Later transferred to Auschwitz-Birkenau. As the chief physician he oversaw incoming transports. Decreed who went straight to the gas chambers, and whose existence was prolonged, however briefly. I take it you also know his medical CV. The experiments with pregnant women, with children, with dwarves. The amputations, the sterilizations, the vivisections without anesthetic, the electric shock treatments. To cite his activities in Auschwitz is to verge on Holocaust porn; in their revolting extremity they can only strike the listener as sensational. Survived the collapse of the Third Reich. Then fled to Argentina. To Buenos Aires. Almost fell into the hands of Mossad. Almost, but not quite. Tell me, Philip, do you know what it's like to be taken off a train, together with your parents, your little brothers and sisters, your uncles and aunts, to be scrutinized by an indifferent doctor, then sent off to the shower room, where, herded together in blind panic with a few hundred strangers, you are gassed?

– Do *you* know what it's like?

– What we do know is that the leader of the spy team resolutely refused his boss's request. That act of defiance took a special kind of conviction. His team had their hands full with Eichmann—another hostage and the whole mission would have been endangered. I often think about that. Because if things had turned out otherwise, we'd have a completely different perspective. Take the way we're talking about this now. How would we have viewed the Nazis without the Eichmann trial? Without Eichmann we wouldn't have the banality of evil and, however often that phrase of Hannah Arendt's is misinterpreted, we wouldn't have had passive participation. Without the soft-center Eichmann we'd only have had the flamboyantly evil Mengele, a doctor who voluntarily carried out monstrous, purposeless experiments, purely out of sadism. A man who didn't afterward submit to the "command of society" like Eichmann, but who set up an illegal abortion practice in South America, causing the deaths of at least two girls that we know of. If we'd only had Mengele, we'd never have had to think about national character, about "only following orders," about how very easy it is for ordinary citizens to become unprotesting cogs in a worse-than-criminal machine.

Here he stopped for a moment and for the first time took a sip of his tea, which by now must have been cold. He took a handkerchief out of his trouser pocket and dabbed his red forehead, and it seemed from where I was sitting that when he folded it up again it was stained with a few drops of blood.

Something welled up in me, something comfortable and languid, and it took a while for me to identify it as a feeling of recognition. This conversation was scarcely any more bizarre than the ones I had every week in my *Sleepwalker* office—how far away that felt! People were forever calling and pitching their ideas, and I would sit there patiently listening to them, responding politely, not getting annoyed by the rabid bullshit they unleashed on me. *Mr. De Vos? Hope I'm not disturbing you. How would you feel about a three-thousand-word article on the popularity of Hitler mustaches in Flanders in the 1940s? It strikes me as perfect for a publication like* The Sleepwalker. *I have access to over fifteen hundred private photos.*

– Philip, could you give me an example of something else we wouldn't have had, if Mengele had ended up in Jerusalem?

The iPhone? I held my tongue. That, too, I'd learned: don't go in for cheap sarcasm. But he remained equally silent.

– I assumed that was a rhetorical question, was all I could come up with.

– Think about all those pet subjects of Josip Brik's. All those films, all those novels, all those sick jokes, all that "imagination" he praised to the skies. Had Mengele been in the witness box, we wouldn't have asked ourselves the question of how "ordinary people," *like you and me,* boo-hoo, sniff sniff, could do what they did. Had Mengele been there, we wouldn't have needed imagination to answer those questions, we'd only have had the deeply dark facts, which could not have been embellished, deepened, or embroidered upon in the fiction to which Brik was so greedily addicted. It would have deromanticized Nazis.

Ever since entering the room I'd been having a sort of out-of-body experience, not the mystical kind, but purely cognitive. "Friso, just look at yourself, creating the most godawful mess." But the moment for revealing my true identity had long gone, that much was certain, and for the first time I felt happy about it. *Josip Brik's pet subjects.* The comfortable, languid feeling vanished abruptly. Burgers was working up to something.

– Tell me, who was Amon Göth?

– Am I being interrogated?

– Philip, please, indulge me.

– The Butcher of Płaszów. Strung up by the Poles. Featured in *Schindler's List*.

– And Paul Blobel?

– Colonel in the SS, responsible for the Babi Yar massacre, condemned to death at Nuremberg.

– Bingo, and tell me, Philip, don't you think it strange that you can come up with all this stuff just like that? That you can instantly fire off facts at the drop of a hat?

– Firstly, I'm a historian, and secondly, this is the kind of stuff you just know, the way you can sing along to Abba songs without ever having bought one of their CDs. You know, just like anyone who watches TV knows, because it's rammed down your throat.

– That's a Brik quote, isn't it? The bit about Abba? I can spot these things, you know. That's the problem with your Brik: whenever he thought of something clever he'd repeat it in every interview and every lecture. My response is: *"Oh yes, at Waterloo Napoleon did surrender."*

– Your point being?

– That Napoleon did *not* surrender at Waterloo. He surrendered a week later at Rochefort, four hundred miles away. How many million boys and girls have gotten that wrong, thanks to Abba?

– But they do sing *"The history book on the shelf is always repeating itself,"* don't they?

– Equally wrong. I gather, Philip, that because of your student loan you're still very much in debt. Forty-three thousand dollars, if I'm not mistaken? Well, I'm prepared to pay off that debt for you.

That was the funniest thing I'd heard all day. So that loser Philip de Vries was in the red to the tune of forty-three thousand dollars! It was so hilarious I nearly forgot to feign indignation and ask how he knew.

– Through certain channels, he said.

– What kind? TV channels, deep sea channels?

As jokes went, it didn't even qualify as pathetic. Apparently I just wanted to put off asking what I had to do in exchange for the forty-three thousand dollars. But I asked anyway.

– I know that Brik left a huge collection of books and art objects. Rare films, old radio recordings, first editions, advertising posters, watercolors. I couldn't give a damn about any of it. What interests me is this.

He held up the second sheaf of papers, the one Winterberg hadn't shown me, and gave it to me.

– This is the inventory. That, too, I acquired through "deep sea channels."

The list was genuine: I'd seen it before, in my inbox, when I'd glanced at it very briefly. Before Brik's house was cleared, an inventory was made of everything he possessed, right down to the last pair of socks.

– You don't have to read it, you know. We'd be here for hours. Besides, I'm looking for something that isn't on the list.

– And what's that?

– I'd hoped you'd know. No little bells ringing? Oh dear, oh dear. Well I'll just have to tell you: I'm looking for Arkady Rossovich. I'm looking for Speer's maquette, which you, Philip, seem to know all about.

I needed to backtrack. Counterattack. I smiled and handed back the inventory.

– I hate to spoil the punch line, but the maquette's a fake. Brik said so himself.

– "Brik said so himself." Golly gosh. But I have reason to doubt that. I have reason to believe that the Speer maquette is all too genuine. And that the fact it's missing from the inventory is no coincidence.

– So who would you say left it out?

– Who would you say broke into Brik's house last month?

– Kids. I was told. Drunk teenagers.

– Perhaps. Perhaps the break-in was supposed to look like the work of drunk teenagers. Perhaps they didn't steal anything valuable, just made a mess—so no one would notice that a little piece of a maquette was missing.

– But I don't see what I can do.

– I want you, Philip, to talk to Mr. and Mrs. Chilton for me. Just test the waters. I know about your connection with them. I saw you at the memorial service. But don't kid yourself, the Chiltons aren't your friends. You don't belong to their social circle. The one percent. You don't owe them anything. I know that Mrs. Chilton's paying for your hotel room, and I'm prepared to bet you owe those new shoes of yours to her too.

– And what if I find out they have the maquette, because that's what you're implying, surely?

– Wrong question. Leave that to me. Do you know what you should really be asking me? You should be asking: "But Mr. Burgers, if you hate Brik and his collection and romanticized Hitler paraphernalia so much, why are you so interested in that maquette?"

– Do I have to ask it in the same squeaky little voice?

– My answer would be: "Philip, it's too early for us to discuss this frankly." Play ball and you'll find out.

I had to ask:

– And what if I say thanks, but no thanks?

Burgers grinned, took out his handkerchief, and started dabbing his forehead again. We'll cross that bridge when we come to it, he said.

– Do you know *The Sleepwalker?*

I wanted to know, I think, whether he'd considered approaching anyone else, namely Friso de Vos, illustrious editor in chief of *The Sleepwalker, Journal of Hitler Studies, Since 1991*, "a one-man Praetorian guard," mentioned by name in at least four of Josip Brik's last five books in grateful acknowledgment of his valuable input as coreader, cothinker, and fixer-cum-fusspot extraordinaire.

– Who's that? Burgers asked.

– Not who, *what*. An academic journal. Of Hitler studies. Brik was involved in it.

– I don't read any journals, he said firmly.

– Why me?

– . . . Lord, asked David. It is what it is.

– "It is what it is."

– Why do you keep staring at my forehead?

– There was this catchphrase a while back: "Everything can break."

– But here's the thing, Philip: everything *can* break.

With one finger he wiped away a drop of blood that was creeping, sickeningly slowly, from his implant to his eyebrow. Where was Google when you needed it? Why weren't these guys on Facebook, so they'd know who they were talking to? And was that a threat, just now?

– I get the feeling that any minute now you'll initiate me with a secret handshake.

– A secret handshake? Shall I show you a secret handshake?

He instantly rolled up his sleeve in a purposeful way, less like a gentleman boxer, I thought, than an old junkie whose community service involves showing his needle marks to kids in the first class of high school. He also undid the leather strap of his watch, giving me a full view of that bit of your wrist that, no matter how much you sunbathe, never goes brown, where the veins show up most and the skin is the thinnest and most vulnerable. On it were five badly tattooed numbers: 82265.

My first reaction wasn't so much surprise, or disgust, but outright naivete: he couldn't be *that* old, surely? Admittedly, with every change of expression, the folds of his face rearranged themselves differently, like an old leather wallet—but he wasn't, couldn't be older than fifty, fifty-five. He waited for me to say something, which I did, in a more strangled voice than I'd expected:

– I'm guessing this isn't a way of remembering your PIN code?

He smiled now, a broad, warm smile, and said, in a much friendlier tone than before:

– Does this mean anything to you, Philip? Do you ever think about it? About the ordinary people, the ordinary victims? This is a daily reminder for me. You people are fixated on the glamour of the Third Reich—the exciting stories that make such great films, the führers and commandants who are so black in their evil that you can't take your eyes off them, as if it were all some gripping horror movie. You're starstruck, you're the paparazzi of historians, only interested in the celebrities, the glitter of the polished skull-emblazoned uniforms. That's what Brik taught you, isn't it? The Great Brik who once so proudly said, proud of his own discovery, that the number of films, novels, artworks, and documentaries made about the war now exceeds the number of people who died in the war? Funny haha, but tell me, Philip, how many of the victims' serial numbers do you know by heart? Where are the victims in that specimen of Hitler prose about your master's little toy?

– I'm not a Nazi fetishist . . . I'm not an anti-Semite, or anything, I said, and before I'd even finished speaking I realized how feeble it sounded. As soon as you voluntarily deny something you've already lost the battle, and my "or anything" was just the icing on the turd.

– I once talked to Edward Said, fascinating man, spoke at this conference years ago. About latent racism in Jane Austen's work. According to him, Jane Austen was an out-and-out racist. But there isn't a single black character in any of her books, surely? I asked. Exactly, he said. *Neglect is the worst form of racism.*

82265. The figures were clearly legible. Don't ask why he's got them, I said to myself. Don't be obliging. Stick to irony, stick to your false persona. It isn't you who's being called into question, but Philip de Vries. Don't ask if it's the number of a relative. Don't defend Brik, don't bite—but he bent toward me with a big smile and patted me on the knee in a way that was both friendly and condescending.

– It's difficult, isn't it, Mr. De Vries, talking to people who take things seriously?

But *what* was being taken seriously? Mossad, Eichmann in Jerusalem? How seriously should you take someone who had a Holocaust tattoo? Someone who couldn't be Jewish? Surely? His name alone, for starters. Why would a non-Jew want to talk me into feeling guilty of anti-Semitism? What did he have against the Chiltons? How did he know them? Was Winterberg his muscle guy? Was Nina his hooker? Did he have access to personal information at the Ministry of Education? What did Eichmann and Mengele have to do with my student debt?

I didn't have any student debt!

Questions, questions. Not that I was in the mood for answers. My mood board was a Rothko painting. I'd been shocked not so much by what he said as the way he said it. One moment he spoke with scornful sarcasm, the next he'd be all smiles, his voice shifted from nasal to deep. He must have really meant everything he said. If it had been fake, if he'd known I was playing him for a sucker, then he'd have said something concrete, he'd have made a speech. Instead it had been a weird, incoherent Second World War collage. And he'd seen me out in such a friendly way, a warm hand on my shoulder. Think about it, Philip. No pressure.

Strange.

My phone groaned in my jacket pocket. It was an American number. The U.S. country code was 01, number one, the country of countries. I hoped so much that it was Pip, I hoped it so much.

– Hello, Friso, how are you today? Mrs. Chilton asked.

I spoke slowly:

– I've been shopping. Got a nice jacket, a nice tie. You can be pleased with me.

– That's just what I wanted to hear. I'm delighted that you're indulging yourself, that you're having a good time. It must be hard for you, with Brik's death still so fresh. You deserve a little pampering.

She sounded more saccharine than usual, there was an element of pastiche in her tone.

– Do you know who I'm lunching with tomorrow? That girlfriend of yours. Pippa, right? I hear she has a magic touch with old paintings.

– That's nice.

– Shall I give her your regards, Friso? Is there anything you'd like to tell her?

I sighed, rubbed my eyes.

– Nothing you want to tell her about Vienna?

Her voice suddenly went down by at least an octave. Dark clouds massed.

– Hasn't anything special happened that you'd like her to know? I'm happy to be your messenger.

– Just tell her lots of love from me, I said, hung up, and threw up the peach sweets over my new shoes.

SEVEN

The first Christmas I spent with Pip we visited her parents, who still lived in her childhood home, a large bungalow in the wooded Utrechtse Heuvelrug. She showed me the manicured back garden, the setting, she told me, of one of her most powerful childhood memories, an almost existential moment. It had been Christmas then, too, she was about five or six, and had wandered outside in pursuit of the dog. From the garden she had looked inside and seen her father next to the Christmas tree, and her mother, brothers, and sister, and had suddenly been overwhelmed by the realization that she *wasn't* in that room. She was outside, she wasn't with her family, and that wasn't a problem. Even without her family, she existed. In all its simplicity it was a feeling that resonated powerfully: I, *too*, am someone.

Just before, over drinks, her parents had proudly shown me photos of her as a girl, and now I saw her standing in that same garden, and I pictured her at age six. As she grew older, her hair turned a darker, more explicit auburn, from latte to Earl Grey. It appealed to me: she was growing older. I wanted to be part of that.

Pippa & me. The problem was that everything went so well. We had the same interests, we did stuff together. Every Saturday we'd go to a farmers' market and buy local produce, then lunch at a little café run by an old couple where the service was very slow, and sit reading the paper in companionable silence. We went to a sing-along session at the local musical club. A couple of her girlfriends came to dinner and I made tapas: prawns, stuffed tomatoes, melon with Serrano ham. Things went swimmingly. When I had to stand in for Brik at a conference in Austin, Texas, Pippa came with me. As I approached the microphone I could see her in the audience, her hair tied up, her hand touching her neck: she was nervous for me, *nervous on my behalf*, and that calmed me. I uttered the sentences that were partly Brik's and partly my own casually, as if I were speaking off the cuff:

– And if you look closely you can see there's something wrong with the Hitler of Bryan Singer's *Valkyrie*. It's not so much his appearance, though his hair's clearly too long, his mustache a little too canine: after 1935 there are no photos in which his mustache extends beyond the tips of his nostrils. The actor plays him plausibly enough: his diction's correct, his eyes bloodshot, like someone who's chronically sleep-deprived. In the scene we're about to see he talks about Wagner, about the task of the Valkyries, he talks in a sufficiently Hitlerish way, with a clear disinterest in the listener—though it's too obviously scripted. What I want you to note is the stooped back. The gait. The trembling right hand. It's familiar, but it's not Hitler. The actor isn't playing Adolf Hitler, he's playing Bruno Ganz in *Downfall* playing Adolf Hitler. The actor is playing the actor playing Hitler. A world within a world.

From Texas we drove to New Orleans, Louisiana, where we stayed a week longer than intended. We ate, made love, and danced arrhythmically to live jazz in little cafés. We resolved to save up for an autumn break, somewhere on a tropical island. There was short- and long-term planning. We had our routines, our modes, our acts, our little two-person sketches.

Me: Hey, Pip, where shall we eat this evening? You can choose.

Her: Uh...

Me: Take your time.

Big smile.

Me: There are no wrong answers.

Her: Perhaps we could have a salad at that Italian place on the corner with all the flowers?

Me: Jesus, Pip, we ate there only yesterday.

These were our set lovers' quarrels. In a little girl's voice: "Do you still love me?" Me, stroking the tip of her chin between my thumb and index finger: "Baby, I've never loved you." Had us in stitches.

Or if she'd said practically nothing all evening, immersed in her work or a book, and then come out with some trivial remark like "This tea's nice," I would respond in mock rage: "For Chrissake, Pippa, can't you keep your trap shut for one minute?!" That was our brand of humor.

There were also moments when she *did* suddenly start to talk about her youth, about the things she'd experienced, her life before she met me, but half the time they were interrupted because of her singular talent for opening up just as the lights on the railroad crossing were turning red or we were passing a barrel organ on a narrow shopping street. Once, on a potholed highway to New York, we were overtaken by six trucks full of scrap iron, and of course that was the moment Pippa picked to tell me how, when she was a little girl, she'd found her grandmother's dead body, clang, crash, bang. And even then she'd tell these stories with an air of uncertain surprise, as if she were talking about someone else and wasn't sure how she knew all these details.

If there were subliminal problems, they didn't manifest themselves sexually. I continued to find Pip as attractive as ever; even the most mundane things still turned me on. People always thought she was too thin: she had a narrow face, a narrow nose, high cheekbones, sinewy hands, and you could encircle her wrists with your thumb and index finger, but when you saw her naked, there was flesh in all the right places. Her body was as white as cream and soft as dough. Her nipples were small, and almost the same color as her skin, but when I kissed them, they glowed red with blood. I could sit there all day thinking about it.

She suffered from an arrogant form of dyscalculia, basically that you couldn't expect her to conclude anything from sums or figures. Me: "I saw in the paper it's going to be seventy degrees tomorrow." Pip: "That doesn't mean anything to me." Her eldest brother announced he'd be earning €90,000 a year in his new job. "That doesn't mean anything to me." Brik read out the findings of a new study: that during Stalin's Great Purge alone, seven hundred thousand people were executed by firing squad. "That doesn't mean anything to me." Brik and I looked at her open-mouthed. She backpedaled a bit:

– Is that, you know, a lot, by comparison?

– Pippa, seven hundred thousand. Suppose Brik and I shoot all your three hundred and something Facebook friends dead, two thousand times in a row. Does that seem a lot to you? If not, you'd be a great apparatchik!

Brik laughed so hard that he nearly fell out of his chair. Pip shrugged: you know me.

She was up to her ears in restoration jobs all over New England, and I wasn't the kind of man to be bothered by her earning more than I did. I was fine with her picking up the tab; even the proprietors of the little family restaurant no longer raised an eyebrow. She spent more too: on thick woolen pencil skirts, on a dozen different white blouses that looked virtually identical to me, on coffee-table books full of glossy photos of abandoned streets and snow-covered branches.

That spring, Pippa's youngest brother, Jim, had officially come out of the closet, an announcement that surprised absolutely no one, not even for a millisecond. In the three years I'd known him he'd switched from a long, androgynous David Bowie–ish hairstyle to a platinum-blond, short-back-and-sides schoolboy cut with side parting à la Draco Malfoy. His polo shirts were so tight that you got a flash of his navel every time he moved his arm. The whole process was clichéd, I felt, but Pippa said she kind of got it: he wanted to belong somewhere and that meant you had to stick to the dress code. In any case, as if a Facebook status update wasn't enough, he undertook a Big Gay World Tour on his father's credit card to explain his Revelation to everyone in person. First to Madrid, where Pip's youngest sister was doing an internship, then to their older brother in Edinburgh, who'd just gotten a fancy job at the Bank of Scotland, and then to New York. Not to our apartment in Ithaca, because traveling all the way upstate by train, *that* was too much for him—*we* had to go to *him*, to his design hotel in Greenwich Village, where he was waiting for us in the bistro, a twenty-two-year-old with an Arafat scarf, a bottle of prosecco, and a little bowl of beluga caviar—it wasn't his money, after all.

But I had no reason to complain. The afternoon was very relaxed. He showed us where you could get the best cocktails in the Village, Pippa bought a dress, I bought a deluxe hardcover box set of Richard J. Evans's three-volume history of the Third Reich. We strolled through the park and ended up wandering into the Metropolitan Museum. His joy and excitement were catching, and the cocktails we'd drunk at lunch made us feel warm and drowsy, and Pip and her little brother listened appreciatively to my orations:

– The almost mystical atmosphere of the painting doesn't just come from the dark, menacing sky hanging over Toledo, shedding a strange silvery gleam over the town—just look how El Greco portrays the buildings: they're cold, lifeless, abandoned, as if they were ruins, as if El Greco weren't painting in his own time, but in the future.

How do you *know* all this stuff, Jim said each time.

– What is John Singer Sargent showing us here? Her body is facing us, but at the same time she's turning her head away. It's about revealing and concealing, offering and withholding; *Madame X* is a masterful take on the game of sexual attraction.

Again: How do you *know* all this stuff?

As a qualified art historian, Pippa probably knew more about that kind of thing than I did, but she would never say so. And it was all a bit of an act, to be honest. I didn't *really* know about it: the trick is to know the language, the vocabulary, the references, to be able to spot a paradox in every contrast, in every black and every white, and present it as the deeper truth of ambivalence, as ambiguity, as competing paradigms. Weren't all artworks and books and films and music just a question of shifting frames of reference?

There was no malice in it, that wasn't in his nature—Jim was just happy with his new life, life in general, and in all his enthusiasm he kept rattling on about our future, which he couldn't see as anything other than rose-colored. When when when are you going to get married? If any couple's ready for it, you are. Friso, *if you liked it then you should've put a ring on it*, and you, Pippa, you'd look so pretty in white. Snow white, white as a princess, white as...

– White as Saruman, I said.

Jim gave a little scream.

– Isn't Saruman the evil sorcerer?

I put my arm around his shoulders and said I'd never been as proud of him as right now, and all three of us laughed so uproariously that the other museum-goers turned to look at us.

The problem about everything going so well was that there was no chance to pause, to get some distance. Since we'd been an item, we'd been on a domestic bliss express that didn't stop anywhere en route. The slightest change of course would have meant putting on the emergency brake. I think that was it.

A few weeks after Jim's visit, Pippa had to go to New York again for a restoration project in an old club, something to do with the UN. I sat on the bed reading while she packed her suitcase, and out of the corner of my eye I saw her packing a few skimpy little dresses that she definitely wouldn't be wearing, because according to the weather forecasts it was going to be freezing. So I took the dresses out again, carefully, so as not to crease them, and Pip stared at me with eyes as big and round as saucers, then suddenly hurled the suitcase at my head. She missed, of course, but all the same, I was perplexed. She exploded:

– I feel like you're always pushing me one way or another and I don't want to have the kind of relationship where I constantly have to push back. And anyway, that only makes you push even harder! Just give me space to live!

– *Lebensraum?* I asked, raising one eyebrow quizzically, a favorite trick.

– Yes, bloody hell, Friso, *Lebensraum*, if you want to put it like that, you horrible bigoted Fascist, because that's all you understand, fucking *Le-bens-raum!*

The discussion ended right there. "Let not the sun go down on your wrath," as the saying goes, and we didn't. We made up, but something still hung in the air. I didn't think her accusation at all fair, but some sort of atonement was required, so in the days that followed I was cheerful, did the cooking, sent thoughtful text messages. But when she got back from New York another of my jokes got her dander up:

– Those jokes of yours, does it never strike you that you're the only one who laughs at them?

I had to think about that. I said it wasn't true.

– No, it isn't true. Brik laughs at them too. He's your audience. But how often do you hear *me* really laughing?

When you're told there are all kinds of things you aren't noticing, the rational response is to wonder what *else* you aren't noticing. Like the fact that I, too, sometimes forgot to laugh. And the nature of our silences: Were they really companionable? People say it's the sign of a good relationship, not having to talk to each other to feel comfortable: I thought this applied to Pippa and me. But when I thought about it a bit more it struck me that it was always *me* who broke our silences, and when I thought about *that* a bit more, I concluded it was because I didn't really trust Pippa's silences—I could never shake off the impression that she wasn't being silent at her ease, but instead biding her time, waiting for something to end.

It wasn't even that we got irritated or angry at each other, but we ended up constantly analyzing and describing all the ways in which we interacted, so much so that they suddenly all felt equally unnatural. It was weird. *One day you're there, and then all of a sudden, there's less of you, and you wonder where that part went, if it's living somewhere outside of you, and you keep thinking maybe you'll get it back, and then you realize it's just gone.*

I looked at Pippa often in those days, looked for something in her glance. A hint of recognition, something that acknowledged our stalemate and that I could interpret as a sign of solidarity. I didn't see it. One evening I sang a snatch of a song: *Where did all the love go / I don't know / I don't know.* Kasabian, I didn't particularly mean anything by it, it just happened to be in my head. But Pip's only response was an irritated twitch of the lip, as if something was stuck between her front teeth, and she said, without really looking at me:

– Don't be such a drama queen.

That's what she said. (She! To me!) Something tipped somewhere, and I stood up and couldn't stop myself from saying something autonomous and final, though I formulated it as a stereotypical member of the stupidest generation of this new century:

– Perhaps you should just do your own thing, and I'll do mine.

And off she went. Within five days, that same Pip, who pretty much needed my help to cross the street, who always confused gross and net, had gotten herself an apartment with parquet floors and ornamental ceilings in the ritziest neighborhood of the old university town for a ridiculously low rent.

THE MACGUFFIN

EIGHT

This was the Viennese waltz so far:

A strapping blond Dutch lad flies to Vienna, Austria, and installs himself in a classy hotel room, knowing that just about every historian, sociologist, cultural critic, writer, philosopher, and journalist who has anything at all to do with his field is in town. Hitler studies is a broad church: its research areas overlap and overtake one another and accelerate further and further away from the original historical object (1889–1945); potential colleagues and competitors will meet here in Vienna. Yet at first this Dutch boy scarcely leaves his hotel room. The tension is palpable: flyers have been printed, websites designed, banners are waving from facades, the research question "What was Josip Brik's contribution to perceptions of Hitler and the War in the twenty-first century?" has been postulated and spoken aloud, and the problem is that he doesn't have a direct answer. Or rather, he has an answer, but he doubts whether there's a consensus. Somehow he can't shake off a premonition that Brik's about to undergo some kind of de-Stalinization. That he will join the forum with the printout of his speech like a burning se-cret in his inside pocket, and that just as he starts to speak people will begin to jeer and bang on the table with their shoes. *Boo! Down with Brik!* He laughs at the idea. This is of course the worst-case scenario. Other scenarios are infinitely more likely. And yet he can't shake off the feel-ing that he must be prepared, must arm himself, have quo-tations, one-liners, observations lined up like bullets in a gun barrel, must be able to parry every argument.

Can he do that alone? Does he need an ally?

This lad met Brik in college. One taught, the other learned. A fair division of roles. A fellow student said he'd once found himself standing next to Brik at a bus stop. It was a hot day in June, not a cloud in the sky. And he dis-covered that if he positioned himself carefully, he could stand entirely in Brik's shadow. Literally. "That guy's colossal—*man*, you can just use him as a sunshade!"

What did he see when he looked at Brik? Because that was the point. As a rational being he should surely be able see something in him that went deeper than the surface. He knew the jokes his fellow students told. Just after the start of the academic year he saw Brik in town and followed him for a while. Like a tiger strolling through the jungle, knowing that no matter what crosses his path he'll always be the victor, the apex predator, the top of the food chain—that's how Brik was walking. He could see him thinking. Something was happening behind those eyes and, though it felt a bit wallflowerish thinking this, whenever he saw

Brik looking at shop windows, at advertisements, saw him observing people, he knew, *he knew!*, that whatever happened, this man would always be able to save himself purely by mental superiority. The apex thingamajig, what was it called again...the apex brain.

Now all that was left was the output of that brain: the books, the YouTube clips, one or two box sets of documentaries, obtainable from niche outlets. Did he doubt his love for Brik? Not for one second. Did he doubt Brik's love for him? Well, it all came down to hierarchy. Brik moved in different circles, saw people in different capacities. Did his favorite student outrank his favorite editor? Who came first: his regular publisher or his regular cameraman? Who did he spend the most time with? Was it the *quantity* or the *quality* of the hours spent with him that counted? So many people had dealings with Brik, in so many different ways.

Now he's dead (mentally he hears his father correct him: *he's passed on*—only common people say *dead*), and people are tentatively trying out a first come, first served approach. Everyone's crowding around that mighty corpus to claim the first rights, just as the Greeks crowded around the fallen Achilles, fighting for his armor. Where do I stand, wonders the lad, can I give myself an advance on the truth, can I appoint myself executor of his legacy, curator of his work (whatever that means), perhaps even *biographer?*

What's with that other favorite student of Brik's? What does he know that I don't?

Bring a pretty girl along, Brik would always say, when he was giving a cocktail party or some other do. That made him feel good: the fact that Brik assumed he just had a supply of pretty girls on tap.

So there he is, alone in his Viennese hotel room with nothing on TV but ski jumping—the commentary in that incomprehensible pseudo-German of theirs—and somewhere out there, like satellites in orbit, people are circling around him. He knows this instinctively. That's why he finds it hard to leave his room. Even though no one's come out of the woodwork and declared their intentions, he knows people are lying in wait, ready to sink their teeth into him, to see how salty his blood tastes.

Mr. and Mrs. Chilton of Brik's home university in the States have been so sickly sweet toward him that he instinctively knows he can't trust them. Can't *allow* himself to trust them, because he'd dearly like to believe in their professed affection, it would make everything so much easier. The comforting feeling that someone's got your back. But he doesn't know what they really want of him. And even supposing it was something concrete, he wouldn't yet dare say how concrete his influence really is.

There's a man with a hat and a knitting pattern of bleeding follicles, who's prepared to lavish serious money and heavy insinuation on acquiring Brik's collection, God knows why. There are blonde girls who smile compliantly at him. He doesn't know the extent to which he's being watched, the extent to which his name's being bandied about. He doesn't know who's out to gain something from him, or what his options are. Whether people would really dare blackmail him, strong-arm him into making certain decisions. He doesn't know whether there are international criminal gangs that film hotel guests on hidden cameras and extort money from them. He knows nothing. There are unknown unknowns. He doesn't know what he doesn't know.

He's not inclined to look for an ally, actually, he'd prefer to defend Brik on his own. But if so many unseen forces are at work, how does he know he has the guts not to deny Brik three times before the cock crows?

He's getting support, of course. Encouraging emails from fellow Brikians. Heartening messages from some of his old lecturers. A few professors send him pointers. There are emails from the editors of talk shows, checking to see if events in Vienna might provide fodder for their programs. The Dutch lad takes note. He tries to see with the eye of the camera, to summarize things that are worth telling hundreds of thousands of television viewers.

And sweet emails from his girlfriend. Affectionate "go-get-'em-tiger" emails from his girlfriend. Tender text messages, "sleep well" messages. Yet more love he'll never have to doubt.

He doesn't attend any of the lectures in his field. Instead, he visits a few museums, but the paintings don't mean anything to him. Bruegel's blue-gray pastoral landscapes, Arcimboldi's silly fruit faces. Of course he's academically trained to perceive a deeper value in such art, but when he sees these pictures all that happens is that a little box is ticked somewhere in his head, of the paintings from his childhood Memory game that he's now seen in real life. *Tower of Babel*: check. Dürer's *Rhinoceros*: check. Then he goes quickly back to his room.

But the outside world mercilessly breaches the safe barrier of his hotel room: when he wakes up someone has pushed something under his door. It's a sheet of paper, folded double lengthwise, like menus tend to be. It's been written on an old-fashioned typewriter, he can feel the profile of the letters with his fingertips.

We are young, love is a battlefield. For too long now, the past has dominated the present. For too long now, gestures that should be timeless have been hijacked by old meanings. As far back as Caesar's day, generals would salute their troops with an outstretched right arm, as a sign of respect and solidarity. An outstretched arm as a mark of unity. Twelve years of German Fascism has tainted that gesture—twelve years in the previous century. The time has come to de-Hitlerize the right arm. We call on teachers to greet their pupils in this way, actors their fans lining the red carpet, TV hosts their viewers. We call on soccer players to raise their right arms after scoring a goal, as a symbol of disengagement from an old drama, as a symbol of a new age. Liberate the right

arm. History can't hurt us. We are the Right Arm
Liberation Front.

Guillaume Beaujolais, École des Beaux-Arts, Paris-Nord
Fatima Meerburg, Rijksacademie, Amsterdam
Robbie Decoster, MoMA Curatorial Program, New York

Up to now *everything* that has happened to him has added
up, but this is over-the-top. The Right Arm Liberation
Front. The letter bears an official stamp with a Facebook
account and a phone number. Initially he hopes it's nonsense, that when you go to their page it'll turn out to be a
commercial stunt: a website advertising a new liqueur with
some macho name like Gladiator's Finest, but instinctively
he knows it's genuine. The straw and the camel's back.
Everything that's happened since Brik's clumsy hotel death
seemed real enough, but the realism is now mounting up
too fast, building up to an excessive, hysterical amount.
Which is exactly what he doesn't want. The accumulation of plausible events contradicts their very plausibility.
Logic is undermining itself. When events start behaving
like a plot, watch out (Brik always used to say). Then they
are no longer events but sets of steps, and you never know
what basement they'll lead you to.

At least, that's how I imagined Philip de Vries's Viennese
days had gone till now.

He must have known the sunshade joke, or if not, a similar one. At least a hundred Brik jokes had made the rounds in Groningen. That he was getting supportive emails was also logical—*he'd* be getting them, because that's what happens when you get your mug on TV. The bit about "dead" versus "passed on" seemed appropriate: he looked so middle-class. The fact that I was on his mind was obvious, otherwise he wouldn't keep trying to contact me. That he felt unsure was also clear, otherwise he wouldn't be so tentative, wouldn't be trying so slavishly to reach an entente cordiale—while I was taking all the mental blows meant for him: the insinuations, the video clips. I was the one who was warding off the Burgers and the Winterbergs and the Chiltons and the Ninas of this world.

That he'd found a manifesto under his hotel room door was easy to deduce, because I'd found one under *my* door, so I assumed all the conference hotels had been flyered. A serious statement or a jokey art project? At first I'd been scared of what Sweder Burgers might do. Oil and fire. If only he and his henchman Winterberg didn't get heavy! But if I thought about it a bit more, which I did, I concluded it might even be a good thing. His camp actually stood to gain from this kind of initiative, I'd tell him. Elite athletes giving the Hitler salute? That wasn't going to go down well with anyone. Extremes of this kind would in fact help to promote his own cause, a cause that, now that I gave more thought to it, hadn't in fact ever been entirely explained.

It would surely be like Philip de Vries to view those paintings purely as a box-ticking exercise, and it would *definitely* be like him to make some classical allusion or other—the armor of Achilles, the betrayal of Peter—just as he did, of course, in that idiotic document about the Bunker and Arkady Rossovich: the heavy symbolism, the Norse myths, death interpreted through images from antiquity. The old misconception that classical references make you look intellectual and well-read, when in fact they just reveal a narrow, predictable, bourgeois view of art.

What else did Rossovich think of? (Or rather: what else did De Vries have him think of?) Of Clausewitz, of Machiavelli—it's easy to score with such solid names, names that conjure up a world of ideas, but who believes that you *really* read them?

I rubbed the sleep out of my eyes. I looked at myself in the mirror, in my boxers, and did a Hitler salute. Then I put the manifesto down and did a Hitler salute while making a diagonal mustache under my nose with my index and middle fingers. It wasn't a good look. I put on a new anthracite suit and a mist gray shirt and a brown-blue woolen tie. I looked touchingly capable.

There had to be more Hitler-saluting people you could think of: weathermen, rock bands. The salute needn't be confined to TV hosts, it could also be given by their guests as they stepped up to the podium (Come on down!), and by directors and actors receiving awards. Train conductors. The Right Arm Liberation Front really needed to press for train conductors. And it would work too. The first few times it would be revolutionary, controversial. People would be called to account, but that was just what was needed here. A rational discourse. That was what it was all about: removing something contentious from the sphere of the irrational. That's what art is for. ("What is art? Art is the possibility of grasping the unreal." *Oh really?* Slogans so freighted with significance they don't signify anything. Abstraction, vocabulary, ambivalence, shifting frames of reference, etc.) Think of all those fourteen-year-old boys who like nothing better than to tell jokes about the Jews, jokes about Hitler, how-many-Jews-fit-in-a-shower-cubicle jokes—you could take the wind out of their sails. If teachers do it, you no longer want any part of it.

I laughed. Rarely had any plan been so doomed to failure. The greater the scale of the Right Arm Liberation Front's operations, the more right arms were stuck in the air, proudly erect and pointing toward a far, far horizon, the more everyone would hate, hate, hate, hate it. The perpetrators would have to appear on all those TV panel shows; the script had already been written.

"Philip de Vries, can you explain, very briefly, what on earth you hope to achieve with this campaign?" It was masterly. I couldn't help myself, fate was smiling on me, I had to call them.

I had no second thoughts as the phone rang three times at the other end. Or when it was answered:

– Hello?

– This is Philip de Vries, I said in English. I'm a hotel guest. I just found something under my door.

– Our manifesto?

– You betcha!

– Have you read it?

– Absolutely, and I was wondering if it would be possible to add something to it. To start with, my name's Philip de Vries. "Philip," as in Philip, and then "de Vries" is spelled *D.E.V.R.I.E.S.* with a space between "de" and "Vries," and I'm Josip Brik's biographer, you see.

– I'm Guillaume.

– Great, Guillaume, the thing is, I totally agree with your campaign. It's a novel way of thinking. And very convincing. Just what we need. And, as I said, I'm the biographer of Josip Brik, the great Hitler philosopher. I'm sure you know him. I'm hoping to finish my biography next year, the working title is *Brik-a-brac: The Life of a Thinking Animal.* Various publishers have already expressed interest, both at home and abroad. So I thought, perhaps you could use my support.

– But…that would be fantastic. Brik was…our hero. As our statement says, we are pressing for a de-ideologization of our soma, a denazification of our loins, we as artists passionately believe that…

– What I was thinking, Guillaume, sorry to interrupt you, was: Could you perhaps add my name to the manifesto? If you're going to be flyering at other hotels in Vienna over the next few days, that is? Because then you could add my name to your list, Philip de Vries, followed by "Josip Brik's biographer," so everyone knows who I am, and what's more, you'd have the weight of Josip Brik behind you—wouldn't that be good?

– Good? That would be fantastic! Guillaume said.

Merveilleux, he added. *Superbe*. He asked if I could spell my name once more and then I had to put my hand over the mouthpiece, as I couldn't suppress my laughter any longer, and I didn't want him to take fright just as he was dutifully telling me they would type out more manifestos today so as to spam the other conference hotels. I hung up and fell back on the bed bellowing with laughter, laughter that sounded surprisingly old and hollow. Josip Brik's biographer. He'd still be allowed to come and talk about Brik on TV, but now no one would ever take him seriously.

Jesus Christ, I thought, when I'd stopped laughing— *Brik* was *their* hero?

The previous evening, after Nina, after the video, after Winterberg, after Arkady Rossovich, after Sweder Burgers and after Mrs. Chilton, I'd gone to bed feeling wide awake. A pointless exercise, I thought. Sleep seemed impossible; too much adrenaline, too much of that feeling that something's about to happen, something that will change everything. But like a child who resolves not to fall asleep before midnight on New Year's Eve and then wakes up with a start at the sound of fireworks, my tormented body wasn't going to let the opportunity slip. I only woke up once, when it was already starting to grow light. I got up to pee and thought about everything in my life. I switched on my laptop and discovered what I'd already suspected, namely that the website of the Burgers Foundation was beautifully designed, with classical music playing in the background, and a page listing all twelve of Sweder Burgers B.A.'s staff with a photo and contact details, and that neither Nina Barth nor Markus Winterberg was among the twelve.

I Googled a bit more and wrote down the addresses of the four Viennese antiques dealers where Arkady Rossovich might conceivably have offloaded his loot. Then I went back to bed and fell asleep the moment my head hit the pillow.

Now I was hurrying across the Heldenplatz—was it possible to walk through this city and *not* cross the Heldenplatz?—with the collar of my covert coat up, like someone who didn't want to be recognized. Because that was my role, that was what I was thinking about the whole time. Events that assume the form of a plot: yes indeed! An accumulation of plausible events: damn right! A plot had been set in motion, one involving treachery and black- mail, in which logical steps would be taken. Someone had set a trap, I had fallen into it, the means of blackmail had been shown, and now all I had to do was wait for the black- mailer to reveal himself. Which in turn would give me the opportunity to shed my Philip de Vries role. As long as Friso wasn't, *I wasn't*, the target, I held all the aces. There was something safe and reassuring about this step-by-step plan. I would stick to my role and everything would auto- matically turn out right.

So it wasn't me who crossed the tram rails, onto the Maria Theresien Platz, where I looked around furtively, as someone would who thought they were being followed—that was my role. It wasn't me who walked, erect and resolute, into the antiques shop, who stood and stared at the old clocks, the heavy wooden figurines of gypsies and knights, it wasn't me who gazed pensively at snowy landscapes by lesser masters, my ears pricked. It wasn't me who expected to hear loud footsteps and feel a hand on my shoulder. Perhaps even a revolver pressed against my back.

How wonderful it was to be an intellectual! To live the life of reason, so you could always see things at this meta-level—it was the culmination of what Brik had taught me, that yes also meant no, white also meant black, here also elsewhere, life also fiction.

Cool, calm, and collected.

But no hand landed on my shoulder, no revolver was poked in my back. The narrative was slow to take off. The first antiques dealer on my list did indeed go back three generations, but had only been based in Vienna for four years—"Why do you want to know, sir?" asked the friendly gentleman behind the till. I merely smiled at him and fled ("It wasn't me who fled...") and made my way to the second antiques dealer, where I also drew a blank. They'd been there for sixty years, in that building, on that street. In good times and bad: sometimes it was a struggle, "but *je maintiendrai*," the owner of the shop told me, quoting the motto of the House of Orange, clearly pleased at his own sharpness—I'd told him I was Dutch. They had sold paintings to Americans, to Russians, to museums, to businesses, to members of royal families—but they'd never sold anything other than paintings and the odd sculpture, and then only as a favor to loyal customers. "Alas . . ."

For the time being, the plot had gotten stuck. Alas. The only other thing worth mentioning was that I saw Philip de Vries, the real one, in the flesh. I was just crossing a shopping street when I saw him, out of the corner of my eye, going into a department store. I followed. He was wearing a long, light coat, with a thin scarf draped nonchalantly around his neck. Tall, slim, with a blond quiff—Goebbels would have liked the cut of his jib. He looked like Ric Hochet, the dauntless reporter hero of the comic strip. He ran up the kitschy, mock–Art Deco staircase of the department store with careless ease, as if it were his second home.

There he was. *Here he was.* Each step he took was a revelation, as if I were seeing things. So he also existed outside my brain. It was like looking out of the window and seeing Santa flying over the roofs in his sleigh. *There he goes*, Josip Brik's heir apparent. His favorite pupil. You could just picture him, sitting in the front row in the lecture room, busily taking notes, hanging around after class, hoping for a minute of private time with Brik. Bless him. His hair was every bit as fair as mine, we were indeed about the same height, probably about the same age. Did we resemble each other? As far as I could see, we had the same laugh lines around our eyes, perhaps even the same nose. Was my smile just as self-satisfied?

It wasn't that I wanted to talk to him, far from it, I always made sure there was a mannequin between me and his line of vision, a buffer of at least two racks of garments, so I could grab a shirt or a pair of trousers from a hanger if he looked in my direction. He paused briefly, and I plucked a pink sweater from a shelf. I held it up and pressed it to my face, pretending to gauge the quality of the wool, while squinting to see if Philip was looking at me. He wasn't. He was just getting his bearings. The only person who'd seen me was a hopeful-looking salesgirl. I folded up the sweater again, faster than I'd ever folded a sweater, and hurried after him, toward the cafeteria; I had to stop myself from running. Though I got to within three paces of him, he only had eyes for an older woman, now getting up from her little table, whom he embraced warmly. I quickly put a soggy sausage roll on my tray, so I could stand close to their table while getting in line for the till. He was telling a long story in flawless Austrian German, and even then it took a while before I realized—first having to recover from the fact that I'd never heard a Dutch person speak such fluent German, so much better than me, so unaccented—only then did the possibility arise in my mind that this wasn't Philip de Vries at all, just some other slim blond guy out of the ten thousand or so at large in this city. Close up he also seemed older, more intelligent.

Was it him? It wasn't him.

In the toilet I splashed water on my face and imagined the water drying as soon as it touched my skin, as if it were falling on a stovetop. Using my fingers, I combed my hair in the same direction as the fake Philip's hair and pushed up my forelock in the same way. I didn't have the same kind of scarf, but I could turn up the collar of my jacket like he did.

Markus Winterberg noticed.

– Your hair's different.

Of course he had to be there, sitting on a bench in the Marcus Aureliusstrasse, just as I was passing. The bench faced away from a little square where children played around a climbing frame, screeching like gulls. He had an unimpeded view of the front door of antiques dealer number three, who with any luck could tell me more about Arkady Rossovich and the Speer maquette. On the other benches women huddled together in little groups, nannies probably, keeping half an eye on their charges while they chatted with each other in a language that wasn't Austrian. Winterberg's head was pale and gleaming, as if he'd put just a bit too much moisturizer on his face. He was peeling an apple while keeping the peel in one piece, something he clearly found satisfying.

– The Indians ate apples to stay awake, I said. An old military trick.

– Do you know many Indians?

– I know a lot of Westerns.

– You don't say. But I've got this to stay awake, he said, and produced a can of Coke from his coat pocket.

– An apple and a can of Coke. A healthy combination. He gestured at me to sit down, and I brushed some snow from the bench. He cut off a few pieces of his apple, transferred them to his mouth with his penknife, and washed them down with a mouthful of Coke.

– When I just a kid, half my intestines were surgically removed, and over the years I've discovered I digest food better if I drink a lot of Coke with it.

A ball bounced onto the narrow street, and a small child dashed after it. One of the nannies had to dive forward to grab her by the scruff of the neck. The child began to wail at the top of her voice. The nanny picked her up and rubbed her back. Winterberg stood up, crossed the street, and retrieved the ball from under a parked car. For a man of his size he moved easily. He was fit; he obviously worked out. The ball was printed with cartoon figures, a sort of blue koala and an Indian princess. He walked toward the crying child and I wondered how she felt, seeing this figure bearing down on her. Was it like standing on the deck of a ship and seeing an iceberg coming straight for you? When she got the ball back at least she stopped bawling.

– Where did you grow up? I asked, when he sat down again.

– Have a guess.

– I'm pretty sure you're not from the Netherlands. So I was thinking... Israel.

– You think I'm a Sabra?

– That sounds like a make of car.

– It's what you call a Jew who was born and bred in Israel.

– So that's what you are? A Sabra?

– Do you think that because of Mr. Burgers's tattoo, by any chance?

– That tattoo . . . I don't quite know what to make of Mr. Burgers.

– Let me reassure you: I don't intend to talk as much as him.

– Mr. Burgers does indeed have a certain talent for oratory.

– He's a man of many talents, certainly.

– And what are *your* talents?

He raised his eyebrows playfully, perhaps even flirtatiously, then described a circle in the air with his penknife, as if he were about to say something. I waited for an explanation, but it didn't come. He put his knife down on his thigh, wiped his mouth on his sleeve, and held up his hands with the fingers spread out, as if he wanted me to count all ten of them.

– I like to use my hands, he said. I can make things, I can break things. If I come up with a plan, I can carry it out myself. No messing around: I can act independently. Which means not having to be accountable to anyone else. I don't need to put up with anybody. I doubt there are many people in this city, at this conference, with hands as callused as mine. That's okay. That's fine. They've got bookcases, I've got calluses.

He took another bite of apple and I waited until he'd finished eating it.

– I don't like artists and I don't like intellectuals, Winterberg said.

– Okay.

– Intellectuals think they're the brains of a nation. In fact, they're not, they're its shit.

I thought for a moment.

– That sounds like something Stalin might have said.

– It was Lenin, in a letter to Trotsky.

Lev Davidovich Bronstein. Again the eyebrows did their little move. He took the apple peel out of his coat pocket and cut it into small pieces, tossing them toward a few pigeons that were idling about under a trash can.

– You people aren't the first to ask me to read something these last few days, I said. *Just making conversation.*

– As long as we're the most important.

– Does the Right Arm Liberation Front mean anything to you? Didn't you get the manifesto from that arty bunch of intellectuals about their initiative?

– The difference between you and me is that when I use the word "front," I'm not talking about an artists' initiative.

I stared, aware of the screeching of the playing children. I realized I was staring, but couldn't help it. Perhaps I was hysterical, but I needed time. Everything he said could be interpreted as a threat, and at the same time, nothing he said could be interpreted as a threat. Israel. Did Israel mean Mossad? Was he a sort of freelance spy like you see in films, the kind who takes time off between deals involving atomic secrets and liquidation contracts to set up editors in chief of academic journals? Each danger that I perceived, each hint of peril, came as much from my own racing brain as from him. And he knew it. He was playing a role just as much as I was: that whole monologue about intellectuals and shit—well, if he wanted to stay in character, that was fine, but then I had to do the same.

– Wow, I said, finally. Wow, what you said about the front, that was a pretty cool thing to say.

Looking at him now, it was difficult to put my finger on it, but there was something feminine about his face. A hint of something. He might well be as gay as a goose.

– There's the antiques dealer's, I said. Why don't you go there yourself?

He smiled at me, broadly, mockingly, and it struck me this was the first time I'd ever seen him really smile. His gums were white, the dark bags under his eyes hung down like little curtains.

– Mr. Burgers is known in the antiques world. He can't simply stroll in anywhere just like that.

– So that's what you've got me for?

– So that's what we've got you for.

The door triggered a little bell. I stepped inside and unbuttoned my jacket (probably to say: Look, I'm wearing a tie, you can trust me) and noticed that my right hand was tingling in an RSI-ish way, just as I'd woken up yet again with a stiff neck and the feeling that my intestines were made of liquorice bootlaces.

The shop was named after the street in which it stood: Marcus Aurelius. You could think of a worse name for an antiques dealer. It consisted of three large rooms, the main one dominated by a black grand piano on which stood a couple of Eastern vases and a Greek nude. A sign propped up on the keyboard said NOT FOR SALE. The rest of the shop was an organized chaos reminiscent of Marlinspike Hall, the home of Tintin's friend Captain Haddock: a promiscuous jumble of suits of armor, busts of composers and deposed monarchs, framed photos of late nineteenth-century and early twentieth-century regiments, bronze statuettes, and Buddhas large and small. There was a cupboard full of porcelain (mainly Delft blue), Persian rugs on the floor, African masks on the walls, still lifes, European landscapes, sabers and knives dating from, I estimated, five different centuries, as if a time machine had gone haywire and beamed up all kinds of random objects.

A little ways off stood a man in a raincoat and a tweed cap talking to a younger man in a sweater vest, who was giving him a mini-lecture on the historic value of the statuettes he was holding. I was greeted by a woman with short gray hair, who was holding a brush. She wore a pale pink pullover; a gold locket hung over the collar.

– Good afternoon.

She had to be over fifty, the skin on her neck hung like wattles. Her eyes were clear and blue and friendly enough, but when she smiled at me her teeth were strangely short and transparent, as if she'd never lost her milk teeth.

– Good afternoon, I said. What a nice shop you have.

– Thank you. Are you perhaps looking for a Christmas present?

– Have you got enough wrapping paper? I said, pointing to a suit of armor.

The woman laughed, clutching her chest (Oh, Friso, you're such a charmer). She put her brush away, on top of a cupboard.

– Are you a collector?

– Not really.

– A connoisseur, though?

– That's a nice term.

– We don't often get people of your age in here. They tend to find old things, well . . . old.

She laughed at her own words, so I laughed along with her.

– Some people come in here just to look around, she said. Other people come to buy something. And others come to buy something on behalf of other people.

– Does that happen much?

She looked at me with a faint smile. She was sizing me up, I thought, trying to place me.

– We sometimes get buyers who are operating on behalf of a third party, because the third party doesn't want to reveal his or her identity to the outside world.

– I'm here in Vienna for a big historians' conference, End of History, perhaps you've read about it.

– Oh, of course. It's been excellent for business, actually, we've had conference-goers coming in all week. That's the appeal of a shop like ours, you know—that sense of history, the feeling of holding something truly old in your hands.

I nodded. Indeed, indeed, that sense of history.

– I'm the editor in chief of a small academic journal, and we recently ran an article about an antique item that was probably sold here, I ventured.

She looked at me uncertainly. Might as well put your cards on the table, I thought.

– The item in question is something you might have sold over two decades ago.

– Okay.

– It's a piece of a maquette.

– Could you be more specific?

– It's a piece of a maquette of *Germania*, designed by Albert Speer, allegedly found in the Hitler bunker in Berlin. It's said to have ended up here after the war. I believe the seller was a Russian. You sold it on about twenty years ago.

Something changed in the way she looked at me. Her mouth closed, her eyes grew smaller, as if something was locking her face.

– That's to say, it's not genuine, apparently, but a fake, I added quickly.

– I can't imagine that we would sell a fake here, said a voice behind me. It was the boy in the sweater vest. He was prematurely bald and had a serious face, with teeth resembling the woman's.

– This is my son. We're a family business, going back over seventy years. If you have more concrete information about your maquette, I could perhaps take a look in our archives, she said, while she gestured with her head at her son. He took himself off, back to the man with the tweed cap, who was now admiring a couple of ornately carved walking sticks.

I followed her to a table with wooden ornaments; on it lay a snoring red tomcat. She opened a drawer and got out a heavy iron box containing hundreds of filing cards.

– And can you tell me anything more about this maquette, or the Russian who sold it?

– I can. It's supposedly just a small fragment, and the person who brought it to your shop was said to be called Arkady Rossovich.

– Any idea what year?

I shook my head. Hopeless. What did I actually know? *Data, data, data, I cannot make bricks without clay.* She, too, must have thought the same thing, because she stopped leafing through the cards and shut the lid of the box.

– Are you a journalist?

– Not exactly, I said.

– Where are you from?

– From the Netherlands. But I work in the States.

– In what field, did you say?

– Well, Hitler studies, actually. We carry out research into, well, Hitler.

– You said you worked for a journal?

– That's right. *The Sleepwalker.* Set up by Josip Brik, if the name means anything to you.

She looked aside and smiled a secret, private smile.

– And may I know your name?

– Philip de Vries, I said.

She wrote the name on a filing card and showed to me.

– Is that right?

– De Vries with a *V* not an *F*. Then it's right.

Her mouth had grown serious again, yet her expression was slightly mocking.

– Tell me, Mr. De Vries: are you here for our German cabinet?

– I am indeed, I said intuitively. Don't say "huh," don't shilly-shally, don't ask "What's the German cabinet?"

She was talking much more quietly now:

– I must say, I thought so from the look of you. Don't ask me how I know, I just do. I can tell immediately. Please follow me.

And why not follow her? Why not? Act as if you always do this, as if it's the most normal thing in the world. Keep smiling. The whole time I'd been in the shop, I'd been smiling, so much so that I was getting cramps in the corners of my mouth. Because this was what I did, this is what I always fell back on: I was blond and Caucasian. I possessed above-average good looks. I was well dressed. I'd had braces on my teeth for three years as a teenager: my gleaming white smile represented thousands of euros' worth of orthodontic care. Who wouldn't want to have me on their side? Just like Mrs. Chilton telling me about her affair—who wouldn't want to confide their secrets to me? Everything about me breathed Europe, the West, the First World—so I took it for granted that wherever I was, people would treat me with the respect and decency associated with the First World. I was my own talisman and I was just going to have to try my luck.

So I followed her down the wooden staircase to the basement. We walked to a large room that was clearly the office. It was full of filing cabinets; an antiquated computer purred on a massive desk. She took a key from the desk drawer and pointed to a wide door with a numeric lock.

– I have to ask you, Mr. De Vries, to be discreet about what I'm now going to show you. Can we agree on that?

– We can, I said.

Using the key, she first unlocked something at knee height, then stood between me and the other lock so I couldn't see the code she keyed in. A little light turned green, followed by a long, approving bleep. The door was under such tension that it sprang ajar.

– We don't show this room to everybody, she said.

She pushed the door open wider, giving me a glimpse inside. The first thing I saw was a flag with an enormous swastika.

– Please go in.

The room measured about twelve by twelve feet, if that. Light came from small windows close to the ceiling. You could only see the feet of passersby; the chance of anyone looking inside was minuscule. Thought had clearly been given to this. Above me I could hear her son's footsteps, but the sound of classical waltz music from the radio had grown much fainter.

– Our shop is apolitical. Our clients have specific interests and we want to meet their needs.

But that wasn't what this was about, I thought. Bullshit. This was a secret church. Holy relics were sold here, and for that you needed believers. If you opened her locket, who would you find? Give you three guesses. I stepped into the room. On the top of a dresser lay ten or more Long Knives, the ones the Night in 1934 was named after. Where the handle ended and the blade began, there was an ornamental swastika. Once again she spoke in dulcet tones:

– See how sharp the blade still is. And look, just above the handle, you can see the serial number. That tells us which soldier it belonged to.

This was somebody who was proud of her wares. A real professional. Next to the dresser was a large bookcase. I ran my fingers along the books. *Racial Science of the German People* by Hans F. K. Günther. *Race and Soul* by Dr. Ludwig Ferdinand Clauss. *The Toadstool*, an anti-Semitic children's book by Julius Streicher. I could feel the profile of the lettering on the spines under my fingertips. The case contained a framed letter, signed by Joseph Goebbels, and a framed, signed portrait of Leni Riefenstahl. The shelves were well dusted; the book jackets stood as straight as a row of soldiers. Between a bronze and a white marble bust of Hitler stood five, ten, fifteen copies of *Mein Kampf*. Old, leather-bound editions, with the kind of yellowing paper that I loved. I could smell it: sweet, this time too sweet.

In the middle of the room stood a wooden showcase the size and height of a billiard table. Under the glass, four Luger pistols lay side by side. The guns rested on red plush, and were lit by special spotlights, as if they were the keys to the city. Two small handwritten price tags were attached to the first two pistols, tucked away so they were quite hard to read, but not so tucked away as to be unreadable: €5,000, €8,500. Placards lay next to them, as if they were museum exhibits:

"Service weapon of *Hauptsturmführer* Dieter Wisleceny, January 19, 1911, Regulowken—May 4, 1948, Bratislawa, SS-number 2.177.889, recipient of the Iron Cross First Class for valor in Operation Barbarossa."

"Service weapon of *Haupsturmbahnführer* Ditrich Ernst zur Lahn, SS number 2.891.626. Born August 22, 1920, Salzburg, German Reich—died for the German people, the Fatherland, and the *Führer* in Königsberg, March 8, 1945."

She gestured to the fourth pistol in the row. I read the short text on the placard: "Service weapon of Field Marshal Otto Moritz Walter Model, Genthin, January 24, 1891—Duisberg, April 21, 1945."

Once again she looked at me with that subservient smile, as if she were a stewardess giving me an extra little packet of cashews:

– I take it that doesn't need any further explanation. This was his personal service weapon, the one he used right to the end. Perhaps you know that in 1945 Field Marshal Model, well... With her thumb and index finger she mimed a pistol, pressing the trigger against her temple. Pow, her mouth said, soundlessly.

– We're very proud of this item. We haven't had it long, but I can assure you we've already had several offers.

– How do you know this was the real pistol, may I ask?

– Discretion prevents me from telling you too much about the exact provenance of our items, but you must understand that this business has been in our family for five generations now. We've built up a regular network of clients and suppliers, so can absolutely guarantee the authenticity of our wares.

What had I said or done to give her the confidence to show me this? What was it in my face that made her think "from the look of me" that I was looking for this? Was

"Brik" the magic word? Once again, questions that I could not ask. The trick is to reduce the riddle.

Next to the pistols and showcase lay an open book, *Mein Kampf*, of course. Something had been written on the title page. A lone letter that looked like a flash of lightning, or a Nordic rune, and next to it a word that had been written diagonally, a capital *J* and *L* next to each other so that together they formed an *H*, an *i* without a dot, a *t* that looked more like an *a*, an *l* that looked like an *I*, and a wiggle that presumably represented an *e* and an *r*.

– That's not for sale, she said smilingly, but firmly. That's a family heirloom.

This was the first time, I realized, that I'd seen Hitler's signature. In real life. Nazis. I was suddenly reminded of what Mr. Chilton had said. They didn't just exist in movies, they were real people, you know. That memory, Brik and I drinking coffee in the sun, just outside our office, laughing, took me away from the present moment. Instead of the book in the showcase, I could now only see the reflection of my face in the glass. I looked so much younger than I felt, my hair just like the fake Philip's. I felt as if I were choking—not a lump in my throat, more like being throttled, as if the oxygen was gradually being sucked out of the room. As if I were grappling with some unseen force. It took a while, but then it hit me. I'd already seen so many swastikas, in all those films, all those novels, all those editions of *The Sleepwalker*, hundreds of thousands of them—Pip had occasionally complained that we had so many books with swastikas on the spines she couldn't bear to look at our bookcase anymore. But that was different. That was out in the open. To suddenly find a flag with a swastika, behind lock and key—that was different. This room, this cellar. The secrecy gave the flag significance. It was the first time I'd ever seen a swastika that meant something. Running into it like that was like coming across a toilet that hadn't been flushed—*that* had been the stench that was sucking away the oxygen.

– If you ever find that maquette from the Bunker, Mr. De Vries, do bear us in mind. I'm sure we could find a buyer for it.

By the time I got outside, Winterberg was no longer sitting on his bench. My neck and my back and my shoulders ached as if I was carrying a menhir and someone had forgotten to give me the magic potion, but I didn't care. The fresh air had seldom tasted so clean.

NINE

Felix was, of course, giddy with excitement when our taxi turned left into the long, illuminated driveway to Schloss Schönbrunn and a handful of policemen in bulletproof vests gestured to us to pull over to the side of the road. One cradled a black machine gun on his chest as if he were suckling a newborn baby, another shone a torch in our faces, straight at Felix's big grin, while another looked under our car with some kind of long-handled device. The driver was given his license back and the officer gestured that we could drive on. Red banners flanked the driveway, showing the faces of the big names of the conference: the Simon Schamas, the Salman Rushdies, the Peter Sloterdijks, the Mathilda Wilsons, the Madeline Steinbergs. Pretzel was there, though he certainly wouldn't be in a position to speak, and so, too, was Brik, his big, faithful dog's face waving in the wind—something that Felix didn't see, because he was almost wagging his tail on the back seat when he saw the metal detector gates at the stately entrance to the palace.

– You know what this means, Friso. Why would there be such tight security otherwise?

The guards looked alert; they took their job seriously. A man with an earpiece frisked us before we could even show our invitations, and only then were we allowed through the detector gates for a second opinion. Felix just kept on chattering away while a second man, with an even broader neck, if that were possible, frisked me again, more roughly, because in my case the metal detector had bleeped, at what turned out to be the buckle of my new belt.

– He's here, he must be. Wow, fancy bumping into a celebrity like him out in the wild. It's like walking down an Amsterdam street and coming face-to-face with a tiger, isn't it?

The guard wasn't too pleased. Sir, I'd like you to step back five paces so that I can do my job.

Felix did so, simply raising his voice so he could go on talking:

– Apparently he's taller. In real life.

The guard's hands felt icy cold as his fingers swept up and down my legs. It had suddenly gotten a lot chillier. The wind sliced through my trousers; it would probably start snowing again any minute. I looked up. Spotlights lit up the butter yellow facade of the Schloss; it stood out flawlessly against the dark sky, glowing like a spaceship that had just landed.

– I'm sure we'll spot him straightaway. That peroxided hair. I wouldn't know what to say to him, though. Ought one to enter into debate with him? One does rather owe it to one's position. As an intellectual. It's the perfect time to discuss that party manifesto of his, in which he talks about the dangers of National Socialism, putting "National" in quotes. In quotes! As if Hitler was actually a Socialist, and National Socialism was just sort of the flavor of the month. Bolognese Socialism. BBQ Ranch Socialism.

We joined a fidgety line. Our view of whatever was going on inside was impeded by the flapping shawls of the women in front of us. They complained in Italian, gesticulated, spoke with exclamation marks. Their handbags were inspected. Two hostesses in shiny gala dresses, their teeth chattering, checked the watermark on our invitations and handed us the guest book to sign.

– What should one say to a man like that, remarked Felix. I mean, what would you ask Hitler if you ran into him?

A tiger in Amsterdam. I took my time, scanning the guest book page for "P. de Vries" or Perhaps "De Vries, Philip," and then for "S. Burgers," "M. Winterberg," or "N. Barth," enemies multiply themselves, but couldn't spot anything and the hostesses were giving me impatient looks. I wrote my name, and seeing it there, *Friso de Vos*, my handwriting struck me as strangely uncertain, as if I wasn't sure of what I'd written. I looked at Felix:

– Munich Hitler or Berlin Hitler?

– Berlin Hitler, Felix answered.

– What would I like to ask him?

– Yes.

– Whether he wouldn't rather have become a painter.

I heard myself say it. Inside we ran straight into the backs of a couple of hundred people who, assembled in the big hall, were being asked to raise their glasses. Apparently we'd just missed the welcome speech. The red conference banners hung on the neoclassical pillars between the state portraits of the Habsburgs, who looked down on us from eternity. On the podium stood a statesmanlike figure with a neat white side parting; he raised his glass of champagne and struck up "*Gaudeamus igitur*" without the least inhibition. I was amazed that anyone would dare ask this gathering of professors and intellectuals and journalists and artists and students to sing along, and even more amazed when they did so—at the tops of their voices, even—so the whole room reverberated. The words were projected on a screen. It had exactly the same effect as a national anthem. Just by opening their mouths and singing the old words, the congress-goers no longer felt numbed by the long lectures or chilled by the cold weather, but instead incorporated into an international brotherhood of minds. *Post iucundam iuventutem / post molestam senectutem, nos habebit humus.* The literary critic who saw the books section in his newspaper shrinking by the year, the professor whose budget for PhD students had dwindled to almost nothing, poets and thinkers, lost souls, they sounded as if they'd looked forward to this moment for weeks; each Latin phrase was sung with full conviction, sincerely, self-assuredly. Under different circumstances this would probably have been exactly what I'd have expected—have hoped—of life, that you could walk into a salon in a palace and find it full of men and women in evening dress, people who all knew their Shakespeare and Tarantino, their Tocqueville and Kissinger, with whom you could have a good long talk about...about any topic under the sun, surely? That was our anthem being sung. This should have been our society, our new republic, a meritocracy of knowledge, all these people, so well read—but under other circumstances. Then I'd have sung along wholeheartedly, then I'd have felt a member of the club, then I'd probably just have fallen into line behind Brik in the conga and felt the pats on his shoulder as if they were on my own. But now I wasn't enjoying it. I felt a distance, and there was more to it than just Brik. All I could see were the backs of people's heads, I tried to distinguish one crown from the other, the tamed quiff of Philip de Vries, the yarmulke hair of Winterberg, the relocated follicles of Sweder Burgers, and perhaps also, why not, the hair helmet of Mrs. Chilton. Felix stood next to me, radiating neurotic energy as he sang along dutifully, programmed always to play the role expected of him, but I saw that he, too, was looking around, searching, in his case, for that peroxided pompadour.

Enter Friso. I'd expected that as soon as the singing stopped, people would turn around, that everyone would look at me, that my name or Brik's, as the former star of this conference, would be on their lips—or actually, deep down, I hadn't expected it at all, but would have liked to have expected it, would so like to have genuinely hoped that people would follow the stage directions of the script in which I'd ended up. Enter Friso. Because actually it didn't surprise me that the only people who had everyone's full attention were the waitresses, whose trays of champagne and hors d'oeuvres were being stormed like the autumn sales. Live music now sounded from another room, a not-very-swinging jazz band with a black singer, who was crooning numbers from the Great American Songbook with an accent that was almost Brikian.

Anodder seashon, anodder reason
For making whoopee.

Felix took me by the arm and led me through a sea of people toward an adjoining room.

– Did you see him? I didn't. But not everyone's here, I bet. This palace has got, what, ten reception rooms? Let's do a tour.

Wherever we went, the vibe was restless. People were talking to each other but not concentrating on what was being said. Everyone was looking around them, in search of better, more famous, more successful conversation partners. Look, there's X! Look, over there, Y! Names echoed all around. Some meant something to me, others didn't.

– Look, there's Nicolas Fokker.

Indeed, there was Nicolas Fokker, small, plump, and celebrated. *Écrivain européen.* An author who looked like a retired bank manager. He lived off caviar and canapés. He would be a personal friend of the queen's. Each year the call from Oslo failed to materialize, and there he stood, hands in his pockets, talking to a boy with unruly curls and mournful eyes, armed with pen and notepad, who looked as if he were from the local school newspaper:

– Well of course, the list of people who *haven't* won it is *much* more impressive.

The boy noted his comment dutifully. As we moved on we passed two women, one young, one older, who were also looking at Fokker. The older lady seemed vaguely familiar somehow. She was diminutive—about a head taller than a shopping cart—with an expensive dress, a weathered face, and teeth that were very white and disproportionately large for her mouth, as if they had belonged to someone else. The girl addressed her:

– Oh my God, those things you wrote about Fokker...

– It wasn't *that* bitchy...

– No I mean, he deserved it, but reading your review made me feel like I was peering through the sights of a sniper's rifle in the mountains above Sarajevo.

People were still coming in out of the cold; despite the late hour, it was open house. The waiters were already struggling to get through with their trays. We heard a woman laugh loudly; somewhere a glass fell to the floor.

– We're not going to find him here, said Felix.

I saw Vikram Tahl talking to a man who was a head taller than him and it was only now, from a distance, that I saw how good his footwork was. Like a boxer. He moved with each movement of the speaker's head, so as to always stand squarely in front of him, unignorable. Tahl was gesticulating; he looked thwarted:

– But how can you *not* be interested in the history of India? he asked, with a forced smile.

– Well, I've just never forgiven those guys for what they did to Ben Kingsley in *Gandhi*.

Wanting to avoid Tahl, I steered Felix toward the window seats, where two mustachioed men who'd commandeered an entire tray of canapés were gobbling miniature meatballs and laughing loudly. ("And you know what the worst thing was? He submitted his volume of poetry to me in Comic Sans!") Next to them were the youngest faces I'd seen up to now, two boys in blazers too big for them.

– What's your favorite war? one asked.

– The Crimean has everything you can expect of a good war, I'd say, the other replied.

Two girls, perhaps their dates, stood a little ways off. They seemed a bit older, a bit more self-assured. One said to the other with a superior smile:

– And then he looked at me and said: "Girl, let's not talk about *les mots*, in your case I'm much more interested in *les choses*."

– Oh wow, like Foucault was trying to chat you up.

In the middle of the room stood a camera crew, and right in front of the camera stood Madeline Steinberg, a scion of the piano family, in a cocktail dress that, given her fifty summers, was shorter than you'd expect at this time of year, or *any* time of year. She was drinking something with an olive in it. This was a woman who had won the Booker Prize with her debut novel, eons ago, and since then had abandoned the genre, had never felt the need to write another novel. Now she wrote books with subtitles like *On the Conscience of Words* or *When Writers Are Silent*. Her neck was long, her eyes old and warm and elfin. A sprinkling of gray highlighted her dark hair. She wore a great many bracelets, enough gold and silver to buy an entire Indian tribe.

Brik had once warned me about her: as vicious as a cat, he said. "And the biggest gossip on the circuit, so watch out. In fact, watch out on two counts, because she's a real cougar. She'll devour you, and I wouldn't like to see that happen to you and that sweet Pippa of yours."

She was speaking in honeyed tones into the interviewer's microphone.

– There was something vulgar about his encyclopedic knowledge. It was as if he was always trying to show you just how much he knew.

Felix was standing on tiptoe, trying to look over the heads of the crowd. He gestured that we should move on. But I went on listening to Steinberg. She continued:

– I mean, he was from some shitty little hamlet in the former Yugoslavia, right? Don't forget that. He must have been overcompensating. *Excusez les mots.*

I grabbed Felix by the arm. Had he heard what she'd said? Did she mean Brik? He shrugged.

– There's live music in the room next door, so he won't be there. Wouldn't it be great if you and I stood up to Wilders—gave him a piece of our minds? Two young intellectuals on the warpath. How about you wait down here, while I run upstairs and have a look, okay?

Felix didn't wait for my reply, but slipped away. I hung around until Madeline Steinberg had finished with the journalists and then walked up to her. That sweet Pippa of mine. Take it easy, I told myself. You can handle this. Get in character just one last time. Play the role just one last time.

– Madeline Steinberg, right? Philip de Vries. I believe Josip Brik once introduced us.

– I'm fairly sure he never did.

She sounded amused, gave me a lingering handshake.

– Can I offer you something to drink?

– Young men like you can always treat me to champagne, she said laughing.

Champagne arrived on a tray. Steinberg looked at me curiously, her eyes wide.

– How strange to find a woman like you here alone.

She smiled again, somewhat uncertainly this time. I was overdoing it on purpose.

– So, Mr. Philip, what brings you to Vienna?

– Brik, of course. I'm here to take part in a debate tomorrow about Brik's legacy, about what made Brik so special. How we can best interpret Brik. What I learned from my close connection with Brik, is that Brik might have come across as an absentminded professor, but that Brik himself was very well aware of how he functioned best.

I tried to use Brik's name as many times as possible in every sentence. Brik, Brik, Brik, she must get the impression that Philip de Vries was the most boastful, name-dropping prole at the conference.

– "Philip," he would say, because that's my name, "Philip, I'm my own worst enemy, because God forbid anyone could do me more harm than I'm already doing to myself."

She couldn't be used to having conversations in which she wasn't asked anything, I imagined, in which she wasn't complimented on her latest book, essay, TV appearance, or *Hello!* magazine home feature, so I didn't ask her anything, just waited.

– So you knew him well? she finally asked, clearly at a loss.

– I did indeed. In fact, I got this watch from Brik, I said, and pulled up my sleeve so she could see the watch my mother gave me as a graduation present. It was simple but elegant, with gold hands and a crocodile leather strap.

– I once told Brik that I didn't have a watch. So he just gave me his! It was like he adopted me as his son.

– Oh really? she said. The son he never had, I take it?

You could see her interest in me waning. She scanned the room for someone more appealing to talk to. This was going well. There wasn't anyone, so she pulled herself together and turned back to me again:

– Tell me, are you also involved in that journal, *The Sleepwalker*?

– No, I said. *Pourquoi?*

I was very proud of myself, coming out with that
"*pourquoi.*"

– Well, I still had a bone to pick with Brik about it. A
year ago I wrote to him, or rather to *The Sleepwalker*, after
Brik wrote a piece on Srebrenica, marking yet another anniversary of the genocide.

– I remember that article well, I said, in the tone of
someone doing a voice-over in a commercial.

– I wrote a letter about it. It seemed fair to approach
him straightaway, rather than wait until he published it in
some essay compilation for the general public, and then
respond in an opinion piece.

– So what did you write?

– That there were some stupid mistakes in it. Hemingway didn't commit suicide in Cuba, but in Ketchum, Idaho.
Klaus Barbie didn't come from Austria, but Prussia. Things
he should have known. But it was mainly about a change
that struck me in Brik's writing. Back in the late 1980s,
when the Wall was still in place, he was already writing
interesting cultural critique pieces, but they were always
quite mild, quite reticent, as if he were restraining himself,
as if there were a truth that could be deferred. After 1991,
that restraint disappeared. Suddenly he was writing with
much more authority and conviction. Much more judgmen-
tally. It took a while before I realized what had changed:
it was the collapse of the Soviet Union, the death of the
Socialist dream. At some level he'd always seen Socialism

as an alternative to Western life. That was what made him noncommittal. When that fell away, first the Wall, then the Soviet Union, there was only one path he could follow. I suddenly noticed it in that piece on the Balkan conflict. That the great, ironic critic of ideology himself had solid ideological foundations. Anyway, I wrote to Brik and got a friendly email back from him, saying how gratified he was that I'd been reading his articles for so long, and that he'd certainly pass on the letter to the editor of *The Sleepwalker*. The letter never appeared in the journal.

It was a sharper analysis than I'd expected of her. I squeezed out a smile.

– I don't know anything about that, I said, and for the first time I was speaking the truth, which tasted like a foreign language.

She looked at me intently with an expression I couldn't interpret. I put on my best poker face.

– Were you talking about him just now, when you were being filmed? I asked.

My attempt at inscrutability didn't seem to have worked. She smiled discreetly, satisfied.

– Very telling that you assume it was about him. Shall I unleash some psychotherapy on you, young man? Do you know what it is—hey look, Nicolas Fokker.

Indeed, he'd just shuffled into the room, perhaps looking for the camera crew. Steinberg filled me in.

– He's one of the guests of honor this week. Got a medal this weekend from the city of Vienna, because he wrote novels about how awful the Second World War and the Holocaust were.

– Glad someone has the guts to make that known, I said.

She laughed. He's such a little shit, she said. I have to say hello to him. Thank you for the champagne, Philip.

She greeted Fokker with three air kisses and she was off. "Do you know what it is?" No, don't tell me, I thought. Now I was alone. Normally you could kill some time by going to the bar, lining up, and ordering something, and then a quarter of an hour had gone by, but here there were staff everywhere, ready to dash forward with whatever you needed.

I was struck by how many other people were alone. Especially men: you hardly noticed them in the crowd, but they were there. They just stood there vacantly, with name stickers on their lapels, stickers that might just as well have said which nursery they should be taken to if they lost their mothers. They didn't go anywhere, they didn't speak to anyone, they drummed their fingers on their wineglasses in time to the music, made a great show of inspecting the paintings on the walls. A man with a Tolstoyan beard was holding one of the curtains, testing the fabric between his thumb and index finger as if he were planning to order a few yards of it from the waiters. The fact that you'd read a lot of books didn't at all mean you could just join in with the rest. I was alone. Would Philip be alone too?

– And you're Friso de Vos.

The answer to my question. I'd once bungee-jumped with Pippa in Thailand, on our first holiday together, because I quite needlessly wanted to impress her by jumping off a crane at a carnival on the beach. The feeling I was having now reminded me briefly of that moment when your freefall stops and the elastic jerks you up again, that moment when you're gripped both by the cord's resistance and by gravity. The face in front of me didn't look as much like mine as I'd feared, a fear I'd never entirely dared formulate, but there was a basic resemblance. His mouth and teeth were different, fuller, larger, his eyes rounder, but we had the same vertical lines, jaw, nose, ears. Our hair was identical, equally fair, the same combination of tufts falling forward and sideways, though his seemed more solid, as if it were all one piece.

A tiger in Amsterdam. I once found myself next to Brad Pitt in a bookshop, and he was smaller than I'd imagined, older too, but he filled the space with a strange sort of energy that made you walk more erect. The energy didn't come from him, I knew that, it was in me, but he triggered it.

– I recognized you straightaway. I'm Philip de Vries. As in Brik.

He stuck out a hand and I reflexively did the same. He wasn't wearing black tie, but a gray suit with a white shirt and a light brown tie, which immediately made me feel a fool for conforming to the dress code.

– I'm Friso.

– I know!

– Friso de Vos. Also as in Brik.

– Of course!

– Oh?

– If there are two dyed-in-the-wool Brikians, it's us.

– Oh really?

– Yes! You rather more than me, of course. It's great to meet you, Friso.

– It is?

– Absolutely. Brik talked about you a lot.

I smiled stupidly. He smiled too, a wide, relaxed Colgate smile, as if he wasn't smiling at me but flashing his teeth, like a scary man in the park.

– No, seriously. I was often jealous of you. All the things you'd done together. He told me about the time you set off in a cheap little rental car to visit his elderly mother, somewhere near Belgrade, and that the engine cut out at the slightest hill, and you had to take turns pushing the car, but you couldn't move it with him inside. Hilarious.

He was still holding my hand and beaming.

– Philip, I said, but was unable to finish my sentence. Not because he interrupted me, but because I didn't know what to say to him, or even where to start. There wasn't a trace of irony in him. Instead he radiated a kind of happy innocence that you usually only see in family dogs. *The master's back, the master!* He was simply happy to be here, truly happy to meet me.

– Call me Flip, he said. All my friends call me Flip.

Flip. "Call me Flip." Please, I thought, please not this.

– I hadn't yet had a chance to call you back, I said. Did you want to discuss our debate tomorrow?

– No, I've got a kind of odd dilemma, he said (his voice had a lilt to it, perhaps West Frisian, it was different from what I remembered from his TV appearance). I got a call, last week, I think it was. From the crematorium. They said no one had left any instructions about Brik's ashes.

I managed to say: "What?"

– Brik was cremated, someplace near Groningen. You know. In Uithuizen. The crematorium called me up to ask who they should send the urn with Brik's ashes to.

Not this, I thought.

– So I said: "No worries, I'll come and pick him up." He gestured to a passing waitress, gave her a broad grin, got one back, and took two glasses of champagne from her tray. He gave one to me and raised his in the air:

– Cheers, he said.

Let's have a toast for the douchebags.

– Cheers, I said. He emptied his glass in a single gulp. Smiled at me again.

– A bit weird, perhaps, but I've got the urn with me. In my hotel room. I thought you'd know better than anyone what should be done with it. Brik was really crazy about you. You'd know what to do, I thought.

– You've got Brik's ashes?

– Yes.

– With you?

– Yes! Just packed him in my carry-on luggage. Had to fill in a special form, go through a separate scanner at Schiphol. No problemo. Did that Liddie Chilton give you money too? She called me later, after New York, you know, the memorial service, wanting to know if she might slip me some cash, so I could buy a nice suit and stay in a swish hotel in Vienna. Pretty chill, eh?

– Super chill, I said.

– Wasn't going to argue with that. Booked something cheap on Hotels.com, figured I'd gotten myself a free vacation. Asked my girlfriend: "Babe, where do you want to go?" Shazam! Booked two tickets to Bali on the spot. We're flying on Boxing Day. Thank you very much! I mean, Brik wasn't the kind of guy who gave a fuck what you wore, so why shouldn't I spend it on something else? You've been to this conference before, right? Is it very different, now that he's no longer with us? Perhaps I'm being naive or too obsessive about Brik, but if the primus inter pares drops away like that, isn't it a bit like the king dying? When that happens, what's left?

– A republic, I said.

– There's always something a bit pathetic about a republic, though. It always comes *after* something. After a kingdom, after an empire. It never just exists spontaneously, as if it's just not a natural state of affairs.

I remembered what Brik had written in *The Red Machine*: when the executioner Sanson held up the dripping head of Louis XVI to the mob on the Place de la Révolution, nothing happened. People simply cheered and went home. The really shocking thing, Brik wrote, was that Paris just went back to the order of the day. The city gates opened again. People went to market, ate in cafés, swept their doorsteps, and went to bed. The republic was ushered in without musket fire or the roar of cannons, without bonfires or dances of joy.

I could still hear him say it: *Who are you, Friso, my Dauphin or my Robespierre?* And if we weren't Dauphins, then what was left?

– Smart thinking, I said, as if I were giving him a present.

He shrugged.

– Apparently the Spanish crown prince is here this evening. He's going to be presented with some forty-volume standard work on the Franco era. That's why there's all this security.

– Hey, Philip, I said, nerving myself, who's Arkady Rossovich?

He smiled.

– Why on earth do you ask?

– Arkady Rossovich. The Hitler maquette. It was stolen from Brik's house.

He put his hand on my shoulder and his smile grew even wider.

– You're joking, right?

– No.

– You know the X-Men?

– Of course.

– Arkady Rossovich is a Russian mutant, Omega Red. A supervillain.

– What?

– I wrote about him for the new issue of *Blondie, Journal of Hitler Studies*. You must know it, surely? Their annual Hitler fiction issue? I wrote a piece of fan fiction about Brik.

– Fan fiction?

– Yes. About Brik. It seemed fun, thinking up a story like that. I have literary ambitions, you know—more literary ambitions than academic ambitions, actually—and the idea of turning Brik's ideas into a gripping tale really appealed to me. Do you like writing?

– I hate it.

– Ha ha, well I don't.

– So the whole story, the whole maquette business, is made up?

– Totally!

I smiled, and he answered my smile with a smile. What a cheerful chap. No conversation with Felix had ever been as easygoing as this five minutes with him.

We wandered from one room to the other, in search of a quieter spot. He told me about the book he was reading, while I kept on looking around, as if having found Philip wasn't enough, as if there might be another Philip still at large. He said he was plowing through the Russian classics in chronological order on Brik's advice, and that he struggled to keep track of all the characters' names. But

I wasn't really listening, I was looking over his shoulder at what was approaching. Markus Winterberg was bearing down on us like an icebreaker cleaving the Barents Sea, parting little knots of guests like ice floes. Behind his fat neck I could see the fedora of his master heave into view.

– Oh, kid, I said to Philip, who gave me a startled look. Oh, dude, you are *so* going to make it as a fiction writer. You'd be amazed at what you can bring to life.

Winterberg stepped aside so that Burgers, in a tuxedo, could join us. The four of us formed a little circle. Everyone looked at everyone else in turn.

– Mr. De Vries, good evening.

– Hallo, Mr. Burgers, I said.

– Have we met? asked Philip.

– You owe me something, I think, said Burgers.

– *A Lannister always pays his debts*, I said.

– We'd agreed you'd give me some more information this evening.

– Information about what? asked Philip.

– Arkady Rossovich, I said, and winked at Philip.

– Arkady? You mean my Omega Red? he asked.

– Does he know about the maquette? asked Winterberg.

– Mr. Burgers, I said, may I introduce a good friend of mine...

– The maquette? Yes, great, isn't it, said Philip, beaming from ear to ear.

– ...far and away the best, the most loyal student Brik ever had.

– Have you read my story?

– What story? asked Winterberg.

– About the maquette!

– ... He is not my brother, yet he is the son of my father, I said.

– So three guesses, who am I? laughed Philip, blissfully unaware.

– Philip de Vries, will you tell this gentleman why you wrote the story about the Rossovich maquette?

– It was commissioned for the fiction issue of *Blondie, Journal of Hitler Studies*. It was fan fiction. But it's only going to be published next month, how do you know ...

– Philip de Vries? said Winterberg.

– That's me, said Philip, why?

– He's Philip de Vries, Mr. Burgers, Mr. Winterberg. The author of fan fiction about Brik. That's what your maquette was, I said. Fan fiction. With the emphasis on "fiction."

– Hey, you don't despise the genre, do you? said Philip.

– Who are *you* then? Burgers asked me.

– Sorry, who are *you* actually? Philip asked him.

– I'm Sweder Burgers. Of the Burgers Foundation, among other things, he said.

– And fucking Mossad or Shin Bet or something like that, I bet, I added, though not aloud. My gaze was fixed on a bare back and a long neck under a perfectly coiffed head of short blonde hair. Her arms were thin but her shoulders angular and muscled, a swimmer's shoulders, I thought. Her ultramarine dress was very low at the back and you could see that her skin was uniformly tanned, carefully bronzed on a sun bed. Her hand found the hand of the man next to her, an older gentleman I'd never seen before. He bent down and whispered something in her ear. He was smiling, clearly flirting. Perhaps he said her name, *Nina Barth*, or perhaps by now she had a new one.

– So you're Philip de Vries? asked Winterberg.

– Yes and he's Friso de Vos. As in Brik, said Philip.

What would she earn on an evening like this, I asked myself. What would I have been worth? The man's hand moved lightly down from her shoulders, his fingertips explored her bare back, while he spoke in her ear. Would she have been sent to him, as she was to me, or would he have approached her? She probably had no idea we were standing ten feet away, was oblivious to the denouement of the train of events she'd set in motion, thanks to the din of the chattering people and the music from the room next door. He drew little circles on her back with his middle finger. How much would he have to pay? A picture flashed through my mind, of me going to a cash machine with Mrs. Chilton's credit card and withdrawing the sum for her. Though my motives were more territorial than noble, I felt if I intervened now, I could save her from this creep.

– Friso de Vos, said Winterberg. I turned back to them.

– Friso de Vos, editor in chief of the *The Sleepwalker, Journal of Hitler Studies, Since 1991*. Nice to meet you.

– But the antiques shop, was that all made up too? Doesn't it have a German cabinet? asked Burgers.

– What are you talking about? said Philip. Why do you think he's me?

– They've got absolutely everything a Nazi would want for Christmas, I told Burgers.

– Jesus, they look so alike, said Winterberg.

– Dammit, that's no excuse, Markus, Burgers snapped.

– Why don't you ask Nina? I said. She's over there.

– Where? Burgers and Winterberg chorused in shock.

But even entropy ends sooner or later. Eventually, things materialize. The abstract becomes concrete. At first I didn't really register it, but I heard it, nevertheless. The music had just died down and instruments were being shoved about on the stage. Burgers heard it too, because he stopped talking and looked at me, pointing at his ear. I nodded.

– Would Philip de Vries come up onstage?

A loud buzzing noise followed, of someone holding a microphone too close to a speaker. Winterberg had gone silent now too, and I put my hand on Philip's shoulder as a sign he should quieten down a bit.

– WOULD PHILIP DE VRIES COME UP ONSTAGE?

He looked at me.

– That's me, he said.

– That's you, I said.

– Do you think I've won something? He laughed and walked off, past the guests, who made way for him. The beautiful woman in the ultramarine dress stepped aside. I saw her face in profile and realized it wasn't Nina. Her forehead was larger, her nose smaller, the balance was lacking. She looked away quickly when she saw me staring at her, much shyer than Nina would ever have been. By now Philip had reached the stage, on which stood two boys and a girl, surrounded by musical instruments. It was a big room. They were too far off for me to see their faces. I walked toward the stage, aware that Winterberg was on my heels. As Philip climbed onto it, all eyes focused on the little group. A lot happened at once. The girl began to recite into the microphone: "We are young, love is a battlefield! For too long now, the past has dominated the present! It's time to wake up! In our own time! For too long now, old meanings have hijacked timeless gestures!" Philip was still looking amused—probably thought he'd been picked out of the audience, like at the circus, to hold up the hoop for the lion to jump through—but his smile vanished at the next words. "An outstretched arm as a mark of unity! Twelve years of German Fascism...!" The two boys next to him, their right arms proudly aloft, stood Hitler-saluting the audience, who immediately began to boo.

– Oh fuck, I said.

Of course Philip didn't play along with this nonsense, annoying one of the boys, who tried to force his arm into the air—"The time has come for the de-Hitlerization of the right arm! History cannot harm us!"—but he wrestled free, knocking the boy over, just as the advancing security guards reached the stage. Philip was the first casualty: the foremost security guard charged him with a shoulder tackle, lifting him straight off the ground and propelling him into the drum kit with an almighty crash. Chaos ensued: blows were exchanged, you could hear cloth ripping, see pushing and shoving, people fell over, the Hitler-saluting boys disappeared under an avalanche of guards in rented black tuxedos, people screamed, a cello broke in two, and the girl with the microphone—"WE ARE THE RIGHT ARM LIBERATION FROOOOONT!"—was picked up bodily by a burly security guard, who tossed her over his shoulder like a small child.

– Markus, let's get out of here, I heard Burgers say. He was fuming with anger.

Out of the corner of my eye I could just see Winterberg. He was holding his hand in front of his mouth, as if he wanted to check whether he had bad breath, but now I saw he was speaking into a tiny microphone attached to a wire emerging from his sleeve:

– Abort mission, I repeat, abort mission. Stand down.

Before he, too, disappeared in the crowd, our eyes met briefly, very briefly, and he pinched my wrist. Not angrily, not aggressively, but amicably, perhaps even with a sort of professional admiration.

The urn, I thought. Brik.

So there it was at last. The plot I'd been waiting for these last two days. The pawns had behaved as expected. Including me. When I went outside, it was snowing again,

and for a moment I thought the morose-looking security guards approaching the castle were heading for me—but they passed me by on their way to the party inside. No one followed me.

The utter calmness I felt made me realize how tired I was. My anger was spent.

In films, the most common line is *"Let's get out of here."* In novels, at scene-setting moments, it's *"Somewhere in the distance, a dog barked,"* or something like that. I looked back at my footprints and counted to see how long it took before they were obliterated by fresh snow—another popular image in fiction, easy symbolism, history being wiped out. Thirty seconds, forty seconds. The prints remained visible.

Should I deduce something from that? Did it represent a deeper truth? Was I doing anyone a service by trying to turn my own footprints into a metaphor?

Enough. Done.

With my fists clenched in my coat pockets I walked on, past the castle's immense gardens, past the clipped shrubs, past the pond. Two swans floated along aimlessly, leaving ever-widening V-shaped ripples in their wake.

Were they real? Didn't swans fly south in winter?

Their eyes were dark, their beaks expressionless, like all beaks. Perhaps that's why you can't ever feel real sympathy for birds: you can't read their faces. They never seem to be truly interested in anything. They could even be fake swans, I thought, with propeller-driven legs and little cameras mounted in their eyes, so security guards could just sit in a room somewhere and keep an eye on visitors by twiddling a remote control. Perhaps that big screw in the sign saying DON'T WALK ON THE GRASS was a microphone.

Thinking up all this stuff made me so tired. Thinkingthinkingthinking.

I was not made to think. I was made to eat.

Even from a distance I could hear the security guards chatting and laughing—apparently there'd been no major panic at the castle, or if there had, it was now once more under control.

"Right Arm Liberation Front *kaltgestellt*. No survivors."

Friso: stop thinking.

The chatter ceased as I neared the exit; the guards wished me good evening in chorus. One told me that if I needed a taxi I'd be sure to find one outside the gates, just on the right.

I liked the way the snow was muting my footsteps, as if I were walking in socks. It would have been nice to linger in the palace gardens, but I had a mission. There were five taxis, and I chose the one that wasn't blasting out pop music or news. The driver was silent, too, as he drove steadily down the city's broad avenues, toward Philip's hotel. To distract myself from my thoughts I concentrated on my body, monitoring all my faculties, trying to register every tiny discomfort. A nagging ache in my lower back, tingling fingertips, burning sphincter, racing heart, and tense, hunched shoulders—complaints that had become normal since Chile, familiar, even. The hotel porters had left their posts and were huddled alongside the staff behind the reception desk, bent over a small television set. Even without seeing the screen you could tell it was a soccer match, probably in injury time; the commentator sounded hoarse and excited.

– Sorry to trouble you, I said. But I lost my room key.

– What's your name, sir?

– My name is De Vries, *D.E.V.R.I.E.S.*

The boy keyed it in apathetically.

– Room number 612?

– That's right, I said.

– Just a second please.

He pressed a few buttons and turned back to the TV for the full twenty seconds it took for a rattling machine to spit out a new key card.

– Have a nice evening, he said.

It went just as easily, just as smoothly as I'd imagined. Let your imagination become reality. Don't trust in security, don't trust in privacy, don't imagine that anyone at all feels responsible for you. To the strains of "The Girl from Ipanema" the elevator took me to the sixth floor. Room

612. I stuck the key card in the slot as if it were the most normal thing in the world, and the little green light flickered on and the door unlocked.

It was the same type of room as Nina's, but bigger. The same familiar, sterile hotel room smell. I walked through the little hallway, just like the one where I'd pulled off Nina's swimsuit. Double bed, beige sheets, white pillowcases. "I want you to go down on all fours in front of me." Nina—where was she now? Would she be doing the same thing in a hotel room in Amsterdam or London? Would she be growing more photogenic with every performance? From a distance, the desk looked like solid wood, mahogany or something, but up close it turned out to be cheap, painted plywood. The round knobs on the drawers weren't really brass. The wooden chair was uncomfortable. In the right drawer there was only hotel stuff: a room-service menu, house rules, writing paper. The left drawer contained a folder with printouts of emails confirming the hotel and flight bookings, a map of the town, some conference papers, lecture schedules. Nothing personal, just documents showing how diligently and enthusiastically he'd prepared for the conference—he must have so looked forward to it.

Where was the urn?

This should have been very easy—if Hollywood has taught you what war looks like, then TV has trained you how detectives operate. Look with "soft eyes," as they said in Pip's favorite series. Look beyond things. Don't just see them for what they are, but for what they might be. See how things relate to each other.

I shut the drawer again softly. Softly, just like my father always told me not to slam the car door. Softly, because I didn't want to shatter the silence of the room. Brik dead, unforgivably dead, and me here, all alone.

History is made by men in back rooms. The minibar contained nothing it shouldn't: a small bottle of Coca-Cola (0.2 liters) for €4.99, a miniature of whiskey (0.125 liters) for €11.99, a bar of milk chocolate (9 ounces) for €3.99. I opened the bottle of whiskey with my teeth, tasting the metal of the cap, and poured it into one of the minibar glasses. I added the Coke, took a sip, and spat it out, partly back in the glass. Sweet and bitter.

An outdoor jacket very like mine hung in the wardrobe. Gore-Tex, water-repellent, hip in a subversive, young-fogeyish way. I checked all the pockets, finding only a receipt for an airport shop. My hand fell on a blue shirt on a hanger. I took hold of the collar and yanked the shirt free with a single movement, tearing off the top button. I did the same with the second shirt. I rechecked the pockets of a suit: jacket and trousers. Nothing, nothing, nothing.

The bathroom was empty except for a toiletry bag: I overturned it in the sink. He had the same brand of surf-look hair gel as I did, salty eco-toothpaste similar to Pippa's.

That left only the chest of drawers. Don't panic. There were three big drawers, three possibilities. Upper drawer:

boxer shorts, T-shirts, shirts, all neatly folded. Three ties, carefully rolled up. I tossed everything in the direction of the wastebasket, mostly missing it, my turn for the Sack of Jerusalem. Among the clothes I came across a book, *The Red Machine*, in Dutch of course. He was reading Brik in translation. Couldn't cope with six hundred pages of English. The title page bore Brik's signature, a date, "Groningen," and underneath, in his scratchy child's handwriting: "For Ph. A promise is a promise. JB." There were a few Post-it notes stuck between the pages, but otherwise it looked brand-new. Perhaps he'd never read *The Red Machine*. The thing in my hands didn't feel like a book, more like something alive. I opened it wider, felt the hard spine of the book resist, the resistance crack. I kept on pressing until the spine snapped—this must be what it felt like to throttle a small animal. A deep groove now ran right through the middle of the *B* of "Brik." I tore out the page with the signature and stuffed it in my pocket. I threw the book away, the front and back cover flapping like impotent wings. It landed somewhere behind the bed.

Second drawer. Socks in all colors of the rainbow. Hip. A pair of sneakers. A hoodie. Nothing interesting.

Bottom drawer, last fucking chance, Philip de Vries. Or should I say: "Last chance for you, Friso de Vos"? The moment I touched the knob and felt how light the drawer was, I already knew. Nothing. Empty. And my head instantly filled up again.

Friso de Vos, Josip Brik's Dauphin, his intended biographer, connoisseur of his work, I should also say "aficionado"—did you feel no pity at all for Philip de Vries?

You mean "Flip de Vries"?

No, really, joking apart, did you feel no pity? Be honest.

Somehow it seemed as if he didn't really exist. As if I'd invented him. That he very much existed was something that I, at that moment, in that hotel room, preferred not to acknowledge.

Why were you so destructive?

It was seeing all his things, I think, they just made it worse.

Because?

They made his existence so concrete. And my intolerance so real.

How did you feel?

Short of breath, actually. I was panting, there in his room.

Why was that? Tension? Fear?

No, I wasn't afraid. It was more like I'd just eaten five plates of stew. As if I was full to bursting. As if I had to unbutton the top button of my trousers.

What were you thinking about?

Back when I was a student in Groningen, a friend in my fraternity told me that when his father died, some hellish document opened in his head, and that everything connected to his father's death, even if only indirectly, was copied and pasted into it and declared sacred. The black wool tie he wore at the funeral, the music that was played—"You Can't Always Get What You Want" and Pachelbel's Canon in D—and via Pachelbel an old film of Robert Redford's because that piece of music featured prominently in it. He remembered someone's daughter crying angrily in the family room of the oncology department and cursing Lance Armstrong for saying that if you keep fighting, you'll win, because you couldn't win this and fuck you, Lance Armstrong—and so Lance Armstrong, too, landed in the document, along with that Dutch sports commentator, because those two went together like a crocodile and one of those little birds that picks the crocodile's scales clean.

Soon after the funeral our fraternity organized an anniversary trip to Venice (paste): he came along, we visited the Peggy Guggenheim Museum (paste) and the distraction did him good, but a year later, when he was playing some PlayStation game in which a hired assassin sprinted and climbed through the streets and canals of Venice, he was suddenly reminded of those days, and it made him almost sick with misery.

He told me that two or three days after the funeral, the son of a famous Dutch writer died in an accident, and that the boy's father later wrote a book about it. Every journalist in the Netherlands wrote how awful it was about the son, and it was, of course, but *his father* was dead too, simultaneously dead, and that was just as awful, but no one damn well devoted any column space to that, so that book was also cut and pasted.

Did the document ever close itself?

Ultimately.

So what was in your document?

Nothing.

Nothing?

I didn't want to open that document, I resisted it.

But isn't it also the idea that you absorb a document like that, incorporate it, so you can—apologies for the cliché—move on?

I preferred to reject it, to put up a fight. I didn't want to make any accommodations, I guess.

It might not have been pasted, but it was all cut, surely? Isn't your clipboard totally clogged up with all that unreleased data?

It's only a metaphor.

You're angry, aren't you?

You can't always get what you want.

Why do you feel the need to blame somebody or something?

Imagine not being able to blame somebody.

What then?

Then none of it matters. Then it's all chance.

A man leans out of a window, the window frame breaks, the man falls and dies. It's a window frame that people have been leaning on for thirty years, perhaps, and yet in his case it breaks. What can you make of that other than chance, than simple bad luck?

You offset chance by making it the punch line of something, by giving Brik's death meaning, fitting it into a story. Even if it means inventing the story.

But all that fiction—isn't that a form of self-deception too?

It was only then that I saw it. It was standing on a bedside table, big, unmissable actually, but the urn looked so industrial it had escaped my attention—I'd taken it to be a lamp, or a meter box, part of the room's equipment. I'd assumed that urns were kind of vase-shaped, but this looked more like a keg.

There was Brik. I put it ("him"!) on my lap, couldn't get the image of a keg out of my head. A beer tender full of Brik.

Did I dare look? Feel?

Unscrewing the lid of an urn, it turns out, doesn't give you immediate access to the contents—the ash was sealed off, like vacuum-packed coffee under silver foil, like that little sliver of silver you have to peel off when you open a new tube of toothpaste. I ran my thumb over the silver, tracing figure eights, and could feel the vacuum, the suction, the unnatural force holding everything together—if I pressed harder, I would press right through the silver, poking my thumb into the ash, into Brik.

The urge was strong; it's always so tempting to break a vacuum, to unseal coffee, experience that split second when the vacuum is released—as if the coffee were breathing, taking a first breath, like something that has just woken up from a cryogenic sleep, a breath of life.

The keg was pleasantly heavy on my lap, like a sleeping child.

I sat there for a while, unaware of time passing, lost in the act of staring. Long enough, at any rate, for the silence of the hotel room to affect me. It began to lull me, to put me under.

Though I didn't fall asleep, I could feel myself getting drowsy. I saw myself sitting there, on Philip's bed, with Brik's ashes on my lap, as if I were looking at someone else, and suddenly I had a vision of myself sitting with Brik's ashes on my lap in Brik's farm in Groningen. Why, I couldn't tell, but all of a sudden I pictured myself sitting with his ashes on that wooden school bench that stood in his kitchen.

And I pictured his friends and colleagues gathered in the garden, pictured how I would get their attention without raising my voice and how I would lead them.

As if in a vision I saw it all clearly. We would leave from Brik's house, two by two, like schoolchildren, down the garden path, past the rose bed and the tree planted to mark the birth of Queen Juliana. We would go over the little wooden bridge across the stream, to the farm of the neighbors opposite, who would be waiting there and silently join the end of our procession. We would walk into their cornfields, which stretched out to where their land ended, a few hundred yards off. The tall cornstalks would rustle in the wind, a sea of gold and yellow seeming to part in front of us. Even if you didn't have them in the Netherlands, we would nevertheless hear the chirping of tree crickets, an invisible wall of sound.

Men would take off their jackets and hang them over their shoulders, women would wear big sunglasses. We would feel the day's warmth on our bare arms, my hand would find Pippa's. Little would be said, but the words that were spoken would be accompanied by familiar smiles, bright faces.

At the end of the cornfields we would climb the stone steps onto the dyke. The Wadden Sea would sparkle in the sunshine. We would walk along the dyke to that bit of the road that jutted out into the sea, where there was a bench, usually with a few cyclists on it, catching their breath and eating sandwiches. Not now, now the bench would be empty. Pippa would hold my hand until we got to the bench, and then place her hand on my back to support me as I climbed onto it.

I wouldn't start speaking right away. First I would look down and take in all the faces: Pippa would be standing at the front, her arms crossed, a look of concentration on her face, lovingly anxious on my behalf. Her parents and her brother Jim would be nearby, her father's hand on her shoulder. Felix would stand with his hands behind his back, patient as a vicar. There would be Mr. and Mrs. Chilton, their faces tanned like vacationers, his arm around her, the Australian art critic leaning on his walking stick, Nicolas Fokker, the little orange ribbon of his medal flapping on his lapel, the police officer from Onondoga

County, his eyes invisible under his hat, the Viennese taxi driver with his foot *kaputt* in plaster. Hitler Lima senior and junior would stand next to each other and you would wonder whether they really shared the same DNA, the one so angular, the other so solid, like the difference between a slice of cheese and a thick beefsteak.

I would look down from the bench and smile, try to make eye contact with everyone, take away some of the tension. Sweder Burgers would be standing there like the big philanthropist, art collector, and uncomplicated Josip Brik fan that he was, his assistant Nina Barth next to him, tall and athletic, obscenely healthy, along with Markus Winterberg, as stately and unmoving as a monument. Vikram Tahl would be shifting his weight from foot to foot, impatient, but too polite to show it, with Yuki Hausmacher next to him to hold his jacket. The historian Maarten van Rossem, dressed in black, would be sweating in the midday sun. Not a hair of Geert Wilders's head would move in the wind. Dame Mathilda Wilson would be wearing a kind of tweed hunting suit and a floppy hat, while Madeline Steinberg would be draped in one of those garments that as a man you never knew what to call, still less how to wear it: a sort of silk shawl-type cape or dress. Beads of sweat would trickle down the forehead of the nurse who'd just pushed Raimund Pretzel's wheelchair up the dyke. The two boys and the girl from the Right Arm Liberation Front would be there, and if I looked closely I would see that something appeared to be growing under the noses of both boys: a strip of downy hair the size of a postage stamp—because apparently mustaches also needed to be liberated.

The dark eyes of the Chilean Susan Sontag would still radiate sympathy and reassurance, but from time to time she would glance aside with a look of concern at Jean-Philippe, the gangling student doing his PhD on Hitlerian Revenge Plays, who'd be clutching his atomizer and plastic bag.

I would slowly scan the rows, so the people in the back would know that I saw them. I would feel the sea breeze in my back, looking out, like a prophet over the flat fields, the promised land, the corn, Brik's house, the windmill, the low country under the unnuanced clear blue sky.

I would spot Brik's mentor Jack Gladney, with his eternal sunglasses and deerstalker. Ilsa the She Wolf of the SS would feel the sun on her long legs, bare below her kinky uniform shorts, her blonde hair braided so severely it looked like a weapon. The host of the TV program would wear a shiny suit that looked at least a size and a half too small for him. There would be the Greek woman from the hotel in Istanbul, with her broad, generous mouth and corkscrew curls ("very, very oral"), as well as Guus Le-Jeune, Erik Lanshof, Omega Red, and Arkady Rossovich. Behind them would be Bruno Ganz, Anthony Hopkins, that actor from *Valkyrie*, that other actor from *Inglourious Basterds*, all having come straight from the set, still in costume. Adolf Eichmann, looking just like his photo on the cover of *Elsevier*, and Josef Mengele, or at least Gregory

Peck as Josef Mengele in *The Boys from Brazil*, because who knew what Mengele really looked like?

Behind them there would be perhaps two dozen students, the same faces you came across at all his lectures, quiet and polite, and in their midst Philip de Vries, taller and fairer than all the rest, the only one who would look me straight in the eyes. "Go get 'em, Friso," his eyes would be saying. "Go get 'em, bro."

All these characters and extras—I'd scan their faces, then address them, resolutely:

"Friends,

"Every now and then I still talk to Brik. I can't help it. As I walk along the leafy lanes of the campus I catch myself saying 'Okay, Brik, what shall we do?' and then I start to talk about some problem, some dilemma, an email I have to write, or something I've seen, a film, a book I've read. Sometimes I repeat conversations we've had in my head, making myself more eloquent than I've ever been in real life.

"No, he doesn't talk back. Don't worry, the only voice in my head is my own.

"I never see him, but I see myself. As if he were standing in the room and looking at me, while I work in our *Sleepwalker* office behind what used to be our desk, I see myself sitting there, through his eyes. I make coffee and read a book and I 'like' an article from some periodical or other so that all my Facebook friends can see I'm an intellectual heavyweight. I see myself doing it, I see Brik laughing at me.

"Brik doesn't talk to me, but I see the world through his eyes. I sit in the cinema and try to watch the film as he would. What would strike him? I don't do it consciously, it just happens automatically.

"They say that's the definition of a genius: someone who makes such a mark on a field that they change it for good. I don't exactly know what Brik's 'field' was—it's a vague term when it comes down to it—Brik did hundreds of things simultaneously. But if my head is a field, a pound and a half of gray matter in my brainpan, Brik changed that for good. However small that is, however personal—that's a legacy. It's a privileged feeling, however individual. In that sense I am his heir. You don't need more than that, I keep telling myself. This is enough."

Then I would pause briefly, I would look at everyone and swallow, and go on in a more strident, impersonal tone.

"There's not a whole lot you can hold against a man like Josip Brik.

"So what if it turned out he didn't forward all the moaning letters he received to his editor in chief. So what if he never quite lost his Communist roots. So what if he came from some shitty little village and didn't know where Klaus Barbie was born and where Hemingway died. In death, Brik owes us nothing. He has no promises he needs to keep, he has no reputation to maintain."

My voice would then grow softer, warmer.

"But Brik has failed us. Of course he has: by dying. By stupidly falling out of a hotel room window he failed himself, ended a life that had by no means ceased to flower. About my grief I can say little, only that his death drew a line under a period of my life—a period of continual inspiration and wonder. But I also missed Brik when he was still alive, and in that respect, Brik failed us all. Brik systematically gave us less than we wanted of him."

I would say "Love that isn't satisfied, hungry love, is the best love. As W. H. Auden wrote: 'If equal affection cannot be, let the more loving one be me.'"

I would keep my gaze fixed on Pippa while I said that.

"He was never there. We wanted to be with him, spend time with him, but his time also belonged to students who barely scraped passing grades. We wanted to have him to ourselves, but he also belonged to outfits like the Right Arm Liberation Front. We wanted him in America, but he had to go and talk to the Hitler family in Chile. We wanted to keep him on campus, but he made just one more trip to a crappy hotel in Amsterdam.

"You know the thing with Brik..."

But I would never finish that sentence. Once again I would pause, this time at greater length, more theatrically. I would open my mouth as if to go on speaking, but then close it again and smile—I would look away and smilingly shake my head, as if I wanted to say something, something definitive, but at the last moment had decided to keep it to myself.

That definitive thing, that thing I wouldn't say—that would be my secret. Even if it didn't exist.

"Anyone who was friends with Brik was forever bidding him farewell, and today we have to do it once again: for the last time. Brik loved this spot, here on the Wadden Sea. We have his ashes with us, here in this urn. I'd like to ask everyone to take a handful and throw it into the water, and then go back to Brik's house, where the drinks are waiting. And *bitterballen*. Because boy, did Brik love a good old Dutch *bitterbal*! Thank you."

And that would be it. I would take Pippa's hand again, worm my fingers between hers and wait as the mourners one by one took handfuls of ashes from the enormous urn, the keg full of ashes, and threw them over the dyke, into the water. The Chiltons, Fokker, Nina, Wilders, Gladney, Lanshof—everyone would take a handful and toss it. It wouldn't blow back, because the ashes would be heavy. Not like loose sand, but more like pellets: black, white, and gray pellets.

No one would think about the fact that they were holding Brik in their hands—was this pellet his nose? That one his eye? No—they would throw him, some would wave as they did so. *"Adieu*, Brik, Godspeed!" And they would walk on, back down the dyke and across the field.

Pippa and I would wait till everyone had gone and then walk to the keg ourselves. There'd be more ashes left than we'd expected. Pippa would throw a handful in the water. Then I'd follow suit.

What shall we do with the rest? she'd ask.

Tell you what, I'd say. You go on ahead, I'll just be a minute.

Pippa would place an understanding kiss on my cheek and walk away without saying anything more.

The keg would be lighter than I'd thought, just as an empty beer bottle crate is always lighter than you think. I'd pick it up with both hands, raise it to chest height, and then upend it in one go, wham, like those winning sports teams throwing buckets of Gatorade over their coach.

The ashes would splash into the sea, and I'd watch to see how the water changed color for a moment, until all the ash sank to the bottom forever and the water became water again in the sunshine, water that sparkled so brightly it looked like it was trying to communicate with the sky, like a radar screen on which all the little lights were lighting up.

The keg was empty. Brik had gone.

And there I was in Vienna, awakening from this funeral fantasy, feeling as if I'd been underwater for a very long time and my face was now finally breaking through the surface, into the air.

The keg was still full. I was sitting on Philip de Vries's bed with it in my lap, but that moment when I emptied the ashes into the water was still wholly with me. I was able to replace the urn on Philip's bedside table without the slightest bitterness. That one vision was worth so much more than whatever I could actually do, no reality could ever match up to this. It was as if something had melted in my stomach, filling me with acceptance—a feeling I hadn't had in months.

I sneaked out of the hotel and walked back into town, every muscle in my body tingling. The Heldenplatz was covered in snow, a white expanse, "as white as Saruman," as white as an unwritten Word document.

My phone pinged and I dug it out of my pocket, surprised. I couldn't remember the last time I'd looked at it. Someone had just tagged me in a photo. I clicked on the link and saw Felix's Facebook page loading.

I looked around me: yes, this is the spot. *That's* the balcony where Hitler must have stood, I saw it now.

It took a moment for the pixels to click into focus, but even while the photo was still blurry and grainy, I could make out the contours of a peroxided hair helmet. Wilders had wrapped one arm demonstratively around Felix's shoulders, there was nothing ironic about their grins. A tiger in Amsterdam. An intellectual on the warpath. Yeah, Felix had given him a piece of his mind all right! I was tagged in the glass of beer he was holding: "Friso de Vos, mission accomplished. Cheers!"

I'd run out of cynicism. My tank of irony was empty; perhaps it had been all along. I just clicked on Like to get rid of the thing.

A motorcade of police cars was slowly approaching the road that bisected the Heldenplatz. There were flashing lights, but no sirens. Flanked by motorcycles driven almost at walking pace by policemen in high-viz jackets, three black limousines glided silently through the snow. I scanned the cars, trying to see through the tinted glass.

I was the only one standing by the roadside. One of the motorcyclists peeled off toward me, probably to show he was keeping an eye on me. When he got close I could see my reflection in the curved glass of his helmet: convex and distorted like in a funhouse mirror.

As silently as they had come, the cars disappeared again. I turned around to face the Heldenplatz and saw— nothing, actually. The place was deserted. I'd already lost sight of Hitler's balcony. All I could focus on was that Word document: I knew the time had come for it to arrive. File (click) New Document (double click) and the white empty page stared at me, and for the first time I couldn't think of a reason why I shouldn't call Pippa, why I wouldn't want to hear her voice. Damn damn damn. I was already holding my phone, wasn't I? Fucking go for it! I don't know how long it took for satellites to connect us, for the G3 networks to do their job, but when I pressed Pippa's name on my phone I was still quite collected and by the time she answered it in America my eyes were swollen and wet and burning, and it felt like I was trying to stop a tsunami in its tracks with just my arms and back. "Hey, Voski," Pip said, and of course she didn't need to say anything else, ever, because just the fact of her being there and her voice being her voice meant so much more than any words ever could.

"Just come, Vos," she said, infinitely understanding, just as understanding as I'd pictured her there by the Wadden Sea. "It's totally okay."

EPILOGUE

The first time I met Pippa's extended family was on a Sunday morning, years ago now, in the function room of one of The Hague's best-known hotels, where all the Lowenberg clan had gathered to celebrate her grandfather's ninetieth birthday. Her grandfather was small and stout, and his bald head had strange dents in it, like an egg before you peel it, and although he still talked with a thick accent like the working-class hero he was, you could see he liked the way the waiters called him "Sir" and darted to his side with hors d'oeuvres and glasses of jenever at the wave of a hand. He'd been in the Resistance; three successive queens had decorated him for his services to the country in the Hunger Winter and afterward. In April 1945 he'd been arrested while carrying illicit documents, but the capitulation was signed before the Germans had time to find a spot in the dunes near Scheveningen where they could decently shoot him.

– So you're our Philomena's new boyfriend?

– I am indeed, I said.

– And you're a historian?

– That's right.

Well, well, he said, and turned away from me again and walked up to someone else he needed to greet.

Pip had warned me. Her grandfather derived a virulent moralism from his status as Knight in the order of Orange Nassau and never scrupled to end every conversation he had with his children and grandchildren—on topics ranging from their choice of university course to immigration policy—with the pronouncement that "something like that would have been unthinkable during the war, young lady," or "you wouldn't have gotten very far in the Resistance with that kind of attitude." A man of deeply entrenched views, Pip told me, he would contemptuously dismiss any historian who dared comment on the war: "What does a whippersnapper like that know about it? He wasn't there." End of debate. So I was primed. But unnecessarily, it soon turned out. That "Well, well," was as much as I'd get out of him—during the hors d'oeuvres he clutched at his chest and collapsed.

He struggled in the hands of the paramedics as if he were a bank robber being bundled into a police van after a long spell on the run, and just before the doors closed we heard his voice one last time, loud enough to drown out the sirens, "And keep your goddamn hands off my organs."

As far as Pippa knew, these were the last words her grandfather ever spoke, because in the ambulance he suffered a second, catastrophic heart attack, blasting every chamber apart, and before they even got to the hospital the ambulance crew had been able to stow away the defibrillation paddles.

Pippa told me that later. I'd walked back to the hotel's conservatory, where I'd ordered another orange juice. No one asked me to join them, and, uncertain of my role in all this, I just stayed put. Three quarters of an hour or so passed, and I could feel the warmth of the sunlight falling through the glass panes on my legs and belly. My body grew heavy and despite the sirens, despite Pippa's family and the hotel guests checking in and out, I felt I could just shut my eyes and fall asleep on the spot. A quarter of an hour later it dawned on me that I was the only one left of the whole party. Pippa had abandoned me there, apparently, had gone to the hospital with her parents without telling me. The head waiter subtly drew this to my attention:

– May I give Sir the bill?

Less than a week later, the men of her family turned out in the same suits they'd worn that Sunday, only this time with more subdued shirts and dark ties.

The church was big, but all the pews were packed, and even though I gathered from Pippa that since the death of his wife, ten years previously, her grandfather had become increasingly intolerant, bullying his sons and treating his daughters like housekeepers, half his grandchildren were crying before the service had even begun. His three sons sat gazing stoically at the floor; his two daughters wore enormous sunglasses. The fifteen grandchildren sat in the second pew. The mourners in the third pew included a lady of about sixty who kept dabbing at her eyes with a white hanky—she was the chief heir. To the surprise and rage of his children, their father had changed his will, making his new girlfriend the beneficial owner of his house on Regentesselaan. Right now she was being cold-shouldered by the children. Later she would be determinedly sued, but I am getting ahead of myself.

Among the mourners in the front row was an older gentleman with a yarmulke and next to him a beautiful girl of about our age, with big brown eyes and thick, dark curly hair. Halfway through the service—after a former queen's commissioner had given a humanist, patriotic eulogy that, with a bit of cutting and pasting, must have been adaptable for all Resistance heroes—she led the man, presumably her grandfather, to the pulpit. He spoke about faith and belief in dark times and about the intrinsic goodness of mankind. "We are born old," he said. "We are born with the weight of all that history on our shoulders. We have a supremely loaded past and a supremely intense present." He talked about his emigration to Israel in the late 1940s. Pippa's grandpa had visited him twice and—another surprise in the lawyer's office—had left his Zionist organization a few thousand euros.

He finished with the announcement that his granddaughter would now join the quintet of conservatory students led by the youngest daughter, Pippa's aunt. They struck up Pachelbel's Canon in D, and because her face was hidden by her violin I couldn't see whether she was proud or tense, but as far as I could tell, every note was played flawlessly, calmly, solemnly, though the performance perhaps lasted a bit longer than intended. When they had finished, Pip's aunt stood up and walked back to her seat with her violin, carefully avoiding any eye contact, and I wondered whose gaze she would normally have sought out among the audience—her father's, probably.

After that the oldest daughter talked about how she used to go to the skating rink with her father, and then Pippa's father stepped up to the lectern. He read a short psalm:

What shall I return to the Lord for all his goodness to me? I will lift up the cup of salvation and call on the name of the Lord. I will fulfill my vows to the Lord in the presence of all his people.

Finally it was Pippa's turn, the elect representative of the grandchildren. What did I see then, when I looked at Pippa? Other things now, but in that spring, a spring that came in the guise of midsummer, in those first pangs of love, I couldn't look at her in public without picturing her during those nights or afternoons when we existed in an almost permanent state of coitus, how she'd bitten my sweaty armpit the first time we fucked, how I'd held my hand under her as she peed, and felt the warm stream run through my fingers—that was what I'd been thinking about during the entire service as I stared at the back of her head, fifteen oak pews in front of me.

It was she who'd banished me practically to the back of the church, while I'd been so desperate to sit next to her, in my role of perfectly trained boyfriend. But Pippa had convinced herself that if I sat too close it would make her nervous. I'd seen her speech and had come up with a few helpful pointers, but when I added some more dashes to her printout, so she'd know where to pause for heightened dramatic effect, Pippa had said she didn't want a prompter.

– The problem is, we're born into a world that already exists. How do we relate to that? Pippa began in a low, unsteady voice.

In the week between the birthday and the funeral I'd had scarcely any contact with her. Not for lack of trying; she just walled herself off. I texted and emailed, but she barely responded. Was at her parents' place in The Hague. Couldn't come to me and didn't give the impression of wanting to. While I, in love, high on hormones, whatever you want to call it, had never been crazier about her than then, when she was *just* out of reach. I lay in bed with a slowly deflating balloon in my stomach. My nights consisted of two- to three-hour catnaps, full of lucid dreams, in which I was aware from beginning to end that I was dreaming. I seized on a book that Pippa had left at my place, an essay by Alain Finkielkraut, who in the introduction alone posed enough questions to keep a dozen intellectuals busy for a year. What is art? What is civilization? What is the ideal? What is essential in life? How do novels help you live? How does fiction form the context of our lives?

In the chapter on Emily Dickinson Pippa had underlined some passages and scribbled comments in the margin. A note in pencil read: "I *never* wonder what someone looks like naked. When I picture people, I *always* dress them," and though I read and reread what Finkielkraut wrote about Dickinson, I could find nothing in the text to which that comment could refer.

The lines and the comments and her fingerprints (she must have been eating something greasy at the time) conjured up Pippa's physical presence so vividly that more than once I found myself holding my phone, on the point of calling an old flame I'd just waved off, sex with your ex, I wanted Pippa so badly I was prepared to hurl myself on her predecessor so I could sublimate my desire, could think of her during my infidelity, could betray her in order to get closer to her. I read Finkielkraut's epilogue three times, and had I read it three times more could still not have found the coherence I sought between the paragraphs, between the sentences. As if his cast of topics threw such a long shadow as to make his discourse invisible. Camus, Dostoyevsky, Blixen, Chekhov blocked the view. The canon, cast in bronze, so safe, so dead.

I thought his message must be something like: literature does not yield truth. There is always friction between one story and another. Our mind is a cinema with a continuous show. We keep on consuming and producing histories. Everything that happens is told, all facts are turned into anecdotes, the purpose of history is to become a story. A veil hangs over everything, a Romanesque veil, Finkielkraut calls it, with a narrative structure.

In the end, desperate, I sent a text, a line of verse I'd once seen on a toilet door in a hall of residence: "*If equal affection cannot be / let the more loving one be me.*"

A day went by. Two days. Three. On the fourth day Pippa finally called to say that she was on the train to Amsterdam, that she wanted to drop by, that everything was all right, that she didn't want me to feel let down. Okay, I said, okay. No worries, take your time.

It was such beautiful weather that week, calling for arms and legs to be bared. Pippa didn't want to, her legs were too shockingly pale, she said, unfit for public view. I kissed them with open mouth. Afterward she lay on the sofa, "as limp as a noodle," as she put it, and I drank Coke out of the bottle and started to tell her what I thought she should say at the funeral—I'd taken the liberty of jotting a few things down, I said, and got out my notebook:

– The problem is, we're born into a world that already exists.

At the funeral she wore her long auburn hair in a side ponytail. Her bare arms looked even paler in her gray-blue dress, as she'd feared, but I'd told her not to worry about it. I read along with her on my own printout and heard how she sometimes swallowed articles and even entirely skipped adjectives. But halfway down page two she stopped in midsentence and folded up the pages, saying it seemed "kind of inauthentic" to just speak from paper.

I wondered what she meant by "speak from paper." That she was reading aloud? Or that she was asking questions she only asked herself on paper, not in her head? And I feared what lay ahead, because she said her grandfather had been her guide to the classics, that he had pushed her through Greek and Latin at grammar school, and that she always thought of him when she wrote poetry. I'd known she had a poetic bent, that she had a notebook she wrote things down in, but since I'd never been allowed to read anything in that notebook, I'd never taken her poetic inclinations very seriously.

There lay the delta, there lay the burning arms of this classical river... The poem she suddenly recited by heart was full of names and words that didn't even mean anything in the context of her sentences, I thought. The Hellespont, Alexandria, Luxor and the old queens, *the blue flicker from the Pylons of Messina*, but in themselves the words conjured up a world: a bygone era. A certain repetition gradually emerged, words and phrases that were repeated like a refrain. Augustus, Jupiter, "*Our beloved Republic, eternally renewed.*" You pictured marching legions, senate chambers, and other manifestations of Roman civilization, and you saw the link with her grandfather, who'd developed a fascination with classical warfare after his retirement and gone to see old battlefields all over Europe. Everybody thought that, I think. But another idea struck me: Pip's poem was about inevitability, about history bearing down on you like a juggernaut and your longing to know its outcome; about everything that you resist, even though in the end things turn out as they must.

She spoke clearly, articulating every word, and after she'd finished she walked back to her seat, also without making eye contact with anybody, least of all me. She crept back like a little mouse and all of a sudden I got it: her poem was about me, about the teleology of her and me, that was it, surely: the new republic—that was her and me, our own statehood.

Afterward I did not, of course, stand next to her, among the partners and cousins, to receive condolences. I joined the row of guests, shook hands with her uncles and aunts, her father and mother, and then got to Pip. I knew better than to give her a significant wink, something to show I'd grasped her double meaning. She looked at me with naked eyes, and I'd never been so convinced I was right.

– Hey, little poet, I said.

I know now, retrospectively, that this is a false memory, that it isn't real. But it still feels real, it feels as if it could be true. Just as flowing water can hollow out stone into a rainbow bridge, I've told this story so many times it's etched itself into my memory. My imagination has imposed a penalty on a random image.

A designer at the periodical where I now work once told me that when she moved house she'd come across a stash of old diaries. She'd opened a bottle of wine, gritted her teeth, and started to read them. The strange thing was, she said, that half of what she'd written ten or fifteen years previously in the sacred one-to-one privacy of her own diary just wasn't true. Stories about lecturers who were supposedly in love with her, housemates who were supposedly ripping her off, boys who stared after her—anecdotes that perhaps had a grain of truth in them, but what she had written, she now knew, was more than exaggerated. It had never been more than a hand on her shoulder, but when she wrote down the story of her day she couldn't resist the temptation to make it noteworthy.

I sometimes think of that, when I think about Brik, but I don't believe it. If I have a self-spun web of fiction, I can't relinquish it—not yet at least.

I would see Brik once more, perhaps eighteen months after the Vienna trip, after I'd left the city on an earlier flight, after the antiques shop on the Marcus Aureliusstrasse had burnt down under mysterious circumstances, and after I got a text message from an unidentified number: "Silence is golden. MW." I saw Brik standing on a low flight of steps on one of the little side streets leading from the Vondelpark to Overtoom, just past the old Film Museum. Although he died there, he didn't like Amsterdam all that much. When he was in the Netherlands he preferred to be in Groningen, where he stayed in a rented farmhouse, near tall cornfields, close to the sea. "The Texas of East Groningen." But there he was. Not the Brik I'd known, perhaps fifteen years younger, a lot thinner, the Brik who hadn't yet slipped discs, who didn't yet stand self-correctingly erect; his hair was darker but at the same time more flaxen than I'd remembered.

Perched on the back of my bike, Pippa pressed against me, her long arms wrapped affectionately around my waist. It was the day we'd registered to get married. She didn't see anything, was facing the other way, and I only saw him in a flash, because perhaps that's the deal between the dead and the living, that they don't really look each other up, but only dwell in that watery region at the corner of your eye, that little chink you can just peep through, but where nothing really comes into focus. I'd like to say he looked happy, but I was cycling too fast to make that out, and I couldn't stop—the turn onto the side street would have been too sharp for our rickety old bike, and there were too many cyclists, mopeds, and joggers to just brake right there. The sun lit up the leaves on the trees, like green gold, and when I took one last look over my shoulder he'd already gone, *exit ghost*, vanished into the light, but even without looking, actually, I'd have known that.

ACKNOWLEDGMENTS
───────────────

When writing the passages on Hitler studies I drew on a
great many publications. Too many, and often too tangen-
tially, to list in full here. But I'd like to mention the follow-
ing: *Explaining Hitler: The Search for the Origins of His
Evil* by Ron Rosenbaum; *The Hitler of History* by John
Lukacs; *Koba the Dread: Laughter and the Twenty Million*
by Martin Amis; "The Hitler Dynasty" by Leonard Haber-
korn; *The Dictators: Hitler's Germany, Stalin's Russia* by
Richard Overy; *Der Untergang* by Joachim Fest; *Europe
Central* by William T. Vollmann; *Hugh Trevor-Roper: The
Biography* by Adam Sisman; the comprehensive *Third
Reich Trilogy* by Richard J. Evans; and the essay "Hitler &
the Sick Joke" by H. J. A. Hofland.

The Jack Gladney character comes from Don DeLillo's
White Noise. Excerpts from *The Republic* have appeared
previously, in a greatly adapted and truncated form, in *Das
Magazin*; in *Agent-provocateurs: 20 onder 35*, compiled
by Thomas Blondeau and Hassan Bahara (Prometheus,

2011); and as an introduction to a new edition of *De SS'ers* by Armando and Sleutelaar (De Bezige Bij, 2012).

The Republic is a work of fiction and fantasy. No identification with actual persons should be inferred.

JDV

CREDITS

p. 1: First epigraph, copyright © 2009 David Mazzucchelli. Used by permission of Pantheon Books, an imprint of Knopf Doubleday Publishing Group, a division of Penguin Random House LLC. All rights reserved.

p. 1: Second epigraph, copyright © 1984, 1958 by Don DeLillo. Used by permission of Viking Books, an imprint of Penguin Publishing Group, a division of Penguin Random House LLC. All rights reserved.

p. 3: *The Surrender of Breda* or *The Lances* (1635). Diego Rodriguez Velázquez (1599–1660). Oil on canvas. Museo del Prado, Madrid. Image copyright Museo Nacional del Prado/Art Resource, NY

pp. 71, 74, 76, 79: From the Web site www.thingsthatlooklikehitler.com

p. 127: "Cosmic Gall" poetry excerpt from *Collected Poems, 1953–1993* by John Updike, copyright © 1993 by

JOOST DE VRIES, born in 1983, studied journalism and history in Utrecht. Since 2007 he has been an editor and literary critic at *De Groene Amsterdammer*. He burst onto the Dutch literary scene with *Clausewitz*, a biblio-thriller inspired by the work of one of his great heroes, Harry Mulisch. In 2013 he was awarded the Charlotte Köhler Stipendium, and his second novel, *The Republic*, won the Golden Book-Owl prize in 2014.

JANE HEDLEY-PRÔLE studied German and Dutch at the University of Liverpool, after which she settled in the Netherlands. Alongside her job at the Ministry of Foreign Affairs she works as a freelance translator. She has translated *Diaghilev: A Life* by Sjeng Scheijen (together with S. J. Leinbach), *The Fetish Room* by Rudi Rotthier and Redmond O'Hanlon, *We Are Our Brains* by D. F. Swaab, and many short stories.